MISSING AMERICAN

absolutely hilarious mystery fiction

JULIE HIGHMORE

Published by The Book Folks

London, 2023

This book is a work of fiction. Names, characters, businesses, organizations, places and events are either the product of the author's imagination or are used fictitiously. Any resemblance to actual persons, living or dead, events or locales is entirely coincidental. The spelling is British English.

ISBN 978-1-80462-075-5

www.thebookfolks.com

THE MISSING AMERICAN is the first standalone mystery in the EDIE FOX DETECTIVE AGENCY series by Julie Highmore. Look out for the second, THE RUNAWAY HUSBAND, coming soon. More details can be found at the back of this book.

For Adam

PROLOGUE

'This is my mother. *Esta es mi madre.*'

'*Esta es mi madre,*' he repeated.

'This is my father. *Este es mi padre.*'

'Este es mi padre.'

'I have two brothers. *Tengo dos hermanos.*'

'Tengo dos hermanos.'

Tedious, he thought. He'd begun with disc one, but it was too easy. He paused Miguel in order to overtake. There was a stretch of straight road ahead, thank Christ. He'd been sitting on the Toyota's tail for miles. Why drive at 48 when the speed limit's 60? You shouldn't be behind a wheel if you're that nervous, braking with every curve in the road. Some old codger with cataracts, or a woman. He got even closer to the car, then swung the steering wheel right, hit the accelerator and shot past. Glancing over, he saw a guy his own age.

'Pussy,' he said, before jerking back to the left.

An approaching car blasted its horn. He gave it the finger, then with the same finger tapped "play".

'My mother has brown hair. *Mi madre tiene el pelo moreno.*'

'Mi madre tiene el pelo moreno.'

* * *

Three houses from home, he pressed the remote to open his garage, then watched the door rise with satisfaction. He'd done all the work himself, a couple of months back, and it was still a novelty.

'You mad, mate?' one neighbour had said. 'Starting a big job like this in November? Get a builder in.'

But he'd enjoyed creating it with his own hands. The physicality of it, the way it had evolved from bare gravelled drive to something tangible and useful. People didn't realise what they were capable of, that was the trouble.

After pulling into the garage, he remotely shut the door behind him, took his jacket and bag from the passenger seat, got out, locked the car, then let himself into the utility room. He dropped the bag, hung his coat up, kicked his shoes off and went through to the hall, where he took the stairs two at a time. In the bedroom he stripped and put on running gear. It was cold, so he went for a thermal-lined hooded jacket. It had "23" on the back. Beckham's number at Real Madrid.

'Number twenty-three,' he said, in the husky voice of Miguel. '*Numero veintitrés.*'

Light was beginning to fade when he set off, taking the side streets for three minutes before hopping over a stile. The footpath would lead him through the spinney, past two ploughed fields, across a grassy one and back on to the busy main road, a third of a mile from his house.

It was colder than he'd expected and patches of ground were frozen and slippery. He could have worn something thicker on his legs, but he'd be warm soon, and sweating. In the meantime, he thought about what he'd cook himself. Something healthy. Fish, perhaps. Green beans would go well, and those Charlotte potatoes. He'd make a sauce, put a splash of white rioja in and lots of butter and garlic. The more he thought about dinner the hungrier he became, but tempting as it was, he didn't take the shorter circuit at the point he could have. You set out to do something, you do it properly.

Back at the house he jogged on the spot under the porch light, checking his phone's stopwatch. Not bad, considering the frost underfoot.

He showered for ten minutes and put on a thick brown robe. Downstairs, he slipped bare feet into loafers and returned to the garage, where he flicked the strip light on and went over to his mother's old chest freezer. What a godsend it had been, since he was so rarely at the house. Even milk could be frozen. He gathered together a fillet of plaice, a handful of green beans and a pack of butter, then closed the heavy lid.

At the door, about to switch off the light, he turned and walked to the space at the rear of his car; the part he never parked on. Cradling the fish, beans and butter, he hunkered down and ran fingers over the smooth concrete. A professional couldn't have done a better job. Beautiful. Once again he focused on the solid grey floor, mentally working his way through to what lay four feet beneath.

'Thees is the loser,' he whispered hoarsely, sounding so like Miguel it made him smile. '*Este es el...*' No, he'd have to look that up.

ONE

Mr Smith was downstairs.

'Could you send him up?' I asked Naz. He was a few minutes early but I couldn't leave him there.

'Yes, miss.'

I brushed crumbs off my lap and drained my tea. I dropped the cup and wrapper in the bin, smoothed my hair, slipped Val McDermid in a drawer and waited for the knock. Even on a Monday in January, I should look busy, I thought. I hit the laptop to wake it up, and there was the personality test I'd done earlier. Result: Idealist Healer.

At the rap on the door I said, 'Come in!' and a man of medium height and build appeared. Our emails had been brief, so I knew nothing about him. I guessed he was early to mid-thirties, and I couldn't say why, but he didn't look British. Too well dressed, or just oddly dressed for his age.

'Scuse me, ma'am,' he said, lifting a black felt hat with a brim. A fedora? His hair was short and blond and parted with precision. He had a round, healthily glowing face, a small nose and full lips. When he smiled he flashed American teeth at me, big and even and whiter than the snow outside. I thought he might ask if I'd accepted Jesus into my life.

'I'm here to see Eddie Fucks?' he said instead.

I stood and inched around my desk. 'That's me. Not Eddie, though, it's Edie. Edie Fox.'

'Oh,' he said, not letting go of the handle. I thought he might reverse and close the door. If you wanted a tough investigator you'd go for an Eddie over an Edie.

'Mike Smith?' I asked.

'Er, yeah.' He continued to hover.

'Do come in.'

He took a small step, then another.

'Pleased to meet you,' I told him, circling my prospective client and shutting the door with my back. We shook hands.

'Likewise.'

'Excuse me,' I said, aware that falafel wrap hung in the air. 'I'll just…' I pointed at the window, then went and lifted the bottom pane. Bits of snow floated in, along with the sound of Ian the *Big Issue* seller. Mike Smith was suddenly beside me, bending to see out.

'You sure know how to do graffiti round here,' he said.

'Thanks. Although we tend to call it street art.'

'That guy Banksy done any?' He spoke slowly, drawing out his words.

'We wish. There are some impressive ones, though. You should check them out in daylight.'

'Sure will.' Our proximity told me he smoked and used grooming products. He sighed, almost in my ear. 'Such a beautiful city.'

Ian stood across the street in his snow-covered hat with ear flaps, his magazines wrapped in polythene. In the doorway of the bank, by the cash machine, was a girl in a sleeping bag and a dog in a neckerchief. Once it had been a working bank, now it was covered in gig posters. There was the discount shop, the betting shop, the pawn shop and the porn shop, and Tesco.

'Yes,' I agreed, guessing he meant the centre, the colleges. I shivered and closed the window. 'Let me take that,' I said, as he undid his coat. I saw now he was on the stocky side. Bit of a tummy. 'Have a seat.'

The coat was black, woollen and heavy. It felt soft and expensive and smelled of cologne. A rich American. My heart sang. I hung Mike's coat and hat next to my parka, then sat at the desk I'd got from Naz's uncle. It was an old pine garden table; very orange, with a hole for a brolly. My laptop covered the hole. Before Christmas an Ikea desk had arrived, all flat-packed and impenetrable and still under the stairs.

Mike rubbed his hands warm. 'Great place you have. Kinda… cosy.'

I laughed. 'Oh yes, definitely cosy. I expect you've had bigger closets?' I was talking too fast, perhaps trying to speed him up.

'No… no.' His eyes drifted to my one hung picture. 'Great artwork, too,' he said, nodding at it, then squinting at the signature with its backwards *f*. 'Alfie,' he said. 'He your kid?'

I paused, not sure what to say. Perhaps Alfie's 'Pollock' should come down. 'No, not mine.' Not quite.

'Anyone tell you, Edie' – his squint had now turned on me – 'you have somethin' of the Lauren Bacall about you?'

'Um…'

'Which is kinda apt,' he went on, 'what with Bogart and Philip Marlowe, and you being a PI. Intriguing woman, Bacall. Had that air of coolness and intellectuality.'

I nodded and smiled, while my head imagined a panic button that would get Naz here in seconds.

Mike placed a hand on his chest. 'My apologies. I'm embarrassing you.'

'Not at all,' I insisted. I worked alone on the first floor, all sounds muffled by two fire doors.

'Pretty cool reception area,' he went on, as though reading my thoughts. 'The food store.'

'Ah, yes, apologies for the locked door. You never know who might wander up.' Someone like you?

'No problem.'

It felt time to end the uncomfortable warm-up. 'So,' I said, fingers clasped on the knotty pine, 'how can I help you?'

He breathed deeply and grew taller in the chair. 'It's my cousin,' he said, his expression turning serious, his hands echoing mine. 'She came over from the States last year to carry out a photography project, basing herself here in Oxford. Something about a comparison between the US and the UK, she told me. Society, nature, industry.'

'Sounds interesting.'

'Yeah. Anyways, that's what she was doing before she disappeared. We've heard nothing from her since Thanksgiving, when she last called. Her cell phone goes to voicemail, no emails, nothing.'

'So, a couple of months?'

He nodded. 'Feels longer, mind. It's been tough for us, what with Christmas and Grandma's birthday.'

I noticed the wedding ring and wondered who 'us' included. 'I take it you've contacted the police?'

'Sure. I called them from the States, late December, and went to see them last week, but they're not taking it seriously.'

'Why not?'

'Well…' he said, 'here's the thing.' He leaned forward, as did I. His eyes were dark brown and his best feature. 'She's still spending money. Cash withdrawals from ATMs, although no card purchases in stores or on hotels, or flights, or any other travel, far as I can see.'

'And you know this from, what, her bank statements?'

'That's right. Initially the cops here checked, but now I do it, since they stopped seeing her as missing. I have access to her accounts, online.'

'She gave you her security details and passwords?'

He sat back and crossed his arms. 'Took some guessing but I thought the situation justified it.'

'I see,' I said, although I didn't. How would that have been possible? 'And where's she making these withdrawals?'

'Before we lost contact, it was Birming Ham, Middlesbo Ro. All over. Since then, they've all been in and around yer beautiful city here.'

'And when was the last one?'

'Four days ago.'

'And where was that?'

'Right over there.' He pointed in the direction of our closed-down bank that had kept its cash machine going. 'Been hanging around there for days, hoping to see her. Reckon if I'd put my hat on the sidewalk, I'd be five pounds richer now.' He smiled toothily, then the serious face came back. 'I have an address for her, here in Oxford, but each time I've swung by there's been no one home. A neighbour told me she'd moved out. It's about a half mile from here. I did an internet search, found you and guessed you'd know the district.'

'I do, very well. And I'd certainly be pleased to help you find your cousin. But do you mind, first of all, if I ask if you had a falling-out with her? A tiff of some kind?'

'A tiff? Cute. I love how polite you Brits are. No, no fights. We've always gotten along well.'

'OK if I jot a few things down?'

'There you go again.'

I reached for my pad. 'I'm not sure we're polite. Just indirect?'

'Whatever, I like it.'

I tried to think how to play this, not wanting to put too much work in without a contract. 'What's your cousin's name?'

'Isabella.'

I wrote it down.

'Isabella Rossoni.'

Mike didn't look remotely Italian. The eyes maybe. I noticed, under the overhead light, just how blond his hair was. Did he bleach it?

'Married?' I asked.

'Me?'

I smiled. 'Your cousin.'

'No. No, she isn't.'

I did a bit of Sherlocking. 'So,' I said, 'she must be your aunt's daughter?'

Mike looked impressed. 'Yeah, she was the daughter of my dad's sister.'

Past tense, I noted with a "PT".

'But her mom died.'

I crossed through "PT".

'Along with her father.'

'OK.'

'And both my parents.'

'Goodness.' I stopped writing and tried to read something in his steady gaze. 'How did…?' I guessed illness, or genetic predispositions. But all of them dead? By, what, their fifties or early sixties?

'They were in an accident,' he said. 'Her parents and my parents. A truly awful accident.'

'I'm so sorry. When did it happen?'

'Oh… let me see, twenny-five, no twenny-six years back. There was this fire… and… well, we were their only kids and we have no other cousins, so our Smith grandparents took us in and raised us. Early on, we'd get visits from Mom's and my uncle Marco's parents, but they were pretty distant, in both senses of the word, and later fell ill, died. We got real close, me and Isabella in our small remaining family. Like brother and sister, only, like I said, without the fighting.'

'That's nice.' It was hardly nice, losing two sets of parents. 'I mean, that you had each other, after such a shocking… well, tragedy. And were able to live a relatively normal… you know, with your grandparents.' I'd never win a prize for counselling, so brought us back to the present. 'Will Isabella's money run out at some point?'

'No,' he said, firmly.

'Never?'

'Pretty much. She and I had this trust set up when we were orphaned, owing to some insurance payouts. The money was well invested, then soon as we could, Isabella and I got into real estate, buying and selling at the right times. Things cooled down during the recession, but she and I sat tight on the properties we had. Came through it OK. Anyways, yeah, she has interest enough alone to get along on. We both do.'

'Sounds like a successful business you and Isabella had. What were you called?'

'It was all pretty low key. We ran it from our homes, kinda quiet. Saved on unnecessary expenses. I've begun adding to our portfolio recently, well mine, buying in stable locations. New York, Stockholm, London. You know, you really can't go wrong with London properties.'

'I've heard,' I said. How young he was to be buying up our capital.

'But I miss doing it with Isabella. She was good at the aesthetics. Had an eye. I asked if she wanted to jump back in the game but she'd gotten into this photography thing and it was kinda all-consuming. Not enough time, she said. Probably, I was a little hard on her. Can't help wishing I'd taken her new interest more seriously.'

He closed his eyes, hands reclasping on the table. He could have been praying, so I stayed quiet. I watched his small nose redden and hoped he wouldn't cry. Then, eyes springing open, he was back.

'Can I get a coffee?' he asked, scanning the room.

In my bottom drawer were a travel kettle, powdered milk, a box of teabags and a Best Gran in the World mug. Also, one glass and a bottle of brandy for distressed clients, half-drunk by me.

'Yes, of course.' I picked up my phone. 'I'll send Naz out.'

'No, no. Please.'

I raised a hand to stop him. 'Hi, Naz. I don't suppose you could fetch Mr Smith a coffee?'

'Sorry!' yelled Naz. 'I have a fare!' The call ended before I could berate him. Naz had taken up taxi driving, while he was meant to be working in his uncle's shop and occasionally being my receptionist.

'I'll go,' I told Mike. It would give him a chance to compose himself. He began to protest but I insisted. 'I could do with a coffee,' I lied. 'It's right next door, so I'll be three minutes max.' I slipped on my parka and picked up my bag.

'Americano?'

'Sure.'

'A pastry? Carrot cake?'

Mike looked down at his midriff and patted it. 'Rain check?'

* * *

It was five or six minutes, by the time I'd queued, then negotiated my way back without a free hand. At the top of the stairs I elbowed the handle, pushed the door with my hip and found the room empty. I thought Mike might be in the toilet down on the half landing, but when my head spun to the hooks they too were empty. The stairwell lacked heating, but it wasn't so cold you'd need a coat and hat for the loo. I put the cups down, opened the window and leaned out dangerously. No sign of him having a smoke in front of the shop, or the ones either side. I took out my phone. Nothing.

'Shit,' I whispered. What an idiot. Me, not him. I should have had a coffee machine, assembled the Ikea desk, been an Eddie. I checked the toilet, then went down to the shop and found pale Emily shelving bread.

'Oh – what, him?' she said. 'He left, like, two minutes ago? Saw him come out your door and, like, hang around by the mangoes for a bit. Picking them up and sniffing them. I don't call that hygienic when you're not buying. Then when you came back, he like shot out?'

It was hard not to stare at her neck, at the tattooed name. Toby. The one time I'd asked, she wouldn't talk about him.

'Naz asked me to keep a look out,' she added, 'cos you were with some dodgy-looking gangstah?'

'I see. Well, thanks, Emily.'

'You're welcome.'

I went around the tall aisles checking Mike hadn't returned, then got distracted by the new broad-ranging stock: seaweed, preserved lemons, haggis, harissa paste, locally sourced meat and organic veg. An entire Polish aisle. Owner Mohammed's new mission – in the shadow of two supermarkets – was to appeal to all ages, all nationalities and all tastes. Capable, if grumpy, Oscar, Emily's older brother, now managed the shop, hence her first ever job, aged twenty-five. Emily and my Maeve had been friends at primary school, but then her left-leaning parents, in a brave but misguided moment, bought a house in the wrong catchment area.

Back upstairs I glared at the guilty-looking cups. I blamed them, and they knew it. I needed clients at the moment. I always needed clients. Where were they? In the past month I'd discovered that, yes, Mrs Murphy was having an affair, and, no, Mr Wilson wasn't. They'd covered the office rental. Just.

My mobile rang. Mike? He hadn't taken my number but it was on the website. I picked it up and saw "Maeve".

'Hey, Mum,' she said. 'How's things?'

'One to ten? Zero.'

'I'm not sure you're allowed that. What's happened?'

'Nothing, I'm being melodramatic. How's the work going?'

'Good, yeah. I just popped out the library to call you. I wondered if you might pick Alfie up. If you're busy, don't worry.'

'I'm not busy. Not even remotely.'

'Cool. I mean, er, sorry to hear that. Things'll pick up, don't worry. I'd better get back, left my stuff. I'll call you when I'm done here.'

'OK.'

'Don't forget Sniffy.'

'Have I ever?' It was Alfie's comforter; an old, grey and grubby T-shirt of Maeve's. 'See you later.'

After pouring the drinks down the sink, I went back to the office to log out of email and shut down. There, still, was my personality test result, only this time I wasn't an Idealist Healer, always seeing the best in people. This time I was a Rational Mastermind, which was odd, since every time I'd done the test, no matter how much I'd bent the truth, I'd got the same result.

I read my new character portrait and discovered that I and my fellow Masterminds make up only two per cent of the population, and that we're thorough-going pragmatists, excellent at complex operations, methodically following one step with the logical next step. As I began to see myself in a whole different light, a scrap of a Post-it note caught my eye. It was tiny and just about covered the Esc key. I looked closer and saw the word "Drawer".

Beneath the table I had a set of plastic drawers on wheels; the kind you stack toys and crayons in. I wheeled my chair back, not quite sure what I was dealing with here. Some oddball the police were looking for… I stretched out, nervously, waiting for a hand to be blown off, then slowly, very slowly, pulled the top drawer out.

There, amongst the chocolate bars, cereal bars, crisps and herbal slimming pills, sat an envelope. I lifted it out and felt its weight. Heavy. Heavy and fat. Heavy and fat like it was full of cash. On the front was a message.

> *Parking lot ticket emergency. Here's a small retainer. Let's talk again tomorrow. Mike Smith, Rational Mastermind – sorry, couldn't resist the test!*

Irritation that he'd used my laptop was replaced by astonishment as I began counting the twenty- and fifty-pound notes. A hundred, five hundred, a thousand, two, three thousand pounds. Jesus. I reread the note and, yes, it did say "small retainer".

What a risky thing to do. I never left anything in this room, let alone a wad of cash. Some lowlife could stray from the shop, even if it was Naz's job to ensure they didn't. But had Mike left the money unattended? Not really. He'd lurked by the fresh fruit, watching the door to the stairs, watching me return, then he'd hurried from the shop. But why? Why not just hand me the cash?

I flicked through it and wondered what he expected of me. I didn't do illegal, not like that dodgy-sounding outfit in Botley, on the other side of town. A retainer? That meant more to come. Could I buy a proper car? I looked at the ceiling and thanked my much-missed policeman dad. I then asked him to keep watch over me, and if I was tempted to hack emails, mobiles, bank accounts or medical records, or attach tracking devices to cars, or any of that illegal stuff Botley International blatantly offered on their website, to please stop me. Unless, I added, it was essential and I paid someone who couldn't be traced back to me.

Tomorrow I'd find out what the deal was. Mike Smith, Rational Mastermind, was a bit overfamiliar. On the other hand, he appeared pleasingly wealthy. He also seemed to have faith in me. But would he, if he knew I'd only been in business nine weeks, and if he knew 'in business' was stretching it?

I kissed the cash with a mix of euphoria and fear and buried it in my bag, then locked up and headed for Twinkle Toes nursery.

TWO

Maeve had her nose in an art tome, while her annoying boyfriend, Hector, was discussing with Alfie the destructive effects of the New World Order.

'And now,' he was saying, all wild sandy hair and intense grey eyes, 'our little family of countries called… do you remember?'

'Yurp?' asked Alfie, continuing to colour in.

'That's right. Europe. Well, ex-family, I should have said. Basically, everything's completely fu– all messed up. Especially us.'

'Why?'

'Tariffs, deregulation, people being sent home just because they're from another country.'

Alfie stopped colouring and looked up. 'Like Bidget?'

'Who?'

'Bridget, his nursery teacher,' I told Hector. 'Well, Brigitta. She's Dutch and Alfie has a crush.'

'Oh right,' said Hector. 'Yes, she'll definitely have to leave.'

Alfie's face crumpled and he reached for Sniffy.

'Enough,' I told Hector. God, he was annoying.

He pulled a what-have-I-done face, and went off to smoke in the snow. Maeve reassured her son that Bridget wasn't going anywhere, then took him for his bath. I put ready meals in the oven, opened a bag of salad and washed up the breakfast things.

* * *

Alfie was asleep when the three of us sat down to overdone M&S lasagne. We all tucked in, or tried to.

After a while Hector said, 'What are those things guys dig up the road with?'

'Jackhammers?' said Maeve. She'd changed for dinner and, having recently moved from the messy layered look to a retro one, was wearing what Granny Fox might have donned if George VI had been popping in, right down to the pillbox hat with netting, perched to one side of her shiny, dark, swept-up hair. I did admire the effort she put in, scouring charity shops and haggling over prices, on top of doing her Masters and being a mother. I wasn't sure about the ethics of haggling over prices in Save the Children, but Maeve had no qualms, just as she had no qualms about posting hangover photos on Facebook. Back in my day, postgrads of both sexes wore shapeless corduroy and stared at the pavement.

'Or maybe that's what Americans call them,' she added. 'Pneumatic drill?'

'That's it, pneumatic drill.' Hector pointed at his plate with a long, thin, annoying finger. 'Edie, you wouldn't happen to have one?'

'Christ,' said Maeve.

'Only kidding.'

I sighed and got up. 'I'll get you a sharper knife.'

'Actually,' Maeve said, 'could I have one too?'

I pulled three blades from the wooden block and handed them out. 'Talking of Americans,' I said, but then immediately decided to keep Mike, and his money, to myself.

'What about them?' asked Maeve.

'Oh, nothing. I was just… thinking… about their elections. And how long they go on for. I mean, no sooner is one over than they're campaigning for the next.'

'That's not entirely true,' said Hector, and then he was off, explaining mid-terms and caucuses, while Maeve sighed and I zoned him out and thought about Mike and Isabella both losing their parents in a fire. As a single mother I'd often worried about what would have happened to Maeve if I'd fallen under a bus drunk; which had, in fact, or so I was told, occurred one night. Luckily, the bus had been idling at the stop and I'd just been trying to get on. But tragedies happen, and Maeve couldn't have gone to live with her dad, since he hadn't known she existed. I'd always assumed my sister would have had her.

'You just think all politics is boring,' Hector was saying.

'That's blatantly not true,' said Maeve. 'But you, Hector, you never actually do anything to make the world better, you just sit on your scrawny private-school-educated arse, being an inverted snob and… I don't know… judging people. You're all opinion and no action, and pardon me for saying so, a bit of a misogynist.'

'That's crap and you know it.'

I stayed quiet. This was all very déjà vu. The young, and how they can let politics get in the way of the important stuff. Me. Terence. Poles apart but shagging against a wall at the ball and creating a person. Which is quite astounding when you think about it. Two relative strangers, two minutes. I was in my first year at Oxford and he'd just done his finals. Terence Casales – Ca-sa-lez – was a mean-spirited Thatcherite, always mouthing off in the JCR and therefore shunned by me and my friends. Unfortunately, Terence had Iberian good looks and his mother's blue eyes, and, unfortunately again, I'd drunk everything handed to me all evening. We danced, we shagged. I'm not sure we even spoke.

All was silent, apart from the sound of lasagne being stabbed.

Maeve put her cutlery down and gazed sympathetically at me. I'd been trying to get used to the new tinted contacts, but it was like someone had surgically replaced her eyes with blue M&Ms.

'Shall I open a tin of beans?' she asked.

'Good idea.'

I hadn't seen Terence since that ball. After graduating, he'd become an army officer, and last I'd heard he'd left the army, following injury in Iraq, and split from his wife. There were children, apparently, two boys, who I tried to think of as charmless little toffs, rather than Maeve's half-brothers.

'Mum?'

'Mm?'

'I said do you want to grate some cheese.'

'Oh, right.' I got up and found cheese, a grater and a plate.

Back home in the holidays, feeling wretched, I'd done a test in the bathroom. Positive. I'd had no experience of babies, never thought about them, didn't know any. Nevertheless, I found myself elated. When I told my parents, claiming I didn't know who the father was, they'd hit the wall and the gin and spent days pressing me to have an abortion.

Maeve handed me beans on toast, knocking the pepper mill on to my plate with an, 'Oops, sorry, Mum,' and sending hot beans into my lap. I quickly scooped them up and dropped them on my plate, then rubbed the stain with kitchen roll.

'Sorry for burning the meal,' I said.

She grinned at me from across the table. 'That's OK.'

I knew she wanted to say she was used to it. My lovely, clever, brilliant, clumsy daughter. Thank God I'd stuck to my guns back then, calmly telling my parents I'd like to have the baby, which I already loved despite its provenance, then go back and finish the degree in a year or so. Mum said did I have any idea how much time and energy goes into mothering, but I'd scoffed. How hard can it be? I'd thought – I found out. My dad announced he wouldn't financially support that plan, and I said OK, and I borrowed money from my sister, packed my things and moved to the safest place I could think of: Ireland.

* * *

We compensated for the food by drinking two bottles of New Zealand's finest, which made Hector more mellow and Maeve more tactile, and around nine, they turned in, leaving me to clear up. I didn't. I helped myself to a Baileys nightcap, and it being so delicious, another. Upstairs, I cleaned my teeth while checking out the mirror.

Lauren Bacall, eh? Perhaps I could go Forties too? I dipped my head, made a side parting and swept mousey-brown, in-need-of-highlights hair across my right eye. Only it wasn't one eye, when I looked in the glass, it was two. There were two left eyes, as well. I may have been drunk but I knew that wasn't right.

THREE

I met Mike in town. Could I recommend a venue for a business breakfast, he'd asked, when waking me with a 7.15 call. Americans, eh? Because I felt like shit, I talked him into brunch at a basic everything-comes-with-toast café, where I now had sauce on my notes.

Isabella Rossoni. Twenty-eight. In the UK since around last July. From small town, North Wilmington, Pennsylvania. Only Mike, Isabella and Grandma left. All other relatives estranged or passed. Grandma ailing now, desperately worried about the missing Isabella, afraid she won't get to see her again before she dies, sent Mike to

UK to search for beloved granddaughter. Arrived six days ago. His wife, Cindy, too busy to join him.

'Where do you and Cindy live?' I asked Mike.

'Oh, we've never strayed far from North Wilmington and my grandparents. Gotta place four miles out now, deep in Amish Country.'

'That must be fascinating?'

'Kind of. And Isabella, she's in the town itself. Used to teach in the liberal arts college. English. Coupla days a week. She didn't need to but got a kick out of it.'

'She stopped, though?'

'Yeah, two, two and a half years back.'

'Why?'

He shrugged. 'Had enough, I guess.'

'And once she got here, how often did you hear from her?'

'Every coupla weeks? She'd call us rather than email. Said it was nicer to hear our voices. Guess she was homesick. Anyways, Cindy, she takes most of our personal calls, since she's a homemaker and I'm often working.'

'You have children then?' I asked.

'Er…' Mike suddenly looked uncomfortable, his eyes darting left and right. I wondered if I'd hit on a delicate subject. 'No,' he said. 'No children.'

'Sorry, I just…'

'Cindy doesn't need to work, not for money. She's involved in several charities, though.'

I smiled approvingly and went back to my notes for a while. 'So... did Isabella send you any of her UK photos?' I asked. 'We might be able to look at them for clues.'

'Strangely, no. I think she felt something of a novice and wanted to hone her skills before going public, as it were. And like I say, we weren't emailing. But, again, I'll ask Cindy if she's gotten any.'

I made a note. 'How about putting more pressure on the police?'

'Seems crazy, I know, but my cousin's recently exceeded her six-month visitor's period. If she's OK, say happy in a relationship or whatever, I don't want to wreck things for her, legally. Cause trouble. Could be she's in hiding from the UK authorities.'

'Maybe that's what this is all about? She's laid low and doesn't want to give herself away by emailing or calling you guys.'

'Yeah, but she coulda written us. An old-fashioned letter. Called from a payphone.'

'That's true.'

Mike had given me two photos of his cousin. One was a posed and formal shot, and in the other grainier one she was outdoors and windswept with a broad smile. Isabella looked nothing like Mike. She had dark hair, a slimmer face and stronger features. Her father, Marco, a second-generation Italian, had owned a restaurant with a club above, which was where all four parents had perished in a fire on Marco's fortieth birthday.

Mike pointed at my grease-filled plate. 'You not eating all yours?'

The very sight of it made me want to retch. That was it, no more drinking. Ever. Me and booze were heading for divorce. Not a trial separation, or let's just try and be friends. We'd end up having a one-nighter and before I knew it the booze would be moving back in, hogging the remote and missing the laundry basket. 'Watching the calories,' I said.

'You're kidding, right? What are you, a hundred ten pounds?' He reached across to my pile of fries, revealing an expensive-looking watch. More bling than I'd have expected of traditional Mike. 'Er, may I?' he asked. 'Full of vitamins, you know, potatoes.'

'Help yourself.' I did a quick calculation, then took a few pounds off. 'A hundred and twenty,' I said, feeling my face warm. I was telling a client my weight?

'Is that all? Reckon I weighed that when I was four. Kinda chunky as a kid.'

I laughed, because he did, and while my blush subsided, I pushed the plate his way. 'OK, back to your cousin. Could you get a copy of her withdrawals since late November to me?' Mike nodded as he munched. 'And I don't suppose luck's on our side and the ATM has a camera? Some do.'

'Not that one,' he said. 'And there are none nearby, far as I can tell. The closest is at the entrance to the big store but the machine's out of range.'

Our plates were taken by a charming guy; a relative, almost certainly, of the Italian founder and owner. The café had been family-run for decades, starting off as a pasta and pizza place, then slowly shifting to an all-day-breakfast menu that students flocked to. If I'd known the circumstances of Mike's parents' demise, I'd have chosen differently.

'Do you have any theories?' I asked. 'Being a Rational Mastermind?'

He looked puzzled, then grinned. 'Oh, that. Shouldna left it on your screen. Makes me sound like a geek. Or a nerd? Never known the difference between those.'

'Isn't a Rational Mastermind just clever and methodical?' I thought about my Ikea desk. 'Likes following manuals?'

He nodded, thoughtfully. 'Guess I am good at that kinda thing.'

No, I decided, inappropriate to ask. I was a bit surprised that he hadn't apologised for using my computer. Maybe it was common practice in Pennsylvania.

Mike gestured to the waiter for another coffee, not knowing you ordered and paid at the counter. 'OK, I'll tell you my thoughts, Edie. First, my cousin would only have stopped communicating with us if she were either under pressure not to, or… if, well, if something had happened to her.'

'You mean, if she's no longer with us?'

Mike flinched.

'Of course there are the cash withdrawals,' I added. 'Those indicate she's alive and well, don't they?'

'That's what I'm praying for, but could be someone's gotten hold of her card.'

'And worked out the pin number?'

'Yeah, I know, but Isabella may've stupidly written that down. Or she could've been forced to reveal it.'

A cup of coffee was placed in front of Mike. 'Just pay on the way out, sir.'

'Thanks,' he said.

Who knew you could do that?

'She wouldn't just disappear,' he went on. 'It's outa character. Good or bad, something's happened to her. Something she's had no control over. A grand passion, or an accident. It kinda makes sense that she's with someone, since no hotel charges have appeared.'

'Or she's staying in places that take cash and don't ask for your card. B&Bs, guesthouses, or some relaxed houseshare.'

'Like the one she was in here? I have no idea why she chose that, when she coulda stayed almost anyplace. Maybe not Bucking Ham Palace, but decent hotels.' He shook his head, as though despairing of her. 'There were roommates, according to Cindy. Could be there was an argument. Isabella has what you might call an Italian temperament. Plus plenty of, you know, *joy de vivra.* Basically, my cousin tends to fit best with your happy, laid-back, easy-going types.'

'You think someone may have upset Isabella and she left in a fit of pique?'

He was grinning again. 'Maybe.'

I got more details from him, such as Isabella's full name, date of birth, mobile number, email, social media, her address in both Oxford and the US and the name of the college she taught at. Plus Grandma's contact details. I asked if Isabella had a boyfriend back home.

'No. Not recently. Not that I knew about.'

'Would she have told you if she'd met someone over here?'

'Yeah, of course. Well, she'd have told Cindy. Like I said, they do the girl-chat thing. Did.' Mike said his wife tended to have her cell phone switched off, which was, 'Annoying as hell, but that's Cindy for ya.'

He told me their home number, which I wrote down then read back.

'Does Isabella have any hobbies?' I asked. 'Apart from photography?' I held up the outdoor photo of her. 'Country walks, for example?'

'I er…' He looked at his shiny watch. 'Listen, Edie, I'm gonna have to split soon. Got another appointment.'

'OK, I'll speed up. Sorry.' Appointment where? I wondered. 'Um, let me see… any friends at home?'

'One or two. There's a Sarah, I think… or is it Susie? Uh, sorry, Edie. I'm pretty hopeless with names. I'll ask Cindy, though.'

* * *

Mike lit up the moment we got outside, taking short puffs as we prepared to go in different directions. The smoke billowed out of his plump lips and shrouded his face, reminding me of the few times I'd seen my mum have a social smoke.

'Where are you staying?' I said.

'Hey, thought you'd never ask.'

Oh dear, bad investigator. 'So long as I have your mobile number and email, I don't need to know where you are.'

'True. It's a charming little hotel on Banbury Road. Great atmosphere and easy to walk downtown.'

'No need for a car.'

'No, no car. I mean… Damn.' He put both hands in the air, as though I had a gun on him. 'OK… ya… got… me.'

'I'm sorry?'

'The parking ticket? My note?'

'Ah.'

'I figured you wouldn't take that amount of cash from me directly, so I disappeared on a pretext.'

'You're right,' I told him. 'I'd have given it straight back.'

Mike cocked his head. 'Oops, I now know that you wouldn't have.'

'What do you mean?'

'You just did that "stating a fact whilst shaking the head" body language thing?'

'I did?'

'Means you're lying.'

'It does?'

Mike dropped the half-smoked cigarette, stubbed it out and pulled his woolly hat down. 'The opposite applies too. Saying no but nodding your head?' He laughed, probably at my expression. 'So, Edie, watch out when you're telling the little white ones. No, your ass doesn't look big, kinda thing.'

I tugged my jacket down over my own. 'Thanks for the tip.'

With a, 'See ya,' and a wave, he trudged off. 'I'll ring you,' he called out, 'mañana.'

'OK,' I said waving, smiling and marvelling at how quickly he'd acclimatised, with his British, 'I'll ring you'. At the end of the street, I stopped, turned around and went back to pay for his coffee.

FOUR

I stayed in town for a couple of hours, looking for warm boots and another good book to move on to. I found the boots but not the book. Lucky then that I had fifty I could reread under my bed; many of them crime novels. In fact, all of them.

Back at the office I made a new doc entitled "Americano" and typed in everything that had happened so far, including my feelings and reactions. What it highlighted, on reading through, was how unsettled Mike made me. I liked him, possibly, but he was definitely in charge. He'd talked me into not bothering with a contract, as he'd already paid me. I didn't even know how much I'd be getting overall, since when I'd brought up my fee, he'd told me not to worry on that front, he'd be passing more my way. 'And I know you Brits find it sordid, talking about money.'

I wasn't about to complain, but carrying chunks of cash around was foolhardy. Yesterday's payment, minus a hundred spent on food, booze and a little package from my man down the road, was scattered around the house. To prevent Maeve happening upon it, a good chunk was in the cupboard under the sink with the cleaning items. Obviously, I intended to deposit all payments in the bank and pay income tax, but I had other things to do first, like visit the Florence Park estate.

I caught a bus on the Cowley Road, which took me from Victorian to Thirties, architecturally. When I reached the address in my hand – a small semi with frosty privet – I, too, wondered why well-off Isabella had chosen this modest accommodation. A pale and bird-like thirty-something woman opened the door. She had a thin nose, lots of strawberry-blonde hair and freckles that joined up. On the end of her black leggings were two tabby-cat slipper boots. She shielded her eyes from the sun and looked me up and down.

'I'm sorry to bother you,' I said.

'Yes?'

I had a business card with my photo on it, inside a leather holder, that I flashed at people, like an LAPD detective. Some examined it, others barely glanced. She was one of the former and peered doubtfully.

'Eddie Fox,' she read out.

'Actually, it's Edie. Edie Fox. I'm a private investigator.'

'Are you licensed?'

'I'm a member of the National Association,' I told her. The National Association of Fibbers. You didn't need to be licensed in the UK, not yet. Sometimes the government made noises about compulsory exams and certification, but if that day ever came, I'd ask for a job downstairs.

She handed back my ID. 'What's it about?'

'Isabella Rossoni?'

Her eyes flickered but that could have been the sun. 'She's not here anymore.'

'I know. Her family's not sure of her whereabouts and I'm helping them find her. We wondered if you'd be able to fill in the picture a little. If it's inconvenient now, I could come back another time?'

She crossed her arms. 'You can come in,' she said, 'but my shift starts at five.' Her accent was local with a hint of whiny. 'I'm Shona, by the way.'

Once inside I took off my snowy boots, as requested, unwound my scarf and unzipped my parka. 'What's your job?' I asked.

She took my things and hung them up, and I followed her slippers into a kitchen-diner full of cats: cat calendar, cat tea cosy, doormat, ornaments galore and two real cats. It was bad, but not enough to make Isabella move out. I held my breath, hoping she wouldn't say policewoman.

'Nurse. I work at the Nuffield Hospital.'

'Orthopaedics?'

'Yes.'

'Do you enjoy it?'

Shona offered me a seat at a table covered in paperwork. I caught handwritten notes and drawings of figures, before she swept the lot up.

'Not when I've got exams,' she said, plonking everything on one chair and sitting on another. 'I'm not sure I'm going to be any help. I've got no idea where she went, or why. I was dead shocked at the time. I mean, she didn't even leave a note.'

'So you weren't here when she left?'

'Away for the weekend. I came back on the Sunday and her room was empty.'

'You must have been quite worried?'

'I was a bit pissed off, to be honest. It just seemed rude, know what I mean?'

'Yes,' I agreed.

'Her rent was all paid, though. You say the family can't find her?'

'They haven't heard from her since the end of November.'

'You mean when she left here?' Shona stared through a window, taking it all in, while I looked around.

'Is this your house?' I asked. 'It's very nice.' It wasn't but it could have been. Places were cheaper in Florence Park than in the heart of east Oxford, plus there was the actual Florence Park with its vibrant borders, miniature golf and original bandstand. If I sold and bought a house there, I'd have money in the bank. A new car.

'Thanks,' said Shona. 'Yeah, I bought it with an ex ten years ago when they were a lot cheaper. Had to buy him out a few years later and that meant taking in lodgers, mostly foreign students. Then I saw Bella's ad in our corner shop. The Londis.'

Again, I wondered why Isabella would have done that, with all her money. 'So, did you spend much time with her when she was living here?'

'Not really. I do these odd shifts, you see, and she was off all over the place with that camera of hers, doing her' – Shona mimed speech marks – '"pro-ject", as she called it.' She pulled a face and smiled apologetically. 'Shouldn't take the mick, in the circumstances. Anyway, she said it was comparing England and America, like different aspects. Sounded interesting, but I never got a chance to see any of her pictures. To be honest, I was either rushing around getting ready for work, or knackered after a shift. Plus, I've got my boyfriend, Matt, living with me. You know what it's like when you're in a relationship.'

I tried to remember. 'Did she share the whole house? The living room too?' I'd glanced in when passing. A mega TV and more cats. 'Did you watch telly together? Eat together?'

'No, we didn't. She'd make something and take it to her room, and it was sort of obvious, I suppose, that the lounge was mine and Matt's. But she didn't seem to mind, not that she'd have said. Feel a bit bad now. It's just that…' She folded her arms, then refolded them the other way. 'Maybe I shouldn't say.'

'Go on.'

She sighed and rolled her eyes. 'I could sort of tell Matt thought she was hot, which didn't exactly make me want us all hanging out. Know what I mean?'

I nodded. Shona was a four or a five, where, judging from the photos, Isabella was a ten. I didn't see Isabella with cats on her feet. 'Did she drive at all?'

'Yeah, she did, occasionally. Mostly, she went places by train or coach, but sometimes she borrowed Matt's car. He pretty much cycles everywhere, and we found we were just using my car. Took her a while to get used to the gears, well, among other things. It was a bit ancient, like twelve years old.'

I wanted to laugh, or cry. I'd have killed for a twelve-year-old car. 'Do you still have it?' I asked, imagining it filled with useful evidence.

'No. Failed its MOT miserably. Matt sold it a few weeks back. Broke his heart, but there you go.'

'So… the weekend she left, she couldn't have driven herself and all her stuff off?'

'Not unless she hired a car, I suppose. She sometimes did that for longer trips. To be honest, she didn't have that much. A taxi would have done the job.'

I made a note to check taxi and car-hire firms. 'And did she ever mention her family?'

'Not that I remember.'

'A cousin called Mike?'

She shrugged. 'Like I said…'

'I know. It's OK.'

Shona kept looking at the wall clock. I needed to get a move on, so took out my pad and galloped through questions. Date Isabella moved in: July 2nd. Visitors: none, but on the phone a lot. Romantic partners: not that Shona was aware of. Names of friends and contacts in the UK mentioned: ditto. General personality: friendly, calm. I asked if mail was still arriving for her, but Isabella hadn't received any at all in those months.

'And did the police ever get in touch with you about her?'

'No? Why?'

'Her cousin said he'd reported her missing at the end of last year, that's all. He felt they weren't taking it seriously, so he's come over to look for her.'

'Oh?' Shona unfolded her arms, scratched her nose, tucked each hand under her thighs and leaned forward. She was on edge, I felt, but then she did have to get to work. 'What's his name?' she asked.

'Her cousin? Mike.'

'And what's this Mike been saying?'

'Only what I've just told you, and some stuff about their family. He gave me your address and asked me to check it out. Said he'd tried calling in, but there's been no one home each time.'

Her hands moved to her lap and clasped each other. 'Well, I'm not going to be able to tell him more than I've told you, so…' Her eyes wandered to the clock again.

There was more to ask. I wanted to know about Matt but Shona was all of a sudden on her feet saying she had to change.

'One last thing?' I said.

'Yes?'

'The weekend you were away, when Isabella left.'

'What about it?'

'Was Matt away with you?'

'No, he wasn't. I went to see a friend in Warwick.'

'Could you tell me this friend's name?'

Shona frowned and her eyes went from side to side. 'Do I have to?'

'No, but…'

She sighed and said, 'It's Nadya, with a *y*. Nadya Erskine.'

'OK, thanks.' I wrote it down. 'So, what, Matt stayed here? In the house?'

'No, he went to his mum and dad's. He came back after I rang him Sunday evening. I was in a bit of a state, wondering if we'd done something to upset her.'

Or if Matt had, I wondered. 'You wouldn't have numbers for both Nadya and Matt's parents? I wouldn't be doing my job properly if I didn't check out…' I wanted to say alibis. 'Everyone.'

She snatched her phone with another sigh and scrolled down. 'This is Nadya's.' I tapped it in as she read me the number. 'But I haven't got Matt's parents', sorry. Never met them. Matt says one day soon we'll go and visit. I don't put pressure on him. Men don't like that, do they?'

Only a certain type of man, Shona. I managed to get her number and Matt's before she started making her way across the room. I got up and thanked her for her help and asked if I could come back some time and look at Isabella's room.

'Do it now, if you want,' she said, 'while I'm changing. It's still empty, apart from Matt's exercise bike. Blokes and their stuff, eh?'

I followed her down the hall and up the stairs, past a gallery. 'Nice cats,' I said, as we ascended. It was like riding an escalator on the Underground, but with kittens flying by. 'Do you know how many you've got?'

'Counting the real ones? About two hundred.' She stopped and looked back at me. 'Matt says it's a cry for unconditional love.'

Matt who ogled the lodger? 'I think you just like cats.'

'Doesn't everyone?'

Five-month Richard didn't. It could have been five-year, or even for-ever Richard, if he hadn't locked Rastus and his litter tray in the shed while I was away. 'All that cat does is take,' Richard had said in his defence, brushing a hand over his very nice rear, 'and moult on the fucking sofa.'

'Here we are,' Shona said, opening the door. 'I'll be ten minutes, so have a quick look and let yourself out the house when you're done.'

'Thanks for your help, Shona,' I said, 'thrusting my card at her. 'Just in case you hear from Isabella, or remember something.'

'OK.'

I was expecting nothing and that's what I got. The room was empty, apart from bed, furniture and the exercise bike. It was nice enough, though. About the same area as my office, which was a good size for a single bedroom, but not for a workplace. There was a narrow, white-painted fire surround, flanked by a wardrobe in one alcove and three shelves above a desk in the other. The bed was a small single. I knelt and looked under it, then lifted the bare mattress and the pillow. One thin pillow seemed stingy. The bedside table had an empty drawer, as did the desk. The chest under the window had three. I looked behind and under all three, then checked behind each curtain. Through the wall I could hear Shona talking quietly on the phone while she changed. Hard as I tried, ear against the woodchip, I couldn't make out her words.

With my back to the window, I tried imagining the Isabella of the photos spending time here. What did she find to do? There was no TV but she could have watched things on a laptop or tablet. Was she lonely, in a strange country with an unfriendly landlady? I guessed a lot of her time had been spent working on the project. Cropping, digitally enhancing, whatever. Maybe some writing.

Who did she talk to on the phone? Mike's wife, Cindy? Expensive to call the States, but then she was super rich. Maybe she'd Skyped friends, telling them how strange the Brits were with their cat slippers and thin pillows. I scanned the magnolia walls and found no desperate jottings – "Help! I'm being stalked and threatened by John Parker, who lives at…"

Shona's freckled face appeared. 'Right, I'm off now.' She looked quite different in her nurse's uniform; more solid somehow.

'All done,' I said, following her down the stairs. 'Thanks.'

I was slipping into boots, doing weather talk with Shona, when a large shadow loomed up to the frosted-glass door and stuck a key in.

I stepped back and in walked a bear of a man I presumed to be Matt, especially when he bent and kissed Shona and said, 'Hello, beautiful.'

Sweat and snow dripped from his face and onto her uniform, but she didn't appear to mind, or even notice. Her cheeks got some colour, her pupils widened, and she was almost beautiful.

'This is… um,' she said. 'An investigator. This is Matt.'

'Hi,' he said.

'Matt works at the Mini plant. He finishes his shift just when I start mine. We get weeks like this, don't we, babe?'

He took off his cycle helmet, then a snug black hat, and handed them to Shona, who put them on a shoe rack.

'Apparently, babe, our missing lodger is, like, really missing.'

'Oh?'

He tugged at a glove, then the other. His reaction felt muted, and I guessed it was Matt that Shona had called. She was in her coat now, holding the door, but I so wanted to talk to her partner.

'You wouldn't have five minutes?' I asked him. 'There are some things I didn't have time to ask Shona.'

Out of all the layers had emerged a very handsome man. He was around six-two, with blondish hair, blue eyes and just enough stubble. A nine. And a half.

'Yeah, OK,' he said, 'if you don't mind me having a quick shower first?'

Only if I could watch. 'Of course not.'

He waved Shona off with a 'Bye, darling. See you in the morning.'

While he was upstairs I had a bit of a nose around: Shona's bizarre diagrams, a dozen cookbooks, a corkboard full of takeaway menus, scribbled phone numbers and Shona's timetable for the week. In less than five minutes, Matt was back, damp-haired and putting the kettle on.

I toured the room once more looking at cats. 'It's quite a collection.'

'It is,' he said. 'Do you take milk and sugar?'

'Just milk, thanks.'

Once we were at the table, I said nice things about Florence Park and asked if it was a good place to live.

'I like it,' he told me. He wore a blue fitted shirt that showed off his shape, and grey jeans. Although we sat at a right angle to each other, he rested the ankle of one leg on the knee of the other, creating an extra barrier between us. His indoor shoes were proper shoes.

'How long have you lived here?' I asked, feeling overly nosy, then remembering I was a detective.

'Since the end of June last year.'

'Just before Isabella moved in?'

'Yes.'

I sipped my very hot tea. It was strong, the way I liked it. 'So, you work at the car factory?'

'I do.'

'On the production line, or…'

'Production.'

'Been there long?'

'Couple of months.'

I waited for him to expand, took another sip. 'I've heard they pay well?'

'It's not bad.'

'What did you do before?'

Matt's ankle started jiggling. Boredom? Irritation? It unsettled me when men did the leg-jiggling thing.

'This and that,' he said. 'I worked on reception at a vet's for a while, which is where I met Shona and her girls. Sporty, Ginger, Baby, Posh and Scary were regular patients.' He pointed at a sleeping Siamese.

'Posh?' I asked.

'Correct. You're here about Bella, though.' My mum would have called him 'nicely spoken'. More Oxford English than Cowley-Oxford English.

'Yes. I've been asked by her cousin to help find her. The family hasn't heard from her since she moved out of here.'

Matt straightened up. 'Her cousin?'

'His name's Mike. I don't know if Isabella ever mentioned him. Mike Smith? They grew up together, after becoming orphaned when both sets of parents had died in a fire.'

Matt looked taken aback, shocked. 'Is he American?'

'Very much so. Apparently, Mike and Isabella's grandma is getting on and she's desperate to see her granddaughter before she passes on. She sent Mike over here to find her.'

'Excuse me,' Matt said.

He got up, went to a cupboard, took out a bottle and a glass and poured himself a shot of something. He knocked it back in one go, then rejoined me.

'Sorry. I got quite chilled coming home on the bike. Oh, er, would you like…' He pointed at the open cupboard. It was packed with bottles. I caught tequila, rum, vodka. 'I make cocktails,' he explained. 'Bit of a hobby.'

'That must be nice for Shona?'

'Not really. She doesn't drink.'

'No? God, I love cocktails.'

'Are you sure you wouldn't like one?'

Of course I wanted one. I stared at a bottle of Gordon's, on the verge of changing my mind. 'No,' I said, 'but thanks.' Better to look professional. 'Anyway… the only piece of information Mike had was this address, so I thought it was a good place to start the search. Shona said you two didn't see a huge amount of Isabella, but I don't know if she ever mentioned people she'd met here in the UK, or particular places she liked?'

'Not that I recall.'

'I'm guessing there were times when you and Isabella were here alone, that's why I'm asking you as well as Shona. Perhaps you and she talked, maybe here in the kitchen?'

He shrugged one shoulder. 'Just polite chit-chat, you know? And not often. I expect Shona told you Bella was always going off places, photographing.'

I nodded. 'Did you see any of her photos?'

'No, she kept herself to herself. She was friendly, but quite a private person.'

'Really?' That hadn't been her cousin's description, but people were multi-faceted. 'Attractive?'

'I suppose so. Why do you ask?'

'Oh… no reason.' I smiled into my mug, deliberately.

'Tell me,' he said.

'I, er, got the impression Shona was a bit jealous?'

'Ah.' He leaned back in his chair, narrowed his eyes, smiled. 'Shona has a vivid imagination when it comes to me and women. Nothing I do or say makes her feel secure. And besides, I don't really go for the Mediterranean look. Bella was gorgeous, don't get me wrong. Just not my physical type.'

I got my notepad out. 'May I?'

'Sure.'

'So,' I said, 'is that what Isabella liked to be called? Bella?'

'She told us her family and friends call her Bella, and she'd like it if we did too.'

'And the weekend she moved out, you were here, is that right?'

'No, neither of us were. Shona was in Warwick and I had a rugby do on the Friday night that sort of morphed into a two-day bender. All a bit of a blur, I'm afraid.'

'Shona said you'd been with your parents.'

'Then why did you ask if I was here?'

'Just doing my job?'

'Fair enough.' He shifted in his chair. 'Yeah, I did tell her that. And I had fully intended to stay with them, but then got this invite… and well, couldn't tell Shona I was hanging out with my rugby mates. She'd have thought there were girls involved, which there weren't. At least, not many.'

'Where do your parents live?'

'Off Woodstock Road. They're both academics, unlike their son.'

Only across town and Shona hadn't met them? 'It's very nice,' I said. 'North Oxford.' Quiet, leafy and filled with Victorian mansions.

'I prefer it here,' Matt said. 'It's more, I don't know, real? As for that weekend, Shona called me on the Sunday evening, telling me Bella and all her things had gone, and I headed straight home.'

'You had no idea she was planning on moving out?'

'None at all.'

'And she hasn't contacted you?'

'No, we haven't seen or heard anything from her since then.'

'Well,' I said, 'I think that's all I need to know for now. Thank you.'

'You're welcome.'

I got a business card out and placed it on the table. 'In case you think of anything else.'

He peered at it and I waited for the 'Eddie' thing.

'Short for Edith?' he asked.

I nodded. 'After my grandmother.'

'Nice name.'

'Thanks. Do you mind giving me your full name?'

'It's Matthew MacNeice.'

'Spelt like the poet?'

'Yes. I believe we're distantly related.'

I wrote it down, together with his phone number, then his mobile rang. Matt took it from his trouser pocket, saw who it was and cut off the call.

'Right,' I said, zipping up my bag and standing.

We walked together to the hall where Matt watched as I self-consciously got into my things.

'So,' he said, 'you're on Cowley Road?'

'I am.'

'Weekdays only?'

'Usually. But I'm always on the end of a phone, if you want to talk or meet up.'

'Come to think of it,' he said, rubbing his chin. 'Bella did show me a photo once, of her and what might have been her cousin. Either brother or cousin, I can't remember now.'

'Did she?' Since she didn't have a brother, it must have been her cousin.

'Yeah, shortly after moving in. You wouldn't happen to have a photo of your client, so I can see if it's the same guy?'

'No, I don't,' I said. It was an odd request and I couldn't see how it would help.

'Just out of interest,' he added, 'and you say there's a grandmother?'

'Yes, Ruth. Lives in Pennsylvania. Isabella's grandparents brought her and Mike up after all four parents were killed in a fire.'

Matt stiffened. 'Christ,' he said, perhaps realising how little he and Shona had known about their lodger. 'And have you arranged to see this Mike again soon? At your office?'

'Not really, but I'm sure I will. Why?'

'I feel bad, that's all. It might be good to meet him and try and help in some way.'

'He could come here?'

'Yeah, yeah. But, you know, we're in and out, doing our shifts. Why don't you text when you're next meeting him and one of us will pop along, if we're free.'

'OK,' I said, reluctantly, puzzled by the sudden keenness to be helpful and worried I might end up getting bypassed.

I reached for the door but his hand beat me to it, and for an awkward but not unpleasant moment, I was nestled in his armpit and smelling whisky.

Well, well, I thought, on the way to the bus. When I'd asked whether he'd known Bella was moving out and if he'd seen her since, Matt had most definitely nodded his head whilst saying no. Either he was lying, and he made daily checks on her under the floorboards, or Mike's nodding-and-shaking theory was complete bollocks.

* * *

Back at my desk I wrote up both interviews, for my benefit rather than Mike's. I'd give him an edited version. I added queries and comments and made notes of things to follow up on, such as Shona's alibi, Nadya, in Warwick. And I made a list of internet searches to carry out, beginning with Bella.

But I couldn't do any of that right then. The adrenaline I'd been running on all day had evaporated, and all I wanted to do was lie in a quiet place and sleep like a psychopath. Apparently, with no remorse, conscience or concern for others' suffering, they fall asleep instantly and rarely toss and turn. When he wasn't incarcerating cats, Richard had done that.

FIVE

I got up early on Wednesday and saw Mike's list of Isabella's cash withdrawals. They were all for either £50 or £100. I'd been expecting a scan of a statement, but maybe for security reasons he'd typed them into an email. The last three were from the machine opposite my office, and the latest had been the previous evening, at 7.24 p.m. I noticed none of the withdrawals had occurred early morning or late evening.

After a shower and some thought I headed straight into town, where I bought thermal underwear from a men's outfitters. I threw in thick socks and a warm hat and gloves, then bussed back to Save the Children and found a large, warm, quilted anorak with frayed seams and cuffs. On arriving at work, I went up to the office and sorted through everything, then typed up a meaningless form on the laptop and printed it out, along with two photos. I called Naz to come up.

He looked horrified at my proposal. 'You mean begging?'

Owing to weak writing skills, and, well, being a boy, Naz had left school with poor A-level results, but his aspirational parents – his father from India via East Africa and mother a British academic – still had high hopes. When not working in the shop, he was retaking through evening classes and being force-fed the *Oxford English Dictionary* by his mum.

'A little extra cash for uni, no?' I dangled long johns and a photo of Isabella in front of him. 'Two hundred for, say, four days, beginning today. Plus what Oscar would have paid you to work in the shop.'

Naz looked underwhelmed. The incentive needed to be big, even for a nineteen-year-old. It was cold and damp out there.

'OK,' I said, 'three hundred to watch the cash machine, very carefully, from a variety of places, again all close by, from say nine in the morning till six in the evening for four days? I think begging will be easiest, and who knows how much people will give you!' I smiled enthusiastically but he didn't.

'And you'll talk to Oscar regarding my absence?'

'I will.'

Naz's body language went from rebellious to thinking about it. 'But if I'm always begging in one location, won't the police arrest me?'

'I suppose they might move you on. In which case, you'll just have to think of something else. Look like you're waiting for a friend.'

'For four days?'

'Or do some pretend browsing, outside the discount shop.'

'I can't spend hours looking at tawdry merchandise.'

'No, no, they've got loads of interesting stuff, Naz. Plates, batteries, poached-egg pans. Smoke alarms.'

'Ha! Would you buy a smoke alarm from there?'

'Of course,' I said. 'I have. And the one in my kitchen works perfectly well.' Daily, I could have added. 'Look, Naz, if you're not interested…'

He gave me a big grin, transforming his face from serious to quite lovely. 'When shall I start?'

'Now would be good?' I took an envelope from my bag and counted out a hundred. 'A quarter now, the rest after four days, unless you spot Isabella and photograph her, and follow her home before then. All inconspicuously, of course. If you pull that off, you might get the full amount and a bonus.'

'Oh, yes?'

'You have to take this task seriously. No moonlighting in the cab. I'm not sure that's even legal. You're nineteen and only passed your test last year.'

'Colin the boss says it's not a problem.'

'I bet he does.' I got up and started pacing. 'So… Isabella. Or rather, Bella. You'll need to look out for disguises. Wigs, dyed hair. A hat or scarf, or both, covering the face.' Sadly, that was every other person in the cold snap. 'Remember the woman in the photos, then concentrate on faces.'

Naz looked at me with hungry brown eyes. 'What size bonus?'

'I don't know… a hundred?'

'Two? If I find her and also where she lives?'

'A hundred and twenty-five.'

'One fifty?'

This was becoming an expensive gamble on a long shot. But, still, easy come, easy go. 'All right.'

'Excellent.'

I gave him my cheap old camera and showed him how to use it.

'But I have my iPhone,' he said.

'No, no, you're meant to be penniless.' I stacked the clothes up in his arms and stuck two copies of the photos on top. 'Ask Oscar for cardboard to sit on, and try to cover your face with a scarf, yeah? Up to about here?' I held my hand below my eyes. 'We don't want your friends spotting you.'

'Or my dad. He'd die with the shame of it.'

'All the more reason to cover up, then.' I directed him to the door. 'Keep me posted.'

'Yes, Miss Fox.'

'Edie,' I said. 'Try to call me Edie.' Eight years ago I'd been his year-six teacher. Life takes strange turns.

'I will, miss.'

I followed him downstairs in order to soft-soap his boss. Oscar said OK but he'd have to pay the remaining staff overtime, and I found myself a further £250 out of pocket. Still, this was barely denting Mike's cash.

At midday I crossed the road and gave the new homeless beggar a pound. 'Fank you, madam,' he said in a pathetic, wobbly voice, and I remembered what a good Navajo chieftain he'd been in my class's assembly. 'You 'ave a lovely day.'

'You too.'

* * *

I popped home to check Maeve had locked up properly and to pick up more cash. On opening the door I saw the usual chaos, made worse by the recent trampling in of wet mud. I remembered a time when the house was an uncluttered joy to return to, back when Maeve was tiny and immobile. The sun always shone and, thanks to my sister Jess, the house smelled of polish and fresh flowers.

Happy days. Jess, bless her, had taken me in when I'd come back from Ireland eight months pregnant, and was with me during the birth. As soon as they saw their week-old granddaughter, my parents melted and forgave me, and so appalled were they by our living conditions that they bought us a house off Cowley Road. They'd just inherited from Granddad Fox, and with prices rising felt it was a good investment. Their plan was that when we moved out, as we surely would, they'd rake in student rent until cashing in at retirement. Three years after graduating, Jess married an Australian doctor and moved to Melbourne, but I never did move out. And my father and his weak heart never did make it to police retirement age. Shortly after he died, my mother packed up and joined my sister on the other side of the world. We Skype.

I stepped over the bills, then wove my way through shoes, boots, clothes, toys, bits of food, a hundred leaflets and a trike. The newel post was a mountain of coats and I had to squeeze past sideways to get on the stairs. Starting at the top of the house, I checked each cash hiding place, then when reaching the final one, under the kitchen sink, where five hundred pounds was layered between J-cloths, I counted out a hundred for Naz and a hundred for me. I paused and stared at the notes, and it suddenly all felt a bit dodgy, this cash. Maybe it was laundered. Was it even real? But then the words 'gift horse' and 'mouth' popped into my head, so I quickly shoved it in my pockets and straightened the J-cloths.

I looked at last night's dishes piled in the sink and decided to tackle them later. According to Hector, who'd not lifted a finger in three months, it was this relaxed approach to housework that made me the successful businesswoman I was.

* * *

Back at the office, I got the landline phone out of my bag and plugged it in. I never left the handset in the office, in case an Australian broke in and decided to call home.

I rang Shona's friend Nadya Erskine, hoping she'd be on her lunch break. If she worked. I just got her voicemail message, in which she sounded a lot like Shona only more upbeat.

Next, I got out the card I'd bought to call the States cheaply. I followed instructions and dialled Grandma's number in Pennsylvania.

'Hello?' came a wobbly voice. 'Is that you, Frank?'

'Ruth Smith?' I asked, and she didn't answer. I told her who I was and that I was working for her grandson, Mike, looking into Isabella's disappearance. I wondered if she'd be so kind as to answer a few questions over the phone, since I was in the UK.

'When will you be home?' she asked. 'Only they haven't delivered the fish and Daddy's coming.'

OK, I thought.

'Frank?' she said, croakily, warblingly. 'Is that you?'

I took stock, then said, 'No, Grandma,' very sweetly. Like Red Riding Hood, only American. I was glad I was alone. 'It's Isabella. Your granddaughter, Bella. I'm calling from England because I know you've been worried about me, Grandma.'

'May I speak with Frank?' she asked. 'I have to tell him about the fish.'

Ruth had a beautifully slow delivery, with vibrato. I could have listened to her all day, but my card wouldn't let me. 'Yes, of course.' I counted to five. 'Hello, Ruth,' I said, now deeper and Frank-like. I hoped she had people dropping in, a carer or neighbour. 'I already have the fish,' I said, 'so please don't worry. I'll see you very soon, my dear.'

The line went quiet, then she hung up.

So, suddenly it was Mike the Bullshitter. His senile gran was more concerned about missing fish than missing granddaughter. Why would he have said all that? To make it appear he'd been sent by someone, rather than coming here on a lone mission? Did he think I wouldn't call her? I tapped my nose with my pen for a while. Perhaps his grandmother had suddenly developed dementia in Mike's absence. No, now I was being silly. I added more to the Americano file, ending with a "WTF?".

Next I got googling.

First Isabella. I typed in her name, the town, the college. There was no mention of her on the college website, but Google told me she'd arranged a talk at the college by an expert on Marlowe in 2009. I tried Facebook; lots with her name, but none were her. Back on Google, I added her date of birth. Nothing new appeared, and there were no references to property at all. I tried "Mike Smith property Pennsylvania" and three tradesmen showed up, all with photos, none of them my Mike. I had no luck with "Michael Smith", either. I should have pressed further for their business name, although Mike had implied they hadn't had one. I included "Isabella" and got all the same results. There was a solitary photo of her in images, and it was the studio shot Mike had given me. It looked as though it had once been on the college's website.

I called the college, and after being transferred twice, ended up with an administrator in the English department. She confirmed that Isabella had taught there. She too referred to her as Bella, but refused to give any personal information, such as anyone Bella was friendly with that I could contact.

'I'm not at liberty to divulge that information,' she said more than once and very politely.

'You don't happen to know if she has a cousin called Mike?' I asked, finally, like a crazed dog digging for a bone.

'I don't have that information,' she said, this time sternly. 'And even if I had–'

'I know, you're not at liberty, blah blah…' I thanked her crossly and ended the call.

I searched for Mike's wife, Cindy Smith and found many, but none in North Wilmington, and none that made sense, age wise, or any other wise. I'd call her, I decided. She'd be a mine of information. Once again I went through the procedure, tapping in the card number, then the number Mike had given me.

‘No route has been found for the number you have dialled,’ said a recorded American male. He pronounced it ‘rowt’. I tried again and got him again. ‘No rowt…’

I found out online that I had the correct country code, and the area code appeared right for North Wilmington, Lawrence County. What Mike had given me was an incorrect landline number, or I’d written it down wrongly. I ought to have asked for her mobile number, even if, as he’d said, she had it switched off most of the time.

I leaned back, stretched, sighed and felt light-headed. Eat, I told myself.

I left the shop with a quick glance Naz’s way, then took a walk along the Cowley Road towards town. Things improved in that direction and the choice of food was almost too much. In the end, I went for a new place called Cat Burger.

It was nice to be eating out without considering the cost, but all the protein and carbs began slowly clearing my foggy head, and I didn’t like what it was thinking. Mike Smith was not Mike Smith. Probably. If you didn’t want to be found online, you’d choose as common a name as you could think of. The work of a Rational Mastermind. He’d been a bit careless with his gran – if she was his gran – but that was something he’d easily wriggle out of. Yes, poor Grandma has a touch of dementia. It comes and goes. A call from a stranger is bound to confuse her.

I dunked fries in ketchup and became more and more fired up. Was there really a wife named Cindy? Had he chosen Cindy Smith because, again, it was common, especially in the States.

Was Mike even Isabella’s cousin? He wanted her found for some reason. And she didn’t want to be found, perhaps for that same reason. I swigged Coke. Mike was a hitman. It was all Mafia-related. The half-Italian Bella had got caught up in something. Mike, who could have been Italian without looking it, was here to take her out. But then what about me? I’d have helped him find her. I ate a chip covered in bloody ketchup. What's more, I'd know stuff. I'd know too much. I dug teeth into the burger. The beef was flesh, my teeth were knives. He'd never let me live. I'd be dead meat.

I got a whiff of cologne before I heard him. 'S'cuse me, ma'am, is this seat free?' I looked up and he grinned. 'I didn't know this was one of your hangouts, Edie? The best burgers in town, don'tcha think?'

I nodded, finishing my mouthful.

Mike took his coat off and hung it on a hook, then sat and perused the laminated menu. 'I'm leaning toward the chicken. You want anything else, Edie?' He was opposite the window, the stark winter sun on his bright white smile.

I dabbed at my mouth with a serviette. 'No,' I said, unable to smile back. I tried but couldn't. My heart raced, the tissue in my hand shook. 'I'm good.'

SIX

'So, got anything for me, Edie?'

Mike had been quiet while eating, either deep in thought or unable to multitask. I didn't mind, since it had given me time to calm down and convince myself that the man opposite, chomping happily and throwing me the odd smile, was who he said he was.

'I called at the house Isabella stayed in,' I said. I'd keep quiet about the 'Bella' thing, and see if he ever called her that, although it might not have been significant. Sometimes a family member can stick with their relative's formal name. I knew a Tom who was still Thomas to his older sister.

'Was anybody home?' Mike asked.

'The owner, Shona. She's a nurse and was about to go on duty, but she let me ask a few questions.'

'And?'

'Apparently, she answered an advert your cousin had put in a Londis window.'

'Londis?'

'A small grocery store. A chain.'

'OK.'

'Isabella moved into the room in early July and spent a lot of time travelling around the country taking photos for her project; sometimes borrowing Shona's boyfriend Matt's car. Which he's now sold, unfortunately. Shona didn't get to see her much because she works shifts at the hospital, and because her boyfriend had moved in just before Isabella did. I think they were a bit couply and Isabella was very much the lodger. When she wasn't away, she tended to stay in her room.'

'Sounds pretty unfriendly, but in some ways that might have suited my cousin. Of the two of us, she was always the quiet studious one.'

That wasn't the impression he'd given before, but I let it go.

'Anyway,' I continued. 'Shona let me look around Isabella's room, which is still unoccupied. Except for the furniture, it was completely empty. No clues, I'm afraid.'

'Find out anything about the boyfriend?'

'He arrived as I was leaving and agreed to have a chat. He works at the car factory making Minis.'

'The Mini? Man, I love that car. You see them in the States sometimes and folks turn their heads and stare. So cool.'

'But also tiny and barely visible to lorry drivers.'

Mike laughed. 'True. Not great for freeways. I had an old Buick called Dammit.'

'Dammit?'

'You know, "Start, Dammit." "No, Dammit, don't cost me more in repairs."'

'Ah.' Old joke but I giggled. 'True?'

'No. I had the Buick, though. My dog, he used to love riding up front with me.'

'You've got a dog? What's his name?'

'Digger. He's long since gone. Kidneys. You like dogs?'

'Yes, but I'm more of a cat person.'

'Is that right? How many you got?'

'None now, but I've had three altogether. They all had decently long lives.'

'I'd imagine you're good with them, Edie. Not that cats need a lotta care, I've heard.'

'Oh, I don't know,' I said. 'They vary, but all my cats liked to be stroked, liked sleeping on a bed at night.'

'Spoiled them, huh?'

'Maybe.'

Mike drifted off for a while, perhaps thinking of Digger and the Buick. Once again I found myself liking him. He was easy to talk to and appeared to be interested in what I was saying. Perhaps it was a well-practised technique, but I wasn't sure you could fake warmth and interest to that extent. Maybe you could. Whatever, it worked on me.

'So,' he said, 'did they say anything else about Isabella? Any mention of friends she made in the UK?'

'I asked, but they didn't know of any.'

'And the weekend she moved out, what happened there?'

'They were both away. She was with a friend in Warwick and he had a drinking weekend with friends.'

'Warwick?'

'It's between here and Birmingham. Has a famous castle?'

Mike shook his head. 'Can't say I've ever… Aah, War Wick. War Wick Castle? Yeah, yeah, famous place.' He leaned back and grinned at me. 'So, you gonna write this up for me, Edie?'

I heard a text arrive so took out my phone and tapped on it. It was from Naz.

'I was planning to,' I told Mike, casual as anything, taking in what I'd just read, slipping the phone into a pocket, thinking, too late, that I should have deleted the message. When the second, promised, 'photographic evidence' ding-donged through, I ignored it.

Mike continued to grin but his eyes were on my cardigan, on the pocket. 'I'd be grateful,' he said, 'for all the information you have. Maybe include physical descriptions too, or better still photographs.'

'Photographs?' My heart began pounding.

He cocked his head. 'You take them with a camera?'

'Yes, but photographs of who?'

'I believe that's "whom", Miss Fox.'

'Photographs of whom?'

'Shona and... what did you say his name was? Matt? Might be useful to know what they look like, in case I happen to bump into them.'

'I see,' I said, but I wasn't sure I did. 'Of course. But I expect they'd be fine about you visiting, too, if you wanted to.'

'And maybe I'll do that. As I say, I tried, but if you give me their numbers in your report, I'll call ahead next time. Not that they're gonna tell me anything new.'

'You never know.'

In spite of my protests, Mike paid me again, under the table, then he paid for both our meals. Outside he said, 'You're doing a great job.'

'Thanks. Oh yeah, one thing I meant to ask, Mike. Did Isabella's name ever get abbreviated?'

I wasn't sure if it was the light, or my imagination, but Mike's face seemed to pale. He pulled a woolly hat from a pocket and slowly put it on, down over his ears. 'Not by me,' he said. 'Such a beautiful name, Isabella, and I've known her by that since she was born.'

'But did some people call her Izzie?' I asked. 'Like other family members and close friends?'

He gave me a strange un-Mike-like look. Fearful, quizzical, I couldn't tell. 'Er… yeah, yeah, I believe they did.'

We said goodbye, then once he'd turned the corner with a final wave, my anxiety came flooding back. Weirdly, I felt safe in his presence, but not out of it. As the knot in my stomach grew bigger and more uncomfortable, I remembered I had something that might help with that.

SEVEN

'You remember twenty-month Greg?' I said.

'Before my time.'

I forgot, briefly, how recently half-Danish Astrid and I had met. It was when she and Maeve were pregnant. I'd thought the two of them would end up good friends, but instead Astrid and I were. She was halfway between my and Maeve's age, so it could have gone either way.

'But I've talked about him, right?'

'Was Greg the skirt-chasing compulsive liar?'

'Yep.'

I was in a garden recliner in her big shed, although she called it her workshop. A heater was making it snug, the spliff was making me relaxed. Astrid decorated objects with bits of broken other objects. There must have been a name for it, but it felt too late to ask. She'd take a plate, vase, or other item and then stick things on – bits of broken pottery, beads, thready stuff, coloured glass. It was probably just mosaic. I liked them but couldn't afford one.

Astrid was gorgeous, as was her four-storey Victorian house, her au pair Eva and her three-year-old son Jakob. She also had a kind and charming husband called Jonathan, who ran a solar-panel business. Alfie and Jakob were in the basement den in the house with Eva watching over them. Maeve would call there in a while to pick up Alfie, leaving me free to indulge in a little weed and recover from lunch with Mike.

'What about him?' Astrid asked.

'Who?'

'God, you get stupid on that stuff.'

'I know, it's great.' Normally Astrid would partake, but today she was working on a commissioned vase. It was gold, silver and white and the client wanted it yesterday.

She sighed. 'Greg?'

'Oh, yeah. Well, for so long I was completely taken in by him, believing every lie he told me. Until I cottoned on, and then I believed nothing. He'd say, "I'm just popping out for a paper," and I'd say, "What woman are you secretly phoning?" It's hard to live with that level of paranoia, I tell you.'

'Hard for both of you.'

'I don't know, I think he got off on my neurosis. Made him feel important. But anyway that wouldn't happen now because my new psycho client taught me how to read the signs, the body language that tells you when someone's lying. This is apart from the obvious stuff like touching your nose.'

'So what are they?'

'It goes like this.' I lifted the armrests and inclined a bit. 'I'll ask you a question and you answer it truthfully.'

'Go on, then.'

'Let me see. OK, in light of what we've been discussing, have you always been faithful to Jonathan?'

'Yes, of course,' she said.

'I believe you!' I told her.

'Why?'

'Well, because you nodded yes, while you were saying yes. If you'd shaken your head, and said yes, you'd have been lying.'

Astrid picked up a piece of broken something and inspected it, turning it in her fingers. Then she peered at me from where she was perched on her stool. 'No,' she said, 'I'm pretty sure I shook my head.'

'I know, but I didn't want to say.'

'I'll tell you about it some time.'

'You don't have to.'

She put the piece down and picked up another. 'So who's this psycho client?'

'Mike Smith.' I told her all about him and his missing cousin, from the moment he walked in my office to the lunch an hour ago, when I'd filled him in on Shona and Matt and he'd slipped more cash under the table. I told her how undercover Naz, despite being forbidden his phone, had texted me while I was with Mike to say he thought I should know that Mr Smith had lurked just inside the discount shop, then followed me from the office. 'Naz then sent a photo as proof,' I added.

I told her about not being able to find Mike, his wife, or his business online, and about the wrong number for Cindy and the call to the supposed Ruth Smith. And how everyone, except Mike, called Isabella 'Bella', and how he'd failed the 'Izzie' test. 'But then,' I added, 'when I'm with Mike he's so normal and nice and believable. I don't know. I don't know what I've got myself into, but I wish I hadn't. I really do.'

Astrid had a tube of glue in her hand and a slack jaw. 'Fuck, Edie, you really are a PI now. Jonathan and I had a bet on when you'd be teaching again. I said the summer term, he thought autumn.'

'Ha!'

'But now you've got this juicy case and you could end up dead. You must find that quite exciting?'

Astrid was not only beautiful, with her long ice-cream hair, but, in a uniquely cruel way, perceptive too. She was right. After years of trying to get kids not to write "would of", I was finally living, being the person I was meant to be. A risk-taker, like the girl against the wall at the May

Ball. 'I think Mike's all right,' I said. 'I'm sure he is. I probably haven't been googling properly.'

Astrid looked sceptical. 'There's a reason he chose you, Edie. This Mike. I'm trying to work out why the hell he did, with all his money.'

'Thanks a lot.'

'Think about it.'

I tried, but left it to her. From across the shed, I could almost hear her brain at work. What Astrid did – her craft – had a certain logic and calculation to it, not just artistic flair. She had to get the little broken bits of china, glass, beads, shells and so on, to fit together cohesively and pleasingly. That involved planning and concentration, then problem-solving when it didn't work. She was stubborn and tenacious by character, and rarely gave up on a piece.

'I bet Mike did his research,' she said. 'He found out that you'd only recently set up shop. Asked around. Discovered, somehow, that you were teaching until last summer. Maybe he found the information online?'

'I'm not on the internet, except for the website. No, not true. I do get one mention in an *Oxford Mail* article, from years back, when I took my class to the Pitt Rivers Museum, all in the costumes we'd made. My one internet image and I'm a burnt-out primary teacher dressed as a squaw. Fake plaits, headband with feather.'

'That's hilarious,' Astrid said without cracking a smile. She picked up something tiny with tweezers, placed it on the vase and leaned back to assess the effect. 'Anyway, that would be enough for Mike, if the school was mentioned. He called the school, or the County Council, and found out when you'd left. Then he'd thought, "Aye, aye, got a green one here," and made his move with what he guessed you needed most, a big fat envelope of cash.'

'But why?'

'Exactly.' She concentrated on her vase for a while, then said, 'You need to find out if he really is her cousin.'

'I know.'

'Did you say Isabella had shown Matt a photo of her with her cousin?'

'Matt was a bit vague, but yeah.'

'So why not forward Matt the photo Naz took of Mike earlier? See if the face rings bells.'

'Hey, good thinking.' I got my mobile out and sent a brief message with the photo. 'I wonder if Mike knows where I live,' I said.

'I'd imagine he does. He's probably followed you home. He's seen you pick Alfie up from nursery and take him to the park, then home. It's possible he watches your house.'

'Steady on, Astrid.'

'He could even know you're here… which to be honest' – she put her bits down and wiped hands on a cloth and dried them on her apron – 'worries me.' She slid off the stool like a Nordic fairy princess. 'I'll just go and check on the boys.'

While Astrid was gone I wrote her a note telling her not to worry, it was just my over-active imagination. I left via the side passage and back at home got into bed fully clothed and counted my latest payment. £2,000. I now had just under £5,000, cash, in my home, and I'd done sod all for it. What if Mike were to come and demand it back? It needed to be somewhere else, somewhere safe. Or better still, spent.

I got the laptop out and went on AutoTrader, but several pages in, when my eyes and my heart glazed over, I decided vehicles were boring when you already had one. Did I need a new car to superstore shop? No. And my inconspicuous Ford was perfect for surveillance.

I switched to email and whizzed down the inbox. Maeve, Amazon, my mum, my sister, casales, Netflix… My eyes paused, then reversed. tcasales234@yahoo.com. What the…? I opened it up and saw a couple of short paragraphs with "Best wishes, Terence" at the bottom. Terence Casales! Bloody hell. I couldn't read it, not yet. Not without carbs.

At the kitchen table, working my way through cereal, I thought back to seeing him on the news that one time. He'd been in uniform, in Iraq, looking oddly working class in a beret. But he'd had some high rank and was talking army-speak about Sunnis and Shiites and ambushes and his men. All I could think, as my eyes zigzagged from the screen to a framed photo of young Maeve, was peas in a pod. The eyes, the nose, the colouring. The way his eyelids slanted downwards, just slightly, just like Maeve's.

I made strong tea in a pot and carried a tray back to the bedroom, closing the door just as Maeve and Alfie crashed into the house. I locked myself in, then rang Maeve to say I had a killer headache and needed to lie still and quiet. The subtext being, please don't tell Alfie I'm home, keep the noise down, don't let him come and disturb me. I'd have liked to give him a hug and jealously listened to news of 'Bidget', but maybe later.

'You don't sound quite yourself,' Maeve said. 'Do you want some aspirin?'

More drugs? If she knew what I'd been up to, she'd kill me. 'No thanks, love. I'll be down later.'

I poured tea, settled on the bed and read the email.

> *Hello Edie, I hope you're well? I did a search for you, wondering if you were still in Oxford, and found your website. Edie Fox Investigators? I have to say, that came as a surprise!*
> *I'm writing because my eldest son, Barnaby, is now a sixth-form boarder in Oxfordshire, and, weather permitting, I'll be driving up to see him this coming weekend. I'm aware it's a bit out of the blue, but wondered if you'd like to meet up, perhaps for lunch? I'd fully understand if you'd prefer not to, but would very much like to see you.*
> *Best wishes,*
> *Terence*

He'd added his mobile number. I read it all again, bewildered and perplexed. Why would he very much like to see someone he'd barely spoken to at Oxford? What did he mean, he'd fully understand? Had he spent two decades feeling wretched about the quickie?

Barnaby the boarder. That would fit, I thought. And he'd no doubt be bright. Easy to be when you've had the best education. Maeve had been declared gifted, aged eight, and I'd worried that the state system would let her down and she'd end up bored and on crack aged twelve. It didn't, and she didn't, and by eighteen she was following in her parents' footsteps with a place at Oxford.

I read the email again and found myself melting. It was actually quite a nice message. And Terence had never been that hateful, just the product of his upbringing, like the rest of us. And young. We were all a bit juvenile back then. And from the tone of the email, I began to rather like him. He was, after all, the father of my child, so didn't that make him special? Of course I'd see him. It was time he knew about his daughter. She knew about him, after all.

Maeve had been desperate to meet him for years, but having done her research she was aware of the hazards of confronting a birth father who'd settled and had a family, with no idea they'd had another child. Maeve always said she felt happy and safe and loved with me, and wasn't ready to go through some awful rejection by her father. 'One day,' she'd say, 'when I'm feeling brave.'

Here goes, I thought. I emailed back, saying yes, and which day and what time, and how about lunching somewhere in town. I said how much I was looking forward to seeing him again and signed it with "Edie x x".

But then Alfie was banging on my door, saying, 'Gan! Gan!' and I did really want a hug and to hear about Bidget, and so the email didn't get sent.

EIGHT

Just after seven on Thursday, after a sublime sleep, I read what I'd written, went cold and quickly deleted it. Jesus. How close I'd got to letting a whole load of danger and chaos into my life. Like I didn't have enough with Mike. Astrid had been right, I got stupid on that stuff.

On my way to the kettle I found a text received the previous evening.

> *It may be the same guy as in Bella's photo. I'm not sure. Matt*

Which really wasn't much help.

An hour later I was in the bath, hiding from the world and reading Lawrence Block for inspiration. It was one of his Burglar series. *The Burglar Who Studied Spinoza.* It was great, but it wasn't helping. What I needed was *The Burglar Who Worked Out What the American Was Up To.*

I dropped the book on the floor, closed my eyes and began working through what had actually happened. Mike had chosen me to investigate. He was surprised to see I was a woman. But was he really? Perhaps I had been singled out, as per Astrid's theory. He'd given a made-up name and possibly a made-up wife. He'd told me a sad family history, which left him, conveniently, with only one senile grandmother and one missing cousin. Most of the details he fed me about Isabella checked out – her former job, her address in Oxford, the photography – but he was hazy on personal stuff. Considering how close to one another they supposedly lived, I'd have expected Mike to know who Isabella hung out with and the reason she'd left her job. However, unlike everyone else, she did actually exist.

What he'd almost certainly invented were Isabella's communications with him and Cindy – if there was a Cindy – and her cash withdrawals. He'd typed that list, when he could have printed out, scanned or even photographed the actual statements. Perhaps she wasn't using that machine at all. Never had. Which meant I could be wasting Naz's time and my money. On the other hand, Naz had tipped me off about Mike following me, so I'd leave him in place for now.

Either Mike wanted to find Bella, or he wanted to appear to be looking for her. If it was the former, he'd have gone to an established agency with a track record, and he wouldn't have made up lies about cash withdrawals – or he'd have been pushier with the police, presuming he had actually contacted them. Something to check? If the search was only for appearances' sake, why was he handing a low-profile rookie wads of cash with no record of payment?

It was all too odd and it was hurting my head. I was beginning to feel overwhelmed and worried that I didn't have the right skills, instincts, or more importantly, contacts for this business. I could do with a dodgy cop who'd take backhanders to feed me info, plus an IT whizz-kid for hacking, and some sly underhand type who'd deal with bugging and tracking. I needed to Botley-up, but had no idea where to begin.

This had been a mad idea. I wasn't Kinsey Millhone, or Precious Ramotswe. Reading a zillion crime novels wasn't going to make me a hot-shot detective, just as Jane Austen hadn't helped my love life. A private eye, how ridiculous. Astrid had more insight than me, and she was a silly-pot maker. Still, I thought, in an attempt to be rational and unemotional, it would obviously take time to get established. Get the name known and the punters coming in. Get the sodding desk assembled.

Perhaps, I thought, it was time to go to the police with this. Get them looking into both Isabella and Mike. I could work alongside them; be useful, but not have all the responsibility.

A bang on the door made me jump.

'Mum, your new hot-sounding American boyfriend's been calling you. Mike? Left a message.'

While she laughed her way down the stairs, I closed my eyes again, took long slow breaths and tried to meditate.

* * *

When I called Mike back, as requested, he didn't pick up, so I left a message saying I'd been in a meeting with a client. I asked him to call again, but he didn't. In fact, I didn't hear from him all day, despite my endless calls. Around ten that night, in a bright chrome-and-white bar in St Clement's, with my third cocktail and well on my way to merry, I tried him again. No answer. I looked at Astrid and shook my head.

'Where's he gone?' I shouted.

'Perhaps Isabella got to him first!' she yelled back, then mimed her throat being cut. She missed my look of horror, while she pulled her coat on and tapped out a taxi number. 'I'll wait outside for it!' she said in my ear. 'Will you be OK?'

'Yeah, yeah.'

Astrid disappeared into the crowd, leaving me with both our drinks. What the heck, I thought, and downed them. This time tomorrow I could be dead in a pool of throat blood.

NINE

When I'd still not heard from Mike by Friday evening, I'd hit the red wine – all alone, unless you counted the sleeping Alfie. As a consequence, I woke up on Saturday feeling rough again. Really, really rough. So much for the alco-divorce. On top of the headache I was horribly sleep-deprived, having woken far too early worrying about Mike. Before going to bed, around one, I'd checked emails and found nothing from him. No calls, texts or emails, and no responses to mine. Mike Smith, I deduced, had either sent me to Coventry or died.

I brewed builder's tea and drank it, then I drank more. It was strong and good. I made another pot. Half an hour later, when I was building a space station in the front room, I reached that inevitable shattered-but-wired stage.

'Don't cry, Gan,' Alfie was saying.

'Sorry, love.' I wiped an eye. Why was Lego so hard these days? 'I'm just not very good at this.'

'Mummy's good at Lego. Can I wake her up now? Pleeeese.'

'But Alfie, it's still very early.' I tugged my phone – his current favourite toy – out of his hands. It was 6.56. That was almost seven, wasn't it? Seven was reasonable, and sod it she was his mother. 'All right, but you might need to give her a big, big shake and make lots of noise.' Maeve had always been a heavy sleeper. 'And, Alfie,' I called out, 'tell Mummy I told you not to.'

* * *

I napped for two hours and sprang from my bed with renewed energy and the determination to find out what the heck Mike was doing. I'd go into the office, despite it being the weekend, and see if he'd left a note. Even if he hadn't, I'd track down the hotel he'd stayed in. Banbury Road, quaint and atmospheric, easy walk into town. I thought I knew the one. I was certain I hadn't offended Mike, so there had to be some other reason for his silence. He'd had his mobile stolen, and his laptop and all other devices. He was in intensive care from all the burgers. Grandma Smith had run off with someone called Frank and he'd had to fly home. Alternatively, having cottoned on to the fact that I suspected he wasn't who he said he was, Mike had done a runner.

I had the hottest of baths as a final detox, dried my hair haphazardly and threw on jeans, a T-shirt and a long fluffy jumper. It was freezing out, so I went for the once-loved purple-puffa-coat-and-Ugg-boots combo. It was Saturday, so what the hell. Everything was topped off with Maeve's pointy Peruvian hat with dangly braids.

I popped into the kitchen and said a goodbye to Maeve and Alfie, who were off to Bristol for two nights to stay with friends. Alfie looked me up and down and asked if I was going to a funny party. I guessed he meant fancy dress.

'Cheeky,' I said, kissing his head.

Maeve told me to enjoy the space and I said not to worry, I would. The truth was, I used to take advantage of Maeve's absences to do things she disapproved of – get wasted, watch romcoms – but since Alfie's arrival I'd tended to clear and clean the house and call her regularly to check they were still alive.

It was a three-minute walk to work, and on reaching the shop I saw not Naz outside the bank but what looked like Emily, wrapped in a blanket and blowing into her cupped hands.

I crossed the road and said, 'Emily? What are you doing? Where's Naz?'

'Oh, he's got pneumonia.'

'What!'

'Or, like, a really bad cold?'

'Oh right. Good. I mean that it's just a cold. So he, what, asked you to stand in here?'

'Yeah. I was supposed to be in the shop today, so Oscar had like a massive strop?'

'I'll talk to him, don't worry. You know what to do here?'

She pulled on a pair of flimsy gloves and nodded. 'Naz gave me the photos of the woman you're looking for?

She's dead pretty, isn't she? I haven't seen her yet, but I know to, like, take a photo with this camera, yeah, if I do? And follow her if I can?'

'That's right. Also…' I took out my mobile and found Naz's snap of Mike. 'Could you look out for this guy too? Let me know if you spot him?'

'The gangstah? Yeah, OK.'

Of course, she'd seen Mike hanging around, then leaving the shop the other day. 'Thanks a lot,' I said. 'Can I get you a hot chocolate or anything?'

'No, I'm cool.'

I noticed the hat beside her. It was filled with coins and there were even a couple of notes, two twenties. 'You're doing well there,' I said. 'That's amazing.'

'I know. I tell the punters I'm like, seventeen, and my stepdad abused me and my mum's a crackhead.'

'That's very creative, Emily.' I wondered if she was an old hand, but she was probably being too careless for a pro. 'Why don't you pocket most of that? Someone might steal it, and you'd probably make even more if you had three miserable coins in there.'

'Don't worry,' she said, 'I was just gonna do that. This old, crippled man gave me most of that lot, just seconds before you got here. Like, two twenties and a whole load of coins.'

'Wow.'

'Said he knew what it was like to go through bad times, and that I should always believe that things would get better.'

'He sounds lovely.'

'He was, he was a really kind old man. We chatted for a bit. He got injured, that's why he's got a walking stick.'

'That's a shame.'

'When he gave me all that money, I started feeling a bit bad. I mean, like I'm not really homeless, am I?'

'That's true, but being generous to you probably made him feel good, so I wouldn't worry.'

Emily lifted her gloved hand and waved at someone.

'Bye, Millie!' a man called out.

'Bye, Terence!' she called back. 'And thanks!'

Terence?

I spun round and saw him leaving the shop with the aid of a walking stick. Terence? Terence Casales? Older, greyer, but definitely him. My heart jammed against my ribs and I quickly turned back. It was the weekend. It was this coming weekend. Shit. Had he recognised me?

'Is that him?' I whispered, mouth drying, knees weakening, pulse racing, perspiration forming under the daft hat.

'Yeah,' she said, waving again.

'Why did he call you Millie?'

'Cos I'm undercover? And cos I like the name?'

I glanced skyward… 'Dad?' I mouthed. 'Tell me what to do?' I looked over my shoulder and saw the lights flash twice on the black car he was approaching. He had a slightly awkward gait and a definite limp, but still moved at quite a pace.

I half turned to watch, a mittened hand covering my face. Was I going to let Terence, father of my child, drive off? He opened the car door but then instead of getting in seemed to reach for something. Next thing, he was upright and the door was shut. The car lights flashed and Terence walked back to the shop, holding what looked like an envelope.

What to do? I decided to let my body make the decision, and it stood perfectly still. It watched him go in the shop and it watched him come out. It watched him get into his car and it watched him drive off. And then it decided to breathe again.

'Bloody hell,' I exhaled.

I hadn't experienced such heightened and mixed emotions since meeting Maeve's flight after her post-Oxford travels. Standing there in Arrivals, all excited, I'd watched her giant tummy come around the corner before her. 'I'm sorry,' she'd said, sobbing on my new outfit. 'I seem to have fucked up the same way you did.'

Terence Casales. Well I never. I felt my chest pound, my stomach was all over the place. To Emily he was a just a generous punter, to me he was the person responsible for my adult life-story arc. To her he was an old man, to me he looked pretty damned good. As good as you could look with a limp and your forties nearing their end. He'd been two years ahead of me. Got a First, of course. But then so had his daughter. Suddenly, I really wanted to tell him that.

I crossed the road and went into the shop with some trepidation. Oscar, manning the till, scowled as he handed me Terence's envelope.

'Oscar, I'm sorry,' I said. 'It was only supposed to be Naz.'

He said nothing, just raised his eyebrows as he packed a customer's items and the queue grew longer. Oscar was a guy of few words.

'Is there anything I can do to help?'

He stopped what he was doing. 'Actually, yes.'

No, please, no. I hadn't meant it. 'What's that?'

He nodded to his left. 'See those crates of Polish bread?'

'You want them on the shelves in the Polish aisle?'

'If you wouldn't mind.'

Polite, but definitely an order. It sounded easy and, really, the least I could do. 'OK.'

'You'll need a gun,' he said.

While I wondered what the neighbourhood had come to, he reached beneath the counter and handed me a large plastic contraption.

'How do I…?'

He sighed heavily and showed me, then gave me a price list. For the next twenty minutes I gradually got into the swing of it: match Polish word on bread with Polish word on list, check price and enter into gun. Fire. Place sticker on bread, place bread on shelf. Repeat. At first I made mistakes and had to peel labels back off items, but I learned to slow down and concentrate. Throughout the task, Terence's letter was pulsating in my jumper pocket. Once finished, I waited until Oscar was busy elsewhere, then placed the gun back under the counter and crept up to my office.

Inside the envelope was no note, just two photos. Of me. In one I was heavily pregnant and walking along the Cowley Road. There was nothing on the back. In the second, I had baby Maeve in a sling, facing forwards. She wore a mop cap and striped tights and looked totally adorable. I turned it over. "I've always wondered", he'd written. And there was his mobile number again.

Who'd taken these? Terence? But hadn't he left Oxford by then and gone to… No, wait a minute, he'd done some postgrad thing. I'd forgotten. Of course, that was why I'd avoided going into town during that last month of pregnancy, when I was back from Ireland, and then with newborn Maeve during the spring and early summer.

But I hadn't managed to avoid him. He'd been secretly taking pictures of me, and not bad ones. I remembered the sling so well. The feel of it, the patches of old baby sick. Both photos had been taken from the other side of the street, but how had I not noticed him? All this time I'd thought Terence had been oblivious, but it wasn't so. He'd always wondered.

Calmness washed over me and I knew what I had to do. I took out my phone and tapped in his number.

'Edie,' he said.

I was already listed? 'Hi,' I said back.

'How are you?' His voice was deeper and more raspy, like he'd smoked or spent time in a desert. Both, probably.

'Fine thanks, and you?'

'I'm well. I take it you got the photos?'

'I did.'

'And my email?'

'Yes. Sorry.'

'I almost phoned earlier but didn't want to appear pushy and intrusive, so this was a last, rather dramatic resort. I'm sorry if I shocked you.'

'You did, but it's OK. Would you still like to meet up?'

'Very much so.'

'Where are you staying?'

'In the prison.'

The old prison was a now a chic hotel with many original features. 'You don't mind the bars on the windows? What if there's a fire?'

He chuckled, deeply, attractively. 'I'm not sure any hotel windows open these days. But listen, I'll come to you.'

'Again?'

'I really don't mind.'

'I look a fright,' I said.

'I always look a fright.'

No you don't, I wanted to tell him. 'I'll wait in the shop.'

* * *

I ran home and changed. Back at the shop, I waited by the entrance, rechecking my face in a small mirror once every thirty seconds. After what felt like an age of nervous pacing, face checking and watching Emily talking to punters, a yellow Mini parked in a loading bay and out got Astrid in a fun-fur coat that matched her hair.

She entered the shop, kissed both my cheeks and said, 'We're completely out of *surströmming*!'

'God, I hate it when that happens.'

'You eat it?' she asked.

'Possibly. What is it?'

'Pickled herring.'

'Only at your house, then.'

'Buy some,' she said. 'It'll do wonders for your complexion. Heard from Mike today?'

'Nope.'

She frowned. 'Isabella may have got in touch, finally. Nice happy ending.'

Had she forgotten what she'd said Thursday night? 'It's possible, but you'd think he'd let me know.'

Astrid checked her watch, as she often did when talking to me. 'I'm going to have to dash,' she said. 'Things to do, a dinner party to organise.'

Another dinner party I wasn't invited to?

She hoicked a capacious yellow bag onto her shoulder; leather, expensive. She never used carrier bags, she'd once said. They made her feel too British.

'That's OK,' I said, full of hurt. 'I'm just waiting for someone.'

She went off to look for herring and I kept an eye out for Terence's car. I wondered if talking to him would bring in a whole new chapter for Maeve, and for all of us. Or perhaps this would just be a one-off, and I'd never see him again. He'd find out, once and for all, about Maeve, and then vanish. Just as Mike had.

As I clocked car after car, I thought back to my lunch with Mike, chatting about cars and his dog, Digger. On top of feeling uneasy about Mike's disappearance, I was quite missing him. Where was he? Had he called in on Shona and Matt and realised he could be doing as good a job as me, if not better? I should call them. At least I wouldn't have to bother getting photos of Shona and Matt for him now. That had been a strange request. A physical description, or better still photographs. 'Shona and… what did you say his name was?' I heard Mike saying. 'Matt?' Had I mentioned Shona's boyfriend's name? Had I actually said 'Matt'? I wasn't sure I had.

No, I told myself, you're wrong. You must, at some point, have referred to him as Matt. A black car pulled up next to the Mini. You're hungover and can't remember clearly. You really must stop the drinking. Really stop. The car door opened and a walking stick appeared. You barely drank when you were teaching. So, what, you think you can't be a private detective without a chequered past, dysfunctional relationships and an alcohol problem? You'll be fine with the first two.

Terence was out of the car now and I finally got a proper look at him. He wore a short brown coat of leather or suede, and a black, grey and brown soft-looking scarf, black trousers or jeans and brown shoes. Everything matched his black, brown and grey hair. He locked the car and walked with the stick, and some awkwardness, towards the shop. It was only then that the nerves kicked in and I suddenly felt queasy about Maeve. What was I doing?

'Edie,' he said, kissing my cheeks. 'You look amazing.'

I doubted that was true but thanked him and led him through the shop, hoping he'd manage the stairs, which he did.

He followed me into my office, stopped, looked around, smiled and said, 'Seriously?'

'Fraid so.'

'It's….'

'Small and ugly?'

'No, no. It's…' He took a step towards the table and pointed at the hole. 'Is that what I think it is?'

'When it gets sunny, I put the parasol up.'

'Even though you're north-facing?'

'How do you know that?'

He grinned, exactly like Maeve. 'One, I'm a guy and therefore have an inbuilt compass. And two, I was in the army.'

'I'm still impressed.'

He went to the window and looked out, perhaps checking on his new homeless friend. It felt uncomfortable, the two of us standing there in my grim workplace. Sort of flat and anticlimactic.

'We don't have to stay here,' I said. 'Let's go somewhere nicer.'

'I'm sorry, Edie. You're upset.'

'Not at all,' I lied. 'It's a bit of a work in progress, that's all. I need to put the Ikea desk together, and then I can start buying orchids and a water cooler, and have modern artwork by young up-and-comings, ha ha.'

'Where is the desk?'

'Down under the stairs.' I pointed, helpfully.

'I'll assemble it, if you like? But not today, I have to see my son later. Tomorrow?'

'That would be fantastic. Are you sure?'

'If you can get someone to carry it up?'

'No problem.'

'Do you have a toolbox?'

'I do.' Along with the house, Dad had given his daughters a fully equipped toolbox and a drill. I'd even used them, until laziness and a salary kicked in.

'Allen keys, just in case?'

'Yep.'

'Now I'm impressed.' When his mouth smiled his eyes joined in, which was disconcerting.

'Do you like burgers?' I asked. It was the one place I might come across Mike. Unlikely, but worth a try.

'Indeed I do,' said Terence. He may have sounded Eton and Sandhurst, but he looked like a deliciously roughed-up Antonio Banderas.

Out on the stairs my phone rang. "Shona", it said.

'I'd better take this,' I told him. 'Sorry.'

'That's fine. I'll be in the shop.'

'Thanks. Hi Shona.'

'Hi,' she said quietly. 'I'm at work, so this'll have to be quick.'

'OK.'

'You said to call if I thought of anything.'

'Go on.'

'OK, well, a few weeks back this man came to the door asking for Bella. Actually, he asked for Isabella. I don't remember the exact date, but I could look it up because we were having a very early Christmas drinks party, me and

Matt, on account of me having to work over the holiday period. I answered the door thinking it was someone arriving late. It was around half eight. The party was meant to be six till eight, but everyone was still there.'

'Did he give a name?'

'No, he just said he was in her photography group, or class or something, and they were wondering if she'd left. The classes, or whatever, were starting up again and she'd always seemed keen, so they were wondering if she was all right.'

'Did she ever talk about this group to you?'

'Never mentioned it, not to me or Matt.'

'Were the classes in the evenings, did he say?'

'Yes, they were. This bloke, he said he'd dropped her off at the house one evening. Said he was passing our house, so thought he'd check on her.'

'And did she go out in the evenings?'

'Occasionally, but usually to see a film, or a play. She was quite, you know, cultured, what with teaching English at a college.'

'Right. I don't suppose this guy left contact details?'

'No.'

'And what was he like?'

'You mean looks?'

'Everything. Can you remember?'

'It's hard. I'd been on the mulled wine, and it was dark outside. I invited him in for a drink but he said he ought to get home. He was in his thirties, I'd say, but you know it's so hard to tell people's ages these days. I look at a patient sometimes, and I look at their date of birth and it doesn't make sense. Anyway, he had this sort of Russian furry hat on, and a scarf, and his collar was up, I think. So there wasn't much to see. He was average size, I suppose, but it was hard to tell because he had a thick jacket on. Oh yeah, I remember he had nice teeth. I noticed them because I'd been to the hygienist that very day, so teeth were on my mind. To be honest, he looked a bit like the guy in the photo you sent Matt.'

'Really?' That couldn't be right, if Mike had only recently flown in. I wandered down the rest of the stairs and into the shop, aware I was keeping Terence waiting. I waved and gestured that I was stuck on the phone.

'Oh yeah, he had a strong Northern Irish accent. My brother married a girl from Belfast, so that's one accent I recognise.'

Not Mike, then.

'We talked a bit about Bella's project, I remember. Well, it was more me doing the talking, what with being squiffy. Anyway, when Matt called out to me, the guy started walking backwards, then he hurried off and shouted, "Sorry to interrupt your party," and that was it. I watched him drive away and thought to myself that was a bit strange. Why hadn't he left a number, like you said, if he wanted her to get in touch. Or details of the new term's classes. He didn't even leave his name.'

'Did you see the car he drove off in?'

'Sorry.'

'And Matt didn't get a glimpse of him?'

'No, he'd gone by the time he got to the door. Listen, I'd better get back on the ward.'

I thanked her and ended the call, then went and found Terence.

'Are you all right?' he asked, while I thought over the conversation. Was there suddenly another person after our Bella?

'Yeah, yeah. It's to do with this mysterious case I'm working on.'

Terence raised one dark eyebrow.

'The plot thickens,' I said dramatically.

'Am I allowed to hear about it, over lunch?'

'I don't see why not.'

Outside, Terence tucked his stick under one arm, put his gloves on and wrapped the scarf around his ears and over his nose. I wondered how tall he was. Five-ten, maybe eleven. He tugged the scarf down under his chin, then looked me directly in the eye and said, 'Is she mine?'

I tried not to appear thrown, although I was, massively. But at least it wasn't going to be the elephant in the room all through lunch. I braced myself, in case he yelled abuse or thumped me. 'Yes,' I told him. 'She is.'

Terence didn't call me names, or hit me. Instead, his eyes welled up and that set me off. For a while we didn't speak, both a bit shell-shocked. An hour ago I'd been skipping to the office concerned only with Mike's odd behaviour. And now this, so unexpectedly. I wanted to give Terence a hug, mainly to stop him getting back in his car and going somewhere to recover, but then he sniffed, pushed his shoulders back and said, 'So. Where to?'

'This way.' I nodded to our left, then glanced at his stick. 'Don't worry, it's only a short walk.'

'I'm fine walking,' he barked, and I suddenly saw the younger Terence. But then he flashed me a smile. 'I'm sorry, but I do rather get that all the time.'

'Sorry,' I said.

'No, I'm sorry,' he insisted, and off we set.

TEN

At midday on Sunday, just a day after the strange reunion with Terence, I found myself, quite alarmingly, heading towards his apartment. Earlier, I'd treated him to brunch to thank him for assembling my desk, and while I'd been putting my coat on he'd suggested I accompany him back to London.

'It would be nice to carry on getting to know each other,' he'd said.

Obviously, my thoughts flew back to what happened the first time I'd been alone with Terence in a secluded spot. 'Um…' I'd said, stalling.

He'd laughed and added, 'Absolutely no strings.'

I'd weighed things up: cleaning my house, or a trip to London with the charming and interesting father of my daughter, plus the chance to check out his home.

I took up his offer and the drive down the M40 had me airing lots of things; not so much about me, more about the Bella case. Things I'd maybe missed or suppressed. Terence was training as a therapist, hoping to specialise in former military personnel, and I'd begun to wonder if he'd been practising his counselling skills to get me to recall things.

'Oh, yeah,' I was saying now, 'then there was Mike's wrist.'

'His wrist?' he asked, as we literally flew past High Wycombe. Once I knew him better, I'd ask him not to drive like a dick.

'Yeah, it was when Mike reached over and pinched some of my fries. I noticed his blingy watch, but what didn't register, until now, were the dark hairs on his arm.'

'And he's not dark-haired?'

'No, blond. But not in a natural way.'

'You're thinking he bleaches his hair?'

'I am. His eyes are dark too, although it's not unheard of to be blond and brown-eyed. His eyebrows aren't dark but he could lighten those too.'

Terence laughed. 'Anything else about Mike that doesn't ring true? Apart from the fact that you suspect he's made up his name, wife, grandma...'

'There's his cousin's name,' I said. 'She told Matt and Shona that her friends and family call her Bella, but Mike always refers to her as Isabella. I put him on the spot and asked if friends and family ever called her Izzie, which as far as I know, they didn't.'

'And what did he say?'

'Actually, he looked a bit… odd, almost panicky. And then he said he thought perhaps people did call her that, only to him she was always Isabella.'

'Which would imply…?'

I felt I was being tested for some investigator's exam, but that was no bad thing. 'It would imply that Mike's seen the name written down, but not heard it spoken in her company, not heard anyone address her. So, I'm guessing he's never met her, not properly.'

'It's possible, I suppose. Do you think he's really American?'

'That's a tricky one. Occasionally, he sounds a bit too American, just as I must have done when I phoned Grandma Smith, pretending to be Bella.' I tittered at the memory. 'And occasionally he'll pronounce something in a Brit way. Like he said "vitamins" once, not "vytamins". All Americans say "vytamins", don't they?'

'I'm not sure. Do it for me, would you?'

'Vytamins?'

'No, do your Isabella phoning her grandmother.'

I looked out of my window, embarrassed now that I'd told him. 'No.'

'Go on.'

'I couldn't. Not without alcohol.'

Terence laughed. 'Later, then.'

'And,' I continued, composed again, 'I still can't work out why Mike would want photos of Shona and Matt. Why not just go to their house again and see them in the flesh?'

'Do you think he ever did call on them?'

'I don't know. He said a neighbour told him Isabella had moved out. Can we assume that he wants to know what Shona and Matt look like, but doesn't want them to see him? I mean, even if he's staked out their place, when they leave the house in this weather they're bound to be wrapped in scarves and wearing hats. Shona's would be some tabby-print affair.' I told Terence about the cat thing. 'Matt thinks it's a cry for unconditional love.'

Terence turned and smiled gloriously. For more than one reason, I wished he wouldn't. One, we were still doing 85, and, two, I just wished he wouldn't.

'I haven't done the women-and-cats module yet,' he said, 'but to me it shouts obsessive-compulsive.'

'Her house was very neat, it's true. Shoes all beautifully lined up. My mum's like that, but I'm the opposite.'

'No kidding?'

'What? Oh, yeah, the office. You should see my house. In fact, no, you must never see it.'

'I hope I will?'

'That might be Maeve's call.'

'True.'

I switched back to Mike again. 'Do you think he's worried that Shona and Matt will recognise him, and not because of some old photo Matt vaguely remembers being shown? They've seen him before, perhaps, not knowing who he was. Do you think he was the photography guy with the Belfast accent?'

Terence shook his head. 'Sounds a bit far-fetched. And if he was the chap from the photography group, he wouldn't need a photo of Shona.'

'Good point. But he might want one of Matt, if he's hoping to follow him without being recognised. I know he's employed me, but he's likely to carry out surveillance of his own. I wonder if that's what he's doing now.'

'I wouldn't worry too much about him going quiet, Edie. I'm not sure PIs are in touch with their clients on a daily basis. I suspect he's leaving you to get on with your search.'

'Yeah,' I said. 'You could be right.'

By the time we'd driven through London and reached Terence's underground parking space, I was almost convinced I should carry on the investigation, with or without communication from Mike. He had paid me, after all.

* * *

'Seriously?' I said, wide-eyed.

'Fraid so.'

'It's…'

I stood taking in the ludicrous amount of space, the oak floors, the original vaulted wooden ceiling, the huge warehouse windows. There was one white sofa in the middle of the, for want of a better word, room. In front of the sofa was a large, square, polished-cement coffee table, and beyond that, some ten or twelve feet away, stood a paper-thin TV as tall as me. There were two abstract sculptures, one black, one white, and on the longest wall, opposite the windows, was a painting remarkably similar to Alfie's, but giant-sized. Around a mile away was a white, white kitchen and white-tabled dining area, and to the side of that, a circular wooden staircase that matched the ceilings and windows. There was another floor?

'It's…' I said, trying to come up with an adjective.

'Ridiculously hip and pretentious?'

'No, no. It's…' I went over to the window and peered out. 'Is that what I think it is?'

'Tower Bridge?' he asked, coming and joining me. 'I have to say, I adore this view.'

'And you've bought this?'

Terence nodded.

'How?'

He grimaced. 'Family money.'

'That's not fair.'

'I know.'

'Your father?' I asked. I imagined some wealthy aristocratic Spaniard, as good-looking as Terence.

'My mother's side. Lancashire cotton mills originally. Made a fortune in lingerie.'

'Huh.'

'Ma fell for a struggling Spanish artist, married him against her family's wishes, and when I was seven, unable to stand the cold, the food and the in-laws, according to my mother, my father left Ireland and returned to Seville.

With appalling timing, I was packed off to boarding school.'

'How sad,' I said, wondering if that early trauma explained his stroppiness at Oxford. I wanted to ask more, but for now just took in the skyline. And while I stood there, soaking up the wealth and privilege, I couldn't help but feel I'd done Maeve out of her rightful childhood; that she could have had so much more. And then I panicked. Once she met Terence and saw the life her half-brothers had led, she could turn resentful. So far we'd been close and happy, but would meeting her rich and really quite nice father drive a wedge between us? It had all been easy up until now, if unglamorous.

'Are you OK?' asked Terence.

'I'm worried about Maeve,' I said, and told him why.

'The truth is, Edie, I wouldn't have been ready before now.'

'No?'

'Too immature and selfish at twenty-two, or, as you put it, an arrogant tosser. Then later, when married and a father to the boys, I wouldn't have dealt at all well with it. My wife's reaction? The army's? No, that would have been a nightmare. It's only been lately, with no wife and no army, and the boys almost grown up, that I've felt in a position to enquire.'

'That makes me feel better.'

'I'm glad. And it sounds as though you've done a terrific job, alone. It's possible I'd have screwed up on a grand scale and Maeve wouldn't be who she is today.'

'You mean a single mother?'

'Maeve's not just a single mother, Edie, but, from what you've said, a great one.'

'True.'

'And on top of that, a first-class Oxford graduate on her way to getting a Masters, then a PhD. Honestly, I really admire you both. Enormously. When I think how easy

Caroline had it with all the domestic help. Au pairs and cleaners and gardeners.'

'Well…' I said, feeling a blush coming on. Was this really the same Terence Casales I'd known – although only in the biblical sense – at Oxford? 'You do what you have to.'

I cringed at the cliché and he laughed.

'Want to see upstairs?' he asked.

'Sure.'

I followed Terence up see-through stairs he obviously found tricky to a wood-floored landing with five doors off it. All closed. Two opened on to dark and shiny wet rooms and three on to spotless and very white bedrooms, all with white-covered king-size beds. I stepped into one and looked around. The walls were bare except for an acoustic guitar, hanging by its strap. 'Whose is this?' I asked, puzzled. It was too tidy to be a teenage boy's room, or possibly any human's.

'Theo's,' said Terence. 'A budding musician.' He hobbled over to what looked like a wall, but which was in fact a row of cupboards with barely discernible grooves where knobs should have been. He slid a door across and revealed a heart-warming jumble of clothes, games consoles, wires, balls, tennis rackets and other boy stuff. 'I've trained them to put it all away,' he explained.

'Ah, well done.' I wish I'd tried that with Maeve, I almost said, but didn't want to paint our daughter in a negative light.

'So…' He slid the door closed and beamed at me. 'Coffee and a slice of something?'

'Yes, please.'

While Terence brewed coffee and defrosted a cheesecake in the microwave, I wandered down to the far end of the flat and poked my nose into his study. The view here was of other buildings, rather than the river, but the room itself was pleasing. Lots of light, a modern chaise longue against one wall and a large whiteboard on another.

Terence was having private tuition to speed up his diploma course. The tutors sometimes came to him, he'd said. I'd have liked a whiteboard to scribble ideas on, but it couldn't be in the office, not where clients would see it.

A photo of two pre-teen boys caught my eye, propped up on the desk, half hidden by a vase of lilies and a landline phone. I stretched an arm over the phone and lifted the framed photo. One of boys, the oldest, bore a strong resemblance to Terence, and the other only a slight one. I guessed he looked more like Caroline, their mother. I'd done an online search for her, but hadn't come across a photo, only the fact that she was a solicitor. I could see bits of Maeve in both boys, so found a photo of her on my phone and held it next to them.

'Yes,' I heard right behind me, 'she's a lot like Barnaby.'

I jumped and apologised for being nosy.

'Don't be silly,' he said with a smile. 'Coffee's ready.'

We sat at a granite-topped island and ate cheesecake and drank strong coffee. Terence told me about his army postings, and how, after a while, the constant moving had negatively impacted family life. 'Caroline dug in her heels, found her dream house in Surrey and made that our base. Better for the boys, of course, but it created a marital gulf that just sort of grew. She resented my rolling up at weekends, or on leave, and disrupting her regime. And then there were the times I was away in combat and would return a little, well, frayed.'

'What a shame,' I said. 'Did you ever consider leaving the army?'

'Occasionally. I knew my mother would support us, should I decide to do something less well paid, or that required training. But, to be honest, as ties to my home weakened, the army became a substitute of sorts. Institutions had been in my blood, remember, from the age of seven.'

How awful, I was thinking, especially for the boys, when Terence suddenly did the gorgeous smile thing. 'Less of this gloomy talk,' he said. 'Tell me what you're going to do about Mike, should he not reappear? Or Isabella?'

I rounded up the last bit of cheesecake with the small fork he'd provided, wondering if Terence had got the whole flat kitted out professionally, right down to cake forks. 'I guess I'll just drop the case. If the person asking me to look for her has buggered off, what would be the point of carrying on the search?' Not entirely true but I didn't want to come across as obsessive.

'Aren't you intrigued?

'Yes, no. I don't know. He's probably found her and hasn't got round to telling me.'

I finished the cake and thanked him, while he stirred his coffee, deep in thought. He was a good person to bounce ideas off. He didn't criticise, or tell me what I should be doing. He got me thinking out loud, which was far more useful. I caught him looking over his shoulder at the wall clock.

'So,' he said, getting off his stool and clearing away our plates, 'what would you like to do before you head back?'

That I was heading back came as news to me. I'd thrown spare knickers and a toothbrush in my bag, just in case, but assumed I'd be the one making the decision, even if the decision had been to sleep in one of the boys' rooms. I tried not to cross my arms defensively, or jiggle a leg, or unknowingly shake or nod my head. I simply smiled and said, 'I'd like to walk off the cheesecake, if that's OK? And maybe grab a bite to eat later, an early dinner? Trains to Oxford run till late.'

'Sounds like a splendid plan,' said Terence. 'I have some work to do for a tutorial tomorrow.'

'Oh, we don't have to do dinner. I can–'

'No, let's. I'd love that. But perhaps an early one. Do you like Thai?'

'I do.'

* * *

Terence ordered me a taxi to take me, not to Paddington, but all the way to Oxford. I'd had three glasses of wine with our early dinner, and was totally fine with being ejected back to Oxford, or so I'd convinced myself. 'No strings' had definitely meant no strings. Perhaps there was a girlfriend he hadn't mentioned and my staying in his apartment would cause problems. Or it was actually to do with the 'pelvic damage' he'd alluded to, when talking about being blown up in Iraq. It could have left him impotent and he was worried I'd jump on him. But this was all very presumptuous of me. The most likely explanation was he just didn't find me that compelling.

'Call me to let me know you're home safe?' he'd asked as he let me out of his building.

Fuck that, I thought, still thirty miles from Oxford and watching endless grey scenery fly by. Once home, I went to bed early in my still-empty house, and out of habit checked the landline beside the bed for messages. Sometimes my mum would leave one, if I hadn't got round to Skyping on a Sunday. But to my surprise, after being told I had a message, I heard Mike's voice.

'Hey, Edie, tried calling you several times the other day to say I was gonna be in Dubai and sorta incommunicado for a coupla days. Spoke to that grandkid of yours once. Cute. Anyways, I called again and left you a message. Kinda odd not to hear back. Thought maybe your cell's playing up, so I'm trying you on this number. Found it on the website. Give me a call, when you can, Edie? Hasta la vista. Soon, I hope.'

I checked my mobile for voicemail messages, but there weren't any. There were, however, several calls from Mike listed for the morning Alfie had been playing with my phone… and presumably deleted the message Mike had left? I vowed my grandson would never touch it again and rang Mike's number. It was only half ten, so he'd most likely still be up.

Not only did I not get through to Mike, but I was told I'd dialled an incorrect number. I tried again and got the same message. Then I hauled my laptop onto the bed and wrote a quick and apologetic email to him, explaining what I thought had happened. But seconds after hitting send, back came a MAILER-DAEMON message. I checked the address and sent it again. Back it came. That was odd. Very odd.

ELEVEN

'No!' Maeve cried, then clapped her hand over her mouth because Alfie had just gone down. 'No!' she whisper-shouted the second time. We were in the front room and she leapt up and grabbed her phone. 'Text me his number? I really want to talk to him!'

'Hey, hey,' I said, 'don't you want to know something about him?'

'Yeah, that's why I want to talk to him.'

'Let me tell you. At least the little I know.'

'But what's to say you won't fill my head with negative preconceptions? He did leave you with a baby to bring up, even though he didn't know about me.'

'Actually, he might have… sort of… guessed.'

'See! You're doing it already! I don't want you telling me he's a prick. He is my dad, after all. Oh wow, this is amazing. Text me his number, please.'

Maeve was at her scariest when spontaneous and determined. I said, 'No,' firmly. I didn't often do that with her. 'Sit down, love, and I'll fetch us both a glass of wine and tell you about my weekend. OK?'

'Aargh,' she said, falling back into the armchair and eyeing my phone on the sofa. I snatched it up and left her staring into the gas fire with manic cobalt eyes.

When I came back, with two safe teas rather than wine, I sat down and told Maeve everything, from Terence's email earlier in the week to the way he'd generously paid for a taxi back to Oxford for me. The only thing I left out was my reaction to being packed off.

'So,' she said, having sat quietly for a while taking it all in. 'I've basically had this quite wealthy dad all this time, who knew I existed, or guessed I was his, and yet he made no contact, and showed no interest and didn't help us financially, until his own perfect little family fell apart?'

'I suppose you could see it that way. But as I told you he claimed he wouldn't have been mature enough initially to take us on, and–'

'Bullshit,' said Maeve, and she got up and left the room.

My stomach knotted as I listened to kitchen noises, then back she came with two glasses of red. She sat crossed-legged in the armchair, looking at the fire and sipping her wine.

'Also,' I continued, 'he thought he might mess things up for you. I don't know, love, people act differently at different points in their lives. For a variety of reasons. Fear, perhaps, in your father's case.'

'You mean cowardice.'

'No, that's different. Fear of doing the wrong thing.'

'So he's weak and indecisive?'

This really wasn't going well. I knocked back wine and said, 'I'd imagine being injured has given him time to reflect on things. And, you have to remember, he didn't know for sure you were his.'

'What, because you were shagging around?'

'Maeve, please. I've told you before I didn't do that.'

'You mean not until after I came along?'

I closed my eyes, wanting desperately to begin this conversation again, or maybe run round to Astrid's for a smoke. I tried putting myself in Maeve's place and felt tears sting at the sense of betrayal and neglect she must be experiencing. I pulled a tissue from a box and blew my nose, while I worked on how to make her feel better. Remind her of how close she and I had been, unlike some of her friends with their parents. Point out that she might have been miserable as an army brat, moving every few years.

'I don't want to see him,' she said, draining her glass and plonking it on the coffee table. She stood up and stretched her arms. 'I'm off to bed. Night.'

'Maeve?' I called out, pointlessly, as she ran up the stairs.

I sat rigidly on the sofa for a while, going over our conversation. 'Shit,' I said. 'Shit, shit, shit.' I went to the kitchen and topped up my glass, then gazed at my stupid self reflected in the window. Why hadn't I just given her Terence's number and left them to it?

* * *

In bed, laptop on the duvet, I checked for emails, and amongst a lot of junk and a message from Mum was one from a guy at Botley International, of all places, suggesting we meet for a mutually beneficial discussion.

> *If there's a convenient time that I might drop into your office, do let me know. Kind regards, Jack Bevington.*

Well, I thought. Mutually beneficial? Perhaps they wanted my help with something. No, ridiculous idea.

I emailed back, saying yes to a meeting, but that I'd rather come to them, if that was all right. This wasn't just self-consciousness about my office. OK, mostly it was. But it would also be interesting to see what a big private investigation outfit looked like, even if it was in suburban west Oxford. I'd checked out the map on their website.

"Excellent!" came a quick and more informal reply. "How about 11 a.m. tomorrow? Directions are on website. Jack."

"OK," I wrote in a similar vein, "see you then! Edie."

I checked the landline for messages – none. I tried Mike's number and it still wasn't available. I tried reading for a bit, then I tried sleeping. But my head was a swirly mix of Terence's pristine bedrooms and Maeve's sad and scary eyes, and Botley International, with its rows and rows of people at desks, covertly listening in to conversations, tracking vehicles on a screen. Men and women flying in and out in long macs with pockets full of devices. One visit to Jack's business and I may well give up on mine. Mutually beneficial. What was that all about?

Excited and nervous, I did begin to wonder if I'd manage to sleep at all. After half an hour, I got up, rolled myself a spliff and smoked it out the window. Then, feeling peckish, I crept downstairs for cereal, listening en route for my daughter sobbing into her pillow. But sobbing into a pillow wasn't Maeve's style. She'd be fine. I'd never known her be cross for more than ten minutes, if that.

TWELVE

Just before eleven, I pulled up outside 14 Noke Road, which, according to the internet, was the business address of Botley International. It was a pebble-dashed semi, like the rest of the houses in the street. Ex-council, I'd immediately thought. Some houses looked uncared for, others had been tarted up by their owners. Number fourteen fell into the second category, and unlike its mirror image next door, had a garage on the side.

Had I made a mistake? I picked up the envelope I'd scribbled directions on, copied from the website. Yes, yes, yes… I had taken all the right roads. I let the engine idle and examined the property. Could it be that this modest façade, with its Venetian blinds and pots of miniature firs, hid an underground labyrinth of offices?

There was no sign of life, not until a young guy appeared from the side of the house, tugging on a suit jacket, then tightening his tie knot. He was tall with dark, vaguely wavy hair and pleasant open features, and as he headed for my car he broke into a smile. I lowered the window.

'Edie Fox?' he asked.

'Yes. Are you Jack?'

'I am.'

I raised the window, switched off the engine, grabbed my bag and got out. We shook hands.

'Thank you for coming,' he said. His voice was as pleasant as his looks. 'Let's go into the office, shall we?'

I locked the car and followed him around the corner to a white half-glazed door between the house and the garage. He used a key to open one of those lever handle locks.

'Excuse the mess,' he said, hitting a switch that lit up a tiny concrete-block room containing a desk covered in paperwork and a large laptop. He opened a fold-up chair and gestured for me to take a seat, then squeezed around the desk and moved an acoustic guitar so he too could sit.

I closed the door behind me and took in the chaos. Were there two Botley Internationals and I'd got the other one?

'We're currently seeking larger premises,' he explained.

We? I wondered, risking the flimsy-looking chair.

Jack reached to his right and twiddled the knob on a convector heater. 'It'll soon warm up,' he told me. 'These things are great.'

I know, I could have said. It was how I heated my office. I undid my coat buttons, feeling overdressed for the occasion. I'd even worn a skirt. 'You wanted to discuss something?'

'I did, I did.' Jack Bevington wriggled in his chair and cleared his throat, then opened the drawer of his cluttered desk. 'I er…' He took out a familiar full-looking envelope.

'I came back from a weekend away and found this on my doormat, hand-delivered and anonymous.'

He passed it to me and I looked inside. I saw a wad of cash and a note, which I pulled out. 'May I?'

'Of course.'

Same writing, I noticed. "There's a PI called Edie Fox" – I flinched at the sight of my name – "contact details below, who could do with your help on a missing woman case. The woman is Isabella Rossoni, known as Bella. Here's a small retainer. I'll be in touch again shortly, telling you where to pick up more cash, which you are to share 50-50 with Edie. Contact her – landline best – and offer your services, particularly the 'specialist' ones you advertise on your website. If she declines, please persist."

There was no signature, but it was clearly from Mike. On top of the shock, I felt insulted, even betrayed. Could he not have mentioned it to me as being a good idea, to join forces with another investigator? Why all this nonsense? I probably would have said yes. Or would I? Maybe Mike thought I'd have said no way am I working with that bunch of crooks, and so he'd changed his mobile and his email, as a way of avoiding the discussion and creating a fait accompli.

'So,' said the smiley young man opposite, looking more like an elongated Alfie than a bunch of crooks. 'Do you know who left it?'

In order to stall, I reread the note and thought about what to do. Tell him? Share the case? Or say no and walk away, then wonder forever what happened to Bella? But was Mike unhinged, and therefore best avoided? Erratic communication, dyed hair… It all pointed to subterfuge, dysfunctionality, danger. The idea of more money appealed, though.

'I need to make a call,' I said.

'Of course.'

Before Jack Bevington could leap up and offer me the room, I made for the exit. Once outside, door firmly shut behind me, I walked to the road and tried Mike's number again. I got the same result: it wasn't available. I tried again, for some reason. More stalling. What to do, what to do. 'Dad?' I whispered, looking up. 'How about a sign of some sort?'

'Are you OK?' called out Jack, and I spun around. 'Would you like a coffee?'

Did I want a coffee? I wasn't sure. I just stood there staring at him; rabbit in the headlights. I ought to say something, I realised, before he thought I was an imbecile he couldn't possibly work with. I was leaning towards a yes to collaboration. Two heads are better than one. And if one of those heads could do a bit of bugging and tracking, all the better. I was also leaning towards jumping in my car and signing up for supply teaching.

'That would be lovely,' I said, and when he went into the house through a side door, I returned to his office for a quick poke around.

I found a lot of handwritten sheet music and a large WH Smith desk diary, which, when I flicked through it, contained no appointments but pages and pages of poetry, or perhaps lyrics. There was an iPod and a card from Dad wishing him "Good Luck with your new business!" Beside the laptop was a messy pile of CDs with handwritten labels on: "Blue Heart Studio Session Oct 16", "Love's a Beach", "Jack and Jill plus misc". Beneath the desk, amid many wires, a music keyboard stood on end. My keen detective's nose told me young Jack was an aspiring musician on the side. Or, looking around at the bare breeze-block walls and the steamed-up door glass, a detective on the side.

* * *

I told Jack everything, and after he'd taken it all in and asked a couple of questions, he picked up a pen and asked for Shona and Matt's address. I then read out various numbers from my mobile and he wrote those down too.

He also tried calling Mike's number and sending him an email, with no luck, obviously.

Jack sat back and tapped his bottom lip with the pen. 'Weird,' he said, leaning forward and dropping the pen on the desk.

'Very.'

'What had you planned to do next?'

I hadn't, so quickly thought on my feet. 'Follow Shona and Matt? I think they know more then they're letting on, especially Matt.'

'But they know you, so that might be tricky. Why don't I surveille them?'

'OK.'

He took a few more details. 'So, how shall we do this? Formal or informal? I mean, have you ever worked in partnership with another agency?'

'Er no. I haven't.

I pointed at his dad's card on the printer. 'I'm guessing you haven't been in business long?'

'A couple of months.'

'And… all that stuff on your website, the services you offer that Mike's keen on?'

'There are devices and services I could access online, but so far I haven't needed them. I've had a couple of errant-spouse cases, which only involved tailing, and one or two potential-employee checks for firms. But that's it. How about you?'

'Ditto. Well, until this crazy client walked in, throwing cash at me.' I told Jack how much I'd received in all.

'No way,' he said with a whistle.

As we finished off our coffees and the two thoughtfully supplied custard creams, I asked him about the music, and yes, it turned out he was more of a hope-filled singer-songwriter than a serious businessman. He told me about his family in Worcestershire, and how he'd lost his mother when he was sixteen and how close he and his dad and sister were. His mum dying had messed up his teens, so he hadn't gone to university and now regretted it. I said it wasn't too late, and told him about Maeve. He asked how long I'd been a single mum.

'Twenty-six years,' I said. 'Although Maeve's father has recently come back into our lives.'

'Cool.'

'For how long, I don't know. He's rather been through it with his other family, not to mention Iraq.' I told him briefly about Terence's injuries.

'We all have our crosses,' Jack said with a shrug.

We agreed that Jack would start following Shona and Matt, and get in touch if he had anything to report, or if he heard anything more from Mike. Otherwise, we'd meet up later in the week. When I stood and buttoned my coat, Jack took the cash from the envelope and made two piles of it.

'A thousand each,' he said, holding out my share.

I almost asked if he was sure; that I'd already had lots from Mike. But I didn't. I took it with a, 'Thank you. Best to follow the instructions of our client, even if he has vanished from sight.' How we'd get information to him was a mystery as mysterious as Mike himself.

I really liked Jack. But driving back along the ring road, I wasn't sure I was going to blindly trust my new partner, since Mike had dented that particular tendency. For all I knew, Jack and Mike were in cahoots in some way. What way exactly, I couldn't imagine. And maybe they weren't. But by going to Jack, Mike had revealed how desperate he was to find Isabella, for good reasons or bad.

THIRTEEN

I was in the children's indoor play centre, up off the ring road; a cavernous, windowless black hole, housing dark purple, dark red and dark blue equipment and virtually no lighting. We'd been there thirty minutes, only it felt like two hours. Alfie loved the place, but only if I went on things with him, which I wasn't always allowed to do. I was currently being kicked off a trampoline by an officious young woman with hair severely pulled into a ponytail. It was like a do-it-yourself facelift. Maybe I'd try it, I thought, as she pointed at a handwritten notice. She watched, dutifully, as we disembarked.

'There's no apostrophe in "adults",' I told her.

She rubbed Alfie's hair, which I felt sure I could report her for, and said, 'Why don't you take Mummy in the ball pit?'

Suddenly I liked her.

'Come on, Gan,' Alfie said, tugging on my reluctant hand. I was sure you could drown in those things and no one would notice. Not in the pitch black.

Maeve was in London lunching with Terence, having managed a change of heart overnight. She'd come downstairs first thing Monday, all bouncy and asking for his number, and before I knew it they'd arranged to lunch at the British Museum the following day, and I'd agreed to collect Alfie from nursery at two. As I worked my way up padded steps and through plastic rope screens and down a short slide into the hideous ball pit, I tried not to think about how it was going for them. What they'd eaten, drunk, talked about. Whether there'd been long awkward silences, or if she'd let off decades' worth of steam. 'Honestly, Dad, all those boyfriends Mum had. I could hardly keep up and I'm not sure she could. Sometimes she'd call them by the wrong name, ha ha. But seriously, Dad, I do think it's scarred me.' A plastic ball hit me in the face, then another.

'Ooh, naughty Alfie,' I said. I'd have thrown one back, lying there on the balls, if I hadn't been clinging for dear life to the rope sides. 'Shall we go soon?'

'No.'

'I'll buy you an ice cream at G&D's?'

'No, Gan. Buy me one here.'

'But they cost a lot here.' Everything did. I heard my phone ringing in the small backpack I'd had to keep with me because notices told me to. That there was a signal in my current location amazed me. I hauled myself up and made my way out of the pit. Luckily, a small boy had joined Alfie in his game and, as is the way with children, and indeed with some men, when something better comes along, I'd become invisible.

The call had come from Jack. I rang him back. 'How's things?' I asked.

'I'm at Bloxham Services.'

'What? On the M40?'

'Yep. Followed Shona and Matt here, then completely lost them. I've been searching the shops, cafés, loos for an hour and they're absolutely not here, but their car still is.'

'They are busy places…'

'No really. They're not here.'

'Are there any other buildings nearby? Isn't there a hotel, or motel, whatever?'

'Yeah, tried that.'

'You mean you searched the hotel bar and restaurant, and asked at reception if they'd checked in?'

There was a long pause before Jack said, 'Yes, Edie. I did.'

'Sorry. Once a teacher…'

'That's all right. Clear communication is good.'

'So… if the car's still parked where they left it,' I said, 'then they'll have to come back some time.'

'I'll stay and watch it, shall I?'

'Is that all right? I'm a bit tied up with… something.'

'So I hear. Where are you, the world's largest kids' party?'

'It's called Mr Playaway.'

Jack laughed. 'Sounds like one of those adultery websites.'

'I wouldn't know,' I said, looking into the gloom, picturing after-work orgies. They'd start once the daytime clients were safely home and getting *In the Night Garden*-ed. That would explain the lighting. I should retrieve Alfie from the balls, I decided. Who knew where they'd been? 'Better go,' I told Jack. 'Let me know if they turn up?'

'I will.'

* * *

Not only had Maeve and Terence got on well, but she'd brought him home with her and given him a name.

'Come and meet Grampy,' she'd told Alfie, as soon as we walked in.

Only half listening, I'd thought she had a new friend round. But when I walked into the front room there was Terence, all good looks and fine clothes, in the oldest and shabbiest armchair, the crust of my late-night bacon sandwich on the table beside him. Worse still was an empty bottle of wine and a solitary glass. There were toys and clothes on every surface and the windows hadn't been cleaned since the Nineties.

'You must be Alfie,' he said. 'Mummy and Granny have told me all about you.'

'Gran,' I said calmly, while wanting to kill him. And Maeve. Mostly Maeve. She didn't see the mess, that was the problem. It wouldn't have occurred to her that this situation might cause me pain. I was tempted to invite Terence upstairs to see how neat, uncluttered and clean my own personal space was, but he was busy throwing Lego together.

'There you are,' he told Alfie, presenting a fully formed tank. He'd had years of experience, of course, with his boys, and the army.

'I'll put the kettle on,' I said. Please don't let him have been in the kitchen.

I left the three of them bonding, while I washed up on fast forward, threw all the wrong things in all the wrong cupboards and answered the door when the bell went. It was Hector, beaming, pupils dilated. I wondered what he was on and whether he'd get me some.

'Is Maeve back from London?' he asked.

'Yes.'

'Can I…'

'Bad time.'

'Hey, Maeve!' he shouted.

God, he was annoying, in his duffle coat and bobble hat; a canvas rucksack dangling from one shoulder, like some throwback radical undergrad. But he wasn't a student, or even employed by a worthy NGO. There was a trust fund, according to Maeve, which was allowing him to write a book on the post-New-Labour right-wing radicalisation of the British working class.

'Hector?' she cried. 'Come and meet my dad!'

'For real?' he asked.

I sighed and let him in. 'Tea?'

Maeve had fallen for her father and she hadn't even seen his home. Or maybe she had. It would be downhill all the way now. I put teas, biscuits and a beaker of juice on a tray and took it to the front room, where Alfie was perched on Grampy's knee and Hector was stroking Maeve on the sofa.

I moved stuff and put the tray down with a 'Here you are!'

When no one responded, I took one of the mugs but could see nowhere to sit, the one free chair being stacked with laundered clothes. The arm of the sofa? I hovered for a while, unnoticed, unneeded, then slipped out of the room.

Back in the kitchen I rang Jack. 'I'm coming to the service station.'

'OK.'

'See you in, what, fifteen minutes?'

'More like twenty.'

'I'll call when I arrive.'

'Cool.'

I left them all a note saying something important had come up, then tip-toed down the hall, jumped in the car and aimed for the ring road. It was churlish of me, I knew.

* * *

I enjoyed motorway driving. I got to listen to Radio Four and my music, and I got time to think. This time, on my race to Bloxham Services, I only did the latter, trying to work out what Shona and Matt were doing, and why. And what Isabella was doing – if she was still alive – and why.

Most days I googled her name, and I'd tried endless missing person sites. I'd called all the local car-hire firms to see if she'd rented something to move house at the end of November, or even since then. I'd tried taxi firms, and none had a record for Isabella's name, or Shona's address. How hard they'd looked, I wasn't sure. Next I was planning on calling a store or coffee shop in her home town and seeing where that got me; hopefully further than the call to her college had. So far, I'd only bookmarked the town's website, but as I drove, I put it on the must-do-tomorrow list in my head.

I parked and rang Jack, telling him where I was, and soon he was in my passenger seat, more casually dressed today and even more handsome. Maeve? I thought. Invite him to dinner?

'Let's get closer to their Citroen,' he said, and I moved us to a spot three spaces along and one row back from a dark red car.

'Any more ideas where they might be?' I asked.

'Nope. The only way out for customers is the entrance. Inside, there are several locked doors that say "private", and you have to tap a number into them. I saw inside one and it was just a cupboard-cum-storeroom. As for the loos, there's no rear exit… if you'll pardon the pun. What you could do is walk into and through the kitchens of the food outlets, and then you'd be out the back of the building where the delivery vans and lorries park, and staff.'

'Shall I take a look around?'

'If you want. I'll go back to my car, in case they reappear and I have to follow.' He pointed to his left. 'Mine's the Audi, two down.'

'OK.'

Having toured the complex, I came to the same conclusion as Jack, that Shona and Matt had either let themselves into a security-coded broom cupboard, or walked out of the building through one of the fast-food outlets' kitchens. One in particular had a view, through an open door, of the kitchen and outdoor delivery area. I went back out the way I'd come in, and through the evening greyness walked around the building to an array of bins, a couple of vans parked beside the doors, and what was probably staff parking. I wandered over to the cars to see if they had permits, but they didn't.

On the far side of the parking area, I spotted a path that led, presumably, to the hotel Jack had checked out. I could see it lit up above a hedge. Thinking I should be thorough, I followed the path through a gap in the hedge, then took a fork to the hotel's entrance. "Welcome to Starlight Inn" said a sign.

I decided against bothering the two young people on the desk, since Jack already had, and wandered across the lobby, following directions to the restaurant and bar. The décor throughout was grey, white and black and dotted here and there were silver stars and the odd new moon. In the lounge-bar area were two groups of guests in armchairs, all middle-aged to elderly. One young guy sat at the bar. Having checked the ladies, I left the hotel through a side exit and soon found myself on the same path back to the rear of the service station.

I was about to go through the gap in the hedge again, when a car pulled into a staff parking space. I stopped and, half hidden by the hedge and the darkness, watched as

Matt and Shona got out; Matt from the driver's side. I didn't know the makes of cars but I knew a white one when I saw it. This wasn't theirs, then. Unless they had two. But then a third person emerged from the back seat. A woman. She was dark-haired and could have been dark-skinned but it was hard to tell in the poor light. My heart stopped. Could it be Bella?

'Bye, Nadya!' Shona called out, as the woman who wasn't Bella headed my way. I stood frozen for a couple of seconds, taking in the approaching grey, black and white uniform. Nadya wouldn't know me, but I didn't want to be ticked off by her for being out of bounds, since I might need to interview her sometime. I spun around and walked back and through the hotel's side door, then out of the main entrance. Weaving my way through lines of vehicles, I finally reached the space where Jack should have been. Shona and Matt's car was gone too.

I got out my phone to call Jack, then decided against it as he'd be driving. There were two texts that I must have missed earlier, one from Maeve and one from Terence, in that order. Was I OK, they asked. I sent them both an apologetic reply saying I was following a lead and would be in touch later.

Terence called me straight back and I let it ring. Although he'd been useful to bounce ideas off, he was slowly becoming family. Mixing family and work were never a good idea, as I'd discovered the one term I'd taught at Maeve's school.

I listened to his message.

'Hi Edie, where are you? I'm so, so sorry about turning up unannounced, but Maeve was rather insistent. You didn't tell me she has a stubborn streak. No, it's not true, she's a wonderful girl, woman, and little Alfie's a delight. I feel blessed, I really do. But we really ought to have consulted you before I visited. Do forgive me, and I hope you won't give Maeve a hard time, as I'm equally culpable. Please call me back, Edie. I'm staying in Oxford tonight, in the prison again, since I'm rather concerned about you, dashing off into the night like that. Call me, please. Bye-bye.'

That was nice. I saved rather than deleted, and then I listened to it again. Such a lovely husky voice. I was about to listen again, when Jack rang.

'I'm following them,' he said, 'but it looks as though they're just heading home.'

'Is your phone hands-free?' I had to ask.

'Only when I drop it.'

I was tempted to hang up but instead told Jack about the three of them arriving in the white car, and Nadya getting out and heading to the Starlight in her uniform. 'If they do this again, we'll need to follow them when they leave in the white car. Nadya's car, presumably. I'll go back now and get the registration and make. Let's meet tomorrow, shall we? Maybe a late breakfast?'

'OK.'

'Is ten too early?'

'No, that's fine. It'll give me time for a run first.'

'Great,' I said, feeling lazy for never having taken up running, the gym, yoga, or any physical activity at all, unless you counted sex, which was very much a past activity.

* * *

As was usual in term time, I had to park two streets away from ours. Couldn't the Victorians have foreseen that students would one day share these small houses with five others and all own Polos? I stayed in the car and called Terence back.

'I've just got home,' I told him. 'Well, almost.'

'Are you OK?' he asked. 'I was worried. The way you rushed off.'

'I got a call from the guy I'm working with now.'

'Oh? Who's that?'

'Jack. He's from another agency. Mike wants us to combine resources.'

'So you've seen Mike?'

'No. Listen, it's complicated. Let's talk about your day with Maeve. How was lunch?'

'Ah…' he said. 'Wonderful.' He went on to eulogise about our daughter, then told me what they'd eaten and what they'd talked about strolling along the South Bank and on the drive home.

He'd driven her home? At the speed he'd driven me to London?

'And as for Alfie,' he went on. 'What an adorable little chap.'

'Yes, he is.'

'I'd absolutely love them to come and visit me, if that would be OK with you? Once little Alfie is used to me, of course. There's so many fun things for kids in London. The aquarium, the parks. Perhaps he'd like the Eye?' I must have gone quiet because he said, 'But listen to me, getting ahead of myself. Sorry, Edie. I'll take it very slowly, I promise.'

'I think that would be best.'

'And if at any point you feel my being around is becoming… detrimental, perhaps–'

'Don't worry,' I said, lightly, cheerfully. 'I'll let you know.'

'Yes,' he said, not quite chuckling. 'I fear you might.'

He apologised again for just turning up, then asked if I'd like to join him for a drink at his hotel. I was tempted. It was only ten to ten. The night was young. But something told me not to be too available.

'To be honest,' I said, 'I'm completely bushed.' I flashed back to trampolines and steep padded ladders. 'It's been a long day. How about meeting up tomorrow, for lunch?'

'Sounds lovely. I'll come to the office, shall I?'

Family and work, I thought. 'No, let's meet in town. The King's Arms at one?'

'OK.'

He said goodnight in his lovely raspy voice. I smiled as I ended the call, turned the engine back on to warm up, then leaned back against the headrest, eyes closed. I heard Maeve proudly introducing her dad to Hector, and Terence looking far too comfortable in our messy home. Was this the end of an era? Me and Maeve, then me, Maeve and Alfie. A unit. Safe and happy. And now there was this disruption, and who knew what would happen. No, no, I was being silly. Worried about my status diminishing. How selfish of me. Terence would add another dimension to their lives. And money, hopefully. That would be welcome. I saw Maeve having no qualms about Alfie going to a private school, and they'd be off on exotic holidays. St Lucia, the Maldives. I had a flash image of our week in Cornwall. Two-year-old Alfie, bored out of his brains in that steamed-up café, singing 'I hear funder' under the table. Somebody else's table. The wettest July on record, they'd said.

FOURTEEN

I realised I didn't want to go home. 'Sorry, Maeve,' I whispered, and knowing Jonathan was away, got out of the car and walked to Astrid's. It was late, but she was a late-type person.

Within half an hour Astrid and I were mildly stoned, not in the shed this time, but in the immaculate showroom she called home. How she did it, I didn't know, but I imagined it took that thing called effort. And maybe a cleaner.

'Let's assume,' she said, tapping a nail on her glass of red, 'that Shona, Matt and Nadya aren't into a threesome thing.'

Since I wasn't Scandinavian, that hadn't occurred to me. 'OK.'

My phone rang, and by the time I'd reached for my bag and rummaged it had stopped. 'Emily,' I told Astrid. A text popped through. 'Call me. Em,' I read out.

'It's quite late,' I said, 'so I probably should.' I sat up, straightened up and braced myself for bad news.

'Hey, Edie,' Emily said.

'Everything OK?'

'Yeah, yeah. Sorry for bothering you so late, only I thought I should tell you.'

'Tell me what?'

'See, I was watching *Midsomer Murders* on the laptop, on like catch-up.'

'OK.'

'I know it's corny and, like, you never see a police station, and thousands of people have been slaughtered in four tiny villages, but it's my favourite programme after *Columbo*.'

'I like it too.'

'Anyway, you know how they don't let you skip through the ads when you watch it online?'

'I do.'

'So this ad comes on for some new floor cleaner mop thing, right?'

'Uh-huh.'

'And they have this bloke cleaning the floor in a suit, like before he goes to work? They're saying this mop's so easy and not messy to use that it wouldn't even splash your business suit. Right?'

If I'd had two free hands, I'd have rolled another smoke, while waiting for the point of Emily's call. Astrid was yawning and checking her watch, then her phone. I wondered if she was expecting someone after my impromptu visit.

'So,' said Emily, 'at the end, he stands holding the mop, all cocky-looking, like he's saying, "What are you housewives moaning about? Cleaning floors is a piece of piss. I can get it done before I go and do a proper day's work." Honestly, men have such a nerve, sometimes.'

'They have.'

'Anyway, he's grinning?'

'Right.'

Astrid was getting out of her chair, either bored or insulted, I couldn't tell.

'And I'm looking at the teeth and the mouth, and the rest of his smug face, and then I'm like what, am I going crazy? I'm thinking, is it really?'

I waited. Astrid was plumping up her cushions, signalling the end of our powwow. 'Was it really what?' I sighed.

'Him. The gangstah?'

'I'm sorry?' I grabbed Astrid's arm as she reached for my cushion.

'What?' she mouthed.

'Mike,' said Emily. 'I know it sounds like seriously like mad, but honestly, Edie, I'd swear it was him.'

'Bloody hell,' I said.

'I think you should watch it yourself and see if you agree? I can pop round like, now, and show you if you want?'

I let go of Astrid and whispered, 'Could Emily from the shop come round? She wants to show us Mike on TV.'

Astrid's eyes twinkled. 'Absolutely. I'm not missing this.' She checked her watch again. 'I might just have to make a call.'

* * *

Emily was standing over us. 'Honestly, you two, don't you realise what drugs do to like your heart and your liver and your... body. And like your brain cells?'

'We do,' said Astrid, 'and we're too old to care. Well, Edie is.'

I nodded in agreement.

'And besides,' continued Astrid, 'research has shown that cannabis can help prevent cancer spreading, decrease anxiety, control epilepsy, relieve arthritic and ulcerative colitis pain, and more relevantly for Edie than myself, slow the progression of Alzheimer's.'

This time I didn't nod. What was she implying?

'Is that right?' said Emily, relaxing her stance and looking for somewhere to put her laptop. 'That's not what they told us when I was detoxing and rehabbing. Maybe I should get some for my nan, cos she's got like all those.'

I took my feet off the coffee table, so she could put the laptop down, then both Astrid and I leaned in towards it, as Emily knelt on the floor, connected to Wi-Fi using the password Astrid had written down, and found *Midsomer Murders*. 'It's buffering,' she said. 'Maybe your broadband's slow?'

'I can assure you it isn't,' said Astrid. 'We are running two businesses.'

'You wanna get it checked out, though.' Emily turned the screen towards us and when the buffering stopped and the programme started, she clicked ahead to the ads. The first was for fabric softener. 'Sorry, can't skip,' she explained. 'They kept showing the same ads over and over, so fingers crossed it's still there.' The second was for 'healthy' kids' drinks – sugar free, aspartame heavy – and then there he was, knotting his tie in the mirror – brown-haired, clean-shaven and besuited.

'Is it him?' asked Astrid.

I nodded. This was weird. Too, too weird. Despite the anxiety-reducing effects of dope, my stomach did a flip.

He was in a kitchen now, looking slimmer than I'd been used to. He didn't speak, he just mopped, with not a droplet of water landing on his shiny black shoes. When he'd finished, the floor sparkling dazzlingly with little stars, the camera panned up to the smug-mug shot; the mop, beside him, now curiously back in its packaging. The mouth, the teeth, the eyes… everything was Mike; all except the hair, which was brown and styled, in that dramatically brushed-forward way that ends with a Tintin peak, fashionable a few years back. I sometimes thought I might have missed a hurricane on the Cowley Road, so much swept-forward student hair was there. It suited him, though. He looked good and a bit younger than Mike, like he'd made the ad some time ago. 'So easy with Soopa Squeezee,' said a southern-English, working-class male voiceover that didn't quite go with the stylish suit.

'Oh. My. God,' I whispered.

'I know,' said Emily.

'Fuck me,' said Astrid. 'That's really him?'

I giggled. It was a kind of release. And I was stoned, of course. Emily giggled too, because she was young and this was shocking and fun. Astrid continued to stare at the screen, pursing her lips.

'Can we watch it again?' I asked. 'I can't make out if the voiceover is Mike.'

'Yeah, I think it might be,' said Emily. 'You know how he says the letter *s*? It's got like a bit of a *sh* sound?'

'Has it?'

'You can hardly notice, but here…'

We watched and listened again. The voice was a shade higher than American Mike's, and yes he did do the slight *sh* thing, and yes, I remembered Mike did it too. The big teeth, I guessed. We watched again, six, seven times.

Emily turned down a drink when Astrid opened a second bottle. 'I don't touch alcohol,' she said, 'these days.' She asked for a fruit juice, which Astrid told her was far, far worse, what with its sugar content.

Astrid tapped her own flat tummy. 'And you can't afford any more weight gain, Emily. As Simone de Beauvoir said, "To lose confidence in one's body is to lose confidence in oneself."'

Emily laughed. 'That's rich, coming from a bloke. All I know is I've never got off my head on apple juice.'

Because she'd been so useful, and because instinct told me she'd be discreet, I filled Emily in on the Bella case. Weed makes me talk more, so she got the whole story.

'That's wicked,' she said, when I'd finished. 'I wonder what DCI Barnaby would do?'

'Who?'

She gave me a disappointed look. '*Midsomer Murders*?'

'Ah, yeah.'

Astrid snorted. 'He'd get the scriptwriters to work it out, of course.' She drained her glass, closed one eye, as though thinking brilliantly, and said, 'The guy from the photography group. Definitely Mike. That's why he couldn't go round to Shona's again. He may be a master of disguise, but he has that distinctive mouth and those worked-on actor's teeth, which, let's face it, are hard to hide.'

'I reckon you need to get in touch with, like, the Soopa Squeezee people,' said Emily. 'See what advertising agency they use. Then the agency might tell you who the actor is?'

'My thinking exactly,' Astrid said.

'Mine too,' I managed.

* * *

'Are you and Terence shagging?' asked Astrid. Emily had gone, as had the second bottle.

I laughed, then told her my theory about his injuries affecting his privates.

'Hmm,' she said. 'Has he mentioned a love interest?'

'No, and I haven't asked.'

'That's not like you, Edie. OK, so… he lives in the coolest of places in whatever they call it, Bankside,

Southwark. And one son is at school in Oxfordshire, but you don't know which school.'

'He hasn't said.'

'And the other is at home with Caroline in Surrey?'

'A day pupil at a private school.'

Astrid nodded and thought for a while. 'Well,' she said, 'I can see why, if he's on his own and desperately lonely in his vast duplex, and possibly unable to have a relationship because he can't get it up, that he'd want to reach out to you.'

I stayed quiet, not sure if I'd just been insulted.

'And Maeve too,' she added. 'They got along today, I take it?'

'Looked like it. He left me a message, said he'd like them to come and stay one weekend soon.' Would I be invited? I wondered. I'd want to be there, of course, to stop Alfie falling in the Thames. That was the worst thing about ageing, worrying about others' safety all the time. No, the worst thing was watching my knees get fatter and wondering why that had to happen, evolutionarily. Bigger laps for grandchildren?

'Are you sure you're up to dealing with all this?' Astrid was asking. 'A missing woman, a creepy and again missing client, and now the father of your child usurping you.'

'I'm not sure,' I said, honestly. 'It's all very... what's the word... different?' I sipped more wine and stared into the middle distance. 'Why exactly did I give up teaching to start a private investigation business?'

Astrid paused and closed her eyes. I knew she remembered everything I'd ever told her, she just had to access it. The eyes opened again, all pale blue and clear-seeing, even after drink and drugs. 'As a teen you wanted to follow in your father's footsteps and join the police, but your mother convinced you that the uniform, and in particular the shoes, would make you a lesbian.'

'Ha! I'd forgotten that.'

'Then, fast-forward several decades, and whilst still teaching, you went to two or three murder mystery weekends, where you had a degree of luck.'

'A detective's nose, the others called it. In the hotel bar.'

Astrid did a slow blink-sigh, which was her version of eye-rolling. 'Plus, you also suffer from an addiction to crime fiction, true crime books and anything on screen containing a dead and mutilated person. And, I hate to say this, Edie…'

No she didn't. 'What?'

'You are quite nosy.'

'Am I?'

'You're always asking people questions about themselves. Haven't you noticed?'

'Well, yes, Astrid, it's called social interaction. Did you have a nice holiday? How's your son doing at uni?'

'You don't think they'd just tell you, if they wanted you to know?'

I laughed. She had, after all, just grilled me about Terence, Maeve and myself. With Astrid, though, it was intellectual puzzle solving, rather than being interested and caring.

'I'd better go,' I told her. It was half eleven and there was washing up to do, and bins to put out and mop makers to contact in the morning.

'Just remember,' Astrid said in her doorway, the hall light creating a religious blonde vision. 'Trust no one. We'd all succumb to evil, if pushed by circumstances.' She tapped at her phone. 'I'm free now,' I heard her say, as the door closed in my face.

FIFTEEN

The following morning Jack and I postponed our brunch so that he could investigate Mike the actor – 'Leave it to me,' he'd said. And then Terence called to say something had come up and he was having to dash back to London. I wasn't disappointed. In fact I found myself smiling and mildly elated after the calls – how blissful not to have to function. I switched off my phone, pulled the duvet over my head and slept until Maeve and Alfie returned from nursery.

After a long bath and a gallon of tea, I was ready to hear Maeve's account of her day with her father. As guessed, it had gone far too well. 'We just clicked,' she said, beaming.

* * *

Jack and I met up two days later for sushi. To me it was like eating raw body parts, but he seemed to like it. I'd spent those days trying various shops in Bella's US hometown, with no luck, and, in disguise, had followed Shona to the hospital and Matt to the factory, twice each. They hadn't repeated the trip to Bloxham Services.

'So,' Jack said, shovelling a bit of knee cartilage in his mouth. He chewed, and chewed some more, and then swallowed. 'Mike goes by the name of Mike Wilder, professionally. Don't know if that's his real one.'

'Sounds made up.'

'It does. Anyway, he missed a three-day shoot in Ireland this week and the agency hasn't been able to get hold of him. Very unusual, according to Marta, the girl I spoke to. Mike Wilder has a reputation for being ultra-reliable, she said. He mostly does adverts and business and training videos, with occasional small speaking parts on TV. We had a nice chat, me and Marta. I told her I'd seen him in an advert and recognised him as my sister's old boyfriend, way back, and that she'd been trying to find him. I said I'd only ever known him as Oscar, on account of his dramatic leanings. A way of getting around not knowing his name.'

'Clever.'

'Marta gave away more than she should have, but that's what my natural charm does to women.'

'This makes sense of him disappearing for those few days, when he gave me the had-to-leave-my-phone Saudi story. He was on a shoot, maybe out of mobile range. Did your natural charm get his address?'

Jack propped his chopsticks on their stand and pulled a notebook from his man bag. 'Lives in Surrey, in a village. Here.' He showed me the address. 'Marta said she really likes him, that they all do, and that they're quite concerned.'

'I think we should check out the address,' I said impulsively. 'Tomorrow?'

'You sure? We'd need to be careful. He might have found Bella and has her prisoner there. He could go on the attack.'

'That's true. But I'm intrigued, I guess, and who knows what we might discover. I don't suppose you found out anything about his past, his family and so on?'

'No, I was supposed to know him, remember. But it might be worth tapping Marta again, maybe even owning up.'

Jack asked if we could go in his Audi, since it was super comfortable and if Mike had been watching us recently, he'd recognise my car.

'As long as you're a safe driver,' I told him.

'Course I am.'

* * *

Later, wearing Maeve's Shakira wig, I sat in my car with a gripping whodunnit; one eye on Shona and Matt's front door. I wasn't expecting anything to happen, and we'd more or less given up on connecting the service station outing to Bella. We felt it best to keep watching them, though. I'd seen them both arrive home within half an hour of each other, which was unusual. I'd jotted down the times – Matt 5.44 and Shona 6.11. It was now coming up to half seven, and I'd promised myself I'd stay until nine. I had a go at a cryptic crossword and didn't do badly, but it was hard to focus on either a book or crossword when I thought I might miss the crucial twenty seconds it would take for them to leave their house and drive off.

It was just before eight, when I was running the engine for warmth, and there they suddenly were, walking down their path, closing the gate and jumping in the Citroen. I panicked, chucked pen, paper and novel onto the passenger seat, strapped myself in and pulled out shortly after they did. I followed them up to the ring road, where at the roundabout they veered off towards the west and north. When they took the turning that led to the northbound M40, I was still close and praying they wouldn't spot me. Suddenly, I was doing real PI work, and it felt both good and bad. I put a music station on to calm my nerves, but it was playing an old Chili Peppers song that reminded me of Bloody Greg. I switched to Classic FM but that was playing Mahler, Richard's hero. What a drag it was being a woman, and therefore having emotional memory. I'd bet my house neither of those exes fell apart when they heard my favourite Verve songs. I hummed *Bittersweet Symphony* while convincing myself I was on a wild goose chase… that Mike Wilder was just a doppelganger, and that Mike Smith had found his cousin and gone back to the States, feeling foolish for having aired his concern to me.

They took the slip road to Bloxham Services and so did I. They parked but I didn't, then when they went into the building through the main entrance, I moved slowly to a spot close to where the white car would appear, if it was going to. In case I was never seen again, I texted Jack and told him where I was and what was happening.

After five minutes or so, the white car crept around the bend. It was still light enough to see there were three passengers. With no training in surveillance, I had no idea how I'd tail them without being spotted. But I knew I couldn't not do it, and soon we were back on the M40 with two cars between us. Whoever was driving did some very last-minute indicating for a turn-off that I'd somehow missed the sign to. I did the same, then had to concentrate hard on the narrow winding roads we were suddenly negotiating, now with no cars between us. Whoever was at the wheel seemed to have the same country-lane competence as me, driving slowly and braking before each bend.

We went through a couple of villages, and then came to one called Middle something, where Nadya, I could see now, took an immediate right into what looked like a modern estate. I turned too, but held back slightly, thinking I could always cruise around and spot the car later. But then she swung abruptly onto the drive of a nearby semi. I parked and quickly turned the engine off, then slumped down in the seat. I could just see them over the dashboard. Nadya got out and stretched, then Matt emerged from the front passenger seat. Shona appeared from the back and before closing her door she scanned the street, looking directly at my car for a while – or so it felt – before helping Matt take several carrier bags out of the boot. The house was lit up. Was it Nadya's, I wondered, and her partner, or whatever, was already there? But no one came to greet them, and it was Matt who led them down a side passage, next to the attached garage, and unlocked the side door.

Well, I thought, getting my phone out to tell Jack all about it.

'Interesting,' he said. 'Maybe it's Nadya's house and she leaves the lights on while she's out.'

'Shona said she lives in Warwick, though.'

'Oh yeah.'

'Unless Nadya's moved. The curtains are closed so I can't casually walk past and peer in, and besides, they might come out at any moment.'

'Right. I suppose all you can do is watch and wait.'

'Yep.'

I told Jack I'd keep him updated and sat in the car for a full forty minutes before the three of them reappeared and I once again slid down in my seat. My car was old enough to have wind-down windows, so I turned the handle until the one beside me was half open. I heard no one calling out 'Bye-bye!' or similar, even though the lights, yet again, remained on.

They drove off and this time I didn't follow. My guess was they were going back to the service station and then home, or in Nadya's case to do a shift at the hotel. No, my plan was to watch the house for a while, see if those lights went off, if there were shadows of anyone walking around, if a cat was put out for the night. Nothing happened, though.

I got out of the car at one point and approached the house, walking purposefully, in case a neighbour was looking. I reached the side door and pretended to press the bell, while I listened out for human occupation. Should the frosted, half-glass door have unexpectedly opened, I'd say I was lost. The inside of the glass was covered by a curtain and there were no gaps to give me even the slightest glimpse. I heard nothing either, so just as casually I walked back to my cold car. At ten thirty on the dot, with ears like frozen shells, I watched the ground floor of the house plunge into darkness. At ten forty-five exactly, the same thing happened upstairs.

I called Jack and we concluded that either a very punctual bed-goer lived there, or the times were a fluke.

'Or,' I added, 'the house is completely empty and the lights are on timers to make it look like someone lives there and is going to bed.'

'Or,' said Jack, 'it could be a double bluff.'

That I had to think about. 'You mean someone is living there, but they're turning the lights of at ten thirty and ten forty-five on the dot to make it look like the lights are on a timer and no one's living there?'

'Just a suggestion.'

'Clever.'

'Thank you. Anyway, are you OK?'

'Better now the car's warming up. I'll head straight home, I think. Are we still going to Mike's tomorrow?'

'Yeah, why not? Investigate all avenues.'

We agreed a time and I strapped myself in and pulled away, passing the house before doing a three-point turn. On my way back I caught something, up in the larger bedroom window. A flicker, then another. It must have been leaking through a gap between the curtain and the window frame. Flicker, it went again. A brief glare. Flicker. A torch? Was someone watching me with a torch? Or was it a reflection? I slowed to a crawl and bent to see through the rear windows, trying to spot a faulty street lamp on the blink. But no… and anyway, it looked more erratic somehow, the flickering. Like a TV, I decided. Or a computer screen. Yes, that was it. Someone was in there, watching a screen. But then, because I was tired and suffering an adrenaline crash, I began doubting what I was imagining. Could you put a TV on a timer, to make it look as though someone was in there… I thought of Jack's double bluff idea, but that just made my head hurt.

SIXTEEN

As Jack whizzed and wove and undertook along the M25, I began to suspect I'd become more timid on the roads as my family had grown. Maeve had slowed me down a bit, Alfie even more. I tuned out my fear and anxiety by thinking about what I'd seen in Middle Thing last night. I felt there had been someone in the house, but couldn't be sure it wasn't all faked for security reasons. It wasn't like I could just ask Shona and Matt. 'Hey, when I was following you guys the other night…'

In an hour and twenty minutes we were entering Langham Green and turning into Field Close, where it finally hit me that we could be taking a massive risk. What if Mike Wilder had been quietly, creepily waiting for us to take this foolhardy course of action?

'You all right?' asked Jack.

'I'm not sure about this,' I said.

'Me neither. Maybe we should send someone he doesn't know. Although I haven't met him, I suspect he watched my movements before putting the package through my door.'

We both groaned at the same time. What exactly had we come here to do? Confront Mike, a potential madman, with what? Pretending to be American? It had been good to put him in context, now we knew who he really was – professionally, at least – but further probing could be irresponsible of me, as a mother, a grandmother and the daughter of a septuagenarian. This all felt too dodgy, and my head filled with nostalgia for my old safe life. Half the class with plimsolls on the wrong feet. The time Bethany wrecked the papier-mâché igloo, showing us how her mum had thrown a chair at her dad. Bradley, with both parents doing time, telling me he loved me.

I took a deep breath and looked around. The cul-de-sac was modern, but not very, and super neat. There were detached and semi-detached houses of varying sizes, with shrubs and creepers and carriage lamps. Someone had gone in for topiary.

Jack checked out house numbers. 'It's that one, four houses down with the green door.'

'OK.' I leaned forward and peered. It was detached and quite large. The front door and garage were painted in a mucky bluey green. Farrow & Ball? I wondered, picturing my own front door that colour, rather than the pillar-box red it had been since Dad painted it when we moved in. Field Close made me feel domestically slovenly, but when your neighbours grew pizza boxes, why bother.

Mike had a small, neat lawn. There were borders filled with winter-dead twiggy shrubs and a couple of holly bushes. The three windows – two up, one down – had semi-closed vertical blinds in them. My heart sped up. Was he watching us through one of those slits?

'I think we should go,' said Jack. 'Let's send somebody else. Do you know anyone who could pose as a meter reader, or something?'

While I thought about this, I spotted a cat sitting by the house, scratching at the front door. 'See that?' I said, pointing.

'Poor thing looks desperate to get in.'

'It does.' I lowered my window and listened out. The cat was mewing, over and over. Scratching and mewing. I looked at Jack. 'I'm guessing Mike Wilder isn't home.'

'What shall we do?'

'I'm not sure,' I said. 'Maybe just sort of cruise by? I could duck down, you could half duck.'

'These windows are tinted, remember. He'd have to have X-ray eyes to spot us.'

'OK, let's do it.' I raised my window, then Jack pulled away slowly and we drifted around the circle of twelve or fifteen houses, observing Mike's place from a variety of angles.

Back at the entrance to the close, Jack pulled over again. We had our backs to the house but watched it through mirrors. No blinds twitched, no lights went on, the door didn't open and a head didn't pop out. The only movement was the cat scratching furiously.

Jack tapped irritably on the steering wheel. 'That's plain neglect, if you ask me.'

'Oh, I don't know, I've had some demanding cats. Ones that whinge and whinge until they hear the tin opener hitting metal. Half an hour later, they're doing it again.'

'But did you see how thin it was?'

I had but I shrugged. 'What can you do?'

'This,' Jack said.

He switched the engine off and got out of the car. Thirty seconds later he returned to his seat and handed me the cat. 'We'll get her some food at the next shop.'

'Jack, I…'

'I'm not leaving her. Sorry. And look, she's already taken to you.' He gave me a peculiar look. 'But then she would. Read the tag on her collar.'

As I stroked at white, black, brown and orange fur, I twisted the silver disc around. "My name is Edie", said the engraving. "If lost please call 01865 612212."

'Isn't that your home number?' asked Jack, but I couldn't speak. 'Edie?'

I was remembering the time Candice smuggled a one-day-old kitten in to show-and-tell and the head had to rush it back to its mother.

'Edie?'

It was odd how children simultaneously loved and abused animals.

'I'm not moving till you say something.'

I turned to Jack and saw him flinch. I probably looked like a white-faced geisha. 'I'm fine.'

'It's just some sick joke of Mike's.'

'Can we just go?'

'We could always give her to Shona.'

'Go!'

'OK.'

We pulled away and turned onto the main road through the village, while the cat, with her bones protruding under her pretty fur, purred contentedly. After we'd stopped and Jack had dashed into a shop and come back with sachets of cat food and a pack of paper plates, we watched her eat noisily on the floor behind my seat.

'She's sweet,' he said. 'Shame I can't have her.'

'Why can't you?'

'Oh… my dad and I co-own the house. Mum had some life insurance, and so we thought we'd put the money to good use. Anyway, Dad's anti pets, wrecking the furnishings and making the place smell.'

'Ah,' I said, half listening, the cat now back on my lap and licking at paws with a cat-food-smelly tongue.

After Jack had cleared away the plate and rubbed the carpet with wet wipes, then got out and binned the lot, we set off for home. I stroked the cat, and while she purred and slept I felt myself calm down. I'd heard pets could do that to you. Oxytocin release. Jack was right, she was sweet. Give her to Shona? I thought not. Having said no to another cat, it looked as though Alfie would have a new playmate.

* * *

'Can we call her Bidget?' he asked. 'Like Bidget at nursery?'

'No.' Bloody Bridget. The child was obsessed. 'Like I said, she's called Edie. You can't just go changing a cat's name, love.'

'Why?'

'Because Edie is the name she answers to. Here, look.' I clapped my hands to get the cat's attention. She was asleep on the laundry pile. 'Edie?' I sang. 'Edie? Hey, Edie?' She remained dead to the world, and no wonder. 'Actually, it's best not to disturb her while she's sleeping.'

'Can she sleep on my bed?'

'Let's ask Mummy, shall we? Tomorrow. We'll leave Edie where she is for tonight.'

Seven o'clock had come and gone, which meant no more CBeebies until the crack of dawn. One terrible day, Alfie would discover you could watch it on iPlayer all evening.

'Time to tuck you up in bed and read you a story, little man.'

Maeve had bathed him early, as she'd been going out with Hector. I got myself, Sniffy and a floppy Alfie out of the armchair and led him by the hand to the door.

'Can I have an ice cream?' he asked.

'Don't be silly, Alfie. I'll warm up a nice cup of milk, as usual.'

'Cats like milk, don't they, Gan?'

'Yes, they do, but not all. We had one once who–'

'Can we give Bidget some?'

'Edie,' I reminded him. 'She's called Edie.'

'Bidget!' Alfie called out, and like a missile the cat flew through the air and landed at our feet.

* * *

I couldn't sleep. Going round and round my head, aside from three glasses of wine, was that conversation with Mike. 'I'd imagine you're good with them, Edie. Not that cats need a lotta care, I've heard…' 'I'd imagine you're good with them, Edie. Not that cats need a lotta care, I've heard…'

Was Bidget – yes, I'd given in – some sort of message? I know you're looking for me, so here's a little something to freak you out and make you stop. Believe me, I'm capable of far worse. Or – a more palatable scenario – Mike Wilder, forced to do a runner and wanting to leave his moggy in safe hands, had used his ingenuity. First he'd brought Jack in on the hunt, in order to support me and prevent me giving up. Then he'd devised a plan for the cat. He couldn't, truly, have predicted that I'd happen upon her on his doorstep, so he'd relied instead on a neighbour or postman contacting me. But forced to do a runner, why? I wondered too why he'd have a cat when he'd often been away on location. Who'd looked after her then, and why weren't they doing it now?

I got out of bed and went downstairs for water, only to find Maeve and Hector having a whispered but heated row. I gleaned enough, by hovering in the hall, to know it was about the planned weekend at Terence's, and Hector's insistence on joining them.

'To repeat,' hissed Maeve, 'I'd like me, Alfie and Dad to do a bit of bonding.'

'But I'm supposed to be your partner,' Hector said, slurring his words. 'We're a unit, you and me… and… and…'

'Alfie?'

'Alfie.'

I walked in, faking a yawn. 'Hi guys. Did you have a nice evening?' Silence. 'Hey,' I went on, regardless. 'Guess what we've got?'

Hector poured some of my wine into a mug and lifted it in an unsteady fashion to his lips.

'Babe, don't you think you've had enough?' asked Maeve.

She was in wide and straight 1940s trousers with rows of gorgeous round buttons down either hip. With a licked finger, she gently rubbed at the wine Hector had splashed on them. Hit him, I wanted to say. Or at least tell him to go home and drink his own booze. And while you're at it, to bring a bottle of wine next time he came to dinner because that was what nice, appreciative people with trust funds did.

'A cat!' I announced.

'Oh, cool,' said Maeve. 'Where from?'

'Long story.'

'Boy or girl?'

'Girl.'

'Where is she?'

'On Alfie's bed.'

'Aw, sweet. I must go and check her out. You coming, Hec?'

He swayed again. 'Course.'

'What's she called?' Maeve said.

I grimaced. 'Alfie named her.'

'Not Bridget?'

'Yep. Well, Bidget. I thought we could sort of morph it into something else, gradually.'

'Like Fidget?'

I laughed. 'Good one.'

'Or Frigid?' suggested Hector, before a ghastly noise left his mouth and he barfed down Maeve's front.

'Arrgh,' went Maeve, backing away. 'Fucking yuck!'

'Shit,' said Hector, still remarkably clean.

When he'd passed out on the sofa and Maeve was showering, and possibly crying, I cleaned up puke on the draining board, cupboard doors and floor, but not before taking a photo of it all, as an incentive for Maeve to dump him.

* * *

Back in bed, having showered, I was now fully awake. Oh, Maeve, I thought. I'd always hoped she'd show better judgement than me when it came to men, but she hadn't got off to a great start, what with Jesus – the guy she'd slept with on her travels, who never replied when she emailed about being pregnant – and Hector. Good strong names, but basically knobs.

I got to thinking of Terence, and my insides did that thing again that I wished they wouldn't. And at my age, too. Would this still be happening in my eighties, I wondered. Meeting someone's rheumy eyes across the wingback chairs, while we all sang …*Baby One More Time* with the staff. It felt adolescent, but perhaps a crush could hit you anytime.

Terence, Terence. Had I been distancing myself from him because of the case, or because my insides did that thing? I got up and went and made chamomile tea, then sat at the table drinking it, listening to fridge noises and trying to ignore the aroma of sick, still in the air despite the bleach.

In bed again I began counting, not sheep, but the loose ends and improbabilities in the crime drama I'd watched earlier.

That worked.

SEVENTEEN

I was in the office, eating the breakfast bap I'd bought next door, waiting anxiously for a call from Naz. He'd taped over the Oxford number on his cousin's vehicle and donned a massive scarf, black-framed glasses and oversized woolly hat, and was pretending to be a called-for taxi at Mike's place in Field Close. Four minutes ago, he'd sent me a text saying he'd arrived outside the house and was about to ring the doorbell, on account, he'd tell Mike, of getting no response from the mobile number he'd been given. There was a chance Mike would recognise Naz beneath the disguise and he'd come to some horrendous harm, and that was why I was nervous. He was a skinny thing, but strong, I suspected, and at least as tall as Mike.

When the phone rang, I jumped. Naz.

'It seems like nobody's home,' he said. 'I looked through the letterbox and there's mail heaped on the floor. Shall I check out the back? There's a low roof I could climb over, between the house and the garage.'

'I don't know,' I said. 'What if a neighbour reports you and the police arrive?'

'You've been here, haven't you, miss? It's pretty isolated. The police would take ages to arrive.'

'Well, OK then, but stay on the phone.' I listened to grunting, clothes rubbing and Naz panting, my fingers crossed on both hands, then after a period of silence, said, 'Naz? You OK?'

'I'm looking through the window into the kitchen,' he said. 'There's a bowl of rotting fruit on the side and two saucers full of crusted food on the floor. Also, there's a vase by the refrigerator filled with dead flowers. It's all a bit spooky, miss.'

'Sounds it. So you think no one's been in the house for some time?'

'I do.'

'Are there any other windows you can look through at the back?'

'Not really, only upstairs. Shall I climb on the sloping garage roof and try the bathroom?'

'No, no, too dangerous. And no time. You'd better get out of there, Naz.'

'Yes, miss.'

I listened to the same noises again, then when I heard Naz open his taxi door and slam it, I began to relax. 'Text me when you're back, and I'll come and pay you.'

'Excellent,' he said and I heard the engine start up.

'Seat belt, Naz.'

'Already buckled, miss.'

'Edie.'

I rang Jack and told him what Naz had discovered and he agreed it was all a bit strange.

'But perhaps he uses other agencies,' I said, 'and something big came up.'

'Or he could have two homes. Say, a base in London that's more convenient for work. Somebody's sofa, even.'

'Then why have a cat?'

'He's a mystery, that's for sure,' said Jack. 'So, how's little Edie?'

'Oh, she's wonderful, and not a scratcher, thank God. Not even the odd gentle nibble. Alfie can practically torture her and she doesn't mind. He calls her Bidget, so we do too.'

The cat, despite fitting in with us immediately, was still puzzling and bugging me. Nothing about Mike made sense, particularly why he'd been searching for Isabella in the first place. And to come up with such an elaborate story, about the fire in the night club, the joint property business and Grandma Smith was ridiculous and unnecessary. Then there was the detailed disguise, right down to posing as a smoker. Had the actor in him got off on the theatricality of it all?

'Shall I pop round this evening?' asked Jack. 'For a chat?'

'Yes, do. In fact, come and have dinner. You can meet Maeve and Alfie.'

'Cool. Tell you what, why don't I make dinner for you all? I miss cooking for someone.'

'That would be lovely. If you're sure? I should warn you that Hector, Maeve's soon-to-be ex, might be there.'

'Warn me?'

'I'm saying nothing.'

Jack laughed. 'I'll be prepared. Speaking of which, I'll bring all the ingredients. Any strong dislikes? Apart from sushi?'

'You could tell?'

'I could tell.'

We hung up and I punched the air.

* * *

'What's that?' asked Hector, in front of the fridge, staring at the photo I'd attached with a magnet. 'Whatever it is, it's er… interesting and quite arty. Did you take it, Edie?'

'I did.'

'Let's have a look,' said Maeve. She put her book down and clomped over in suede peep-toe shoes. When Maeve went retro, I always fantasised about who'd originally worn the skirt, hat, shoes… if she'd worked in a munitions factory, jitterbugged at the weekend, lost her husband in the war, watched the Coronation wearing that very item.

When Maeve got to the fridge she roared with laughter.

'What?' said Hector.

'I think you should give it a title, Mum.'

'Vomit?' I asked.

'Oh,' said Hector, realising. He moved in closer. 'Impressive range, eh?'

The doorbell rang. 'That'll be Jack,' I said.

'I'll go!' sang Maeve, and off she tottered looking stunning.

I'd given her a one-word description of Jack earlier – 'Gorgeous' – and her face had lit up and the lipstick had come out. Now I could hear her talking and giggling in the hall. Maeve wasn't generally a giggler.

I watched Hector's eyes dart from side to side as he listened. 'Who?' he asked.

'My associate, another investigator. We're working on a case together.'

'Oh,' he said, visibly relieved.

But then Jack entered the room, all height and handsomeness and laden with ingredients. 'Hey, Edie,' he said, 'sorry I'm a bit late. I couldn't find tamarind paste, so had to stop off at your shop. Is Alfie OK with spicy food, because I can make something separate for him?'

'That's a kind offer,' said Maeve, 'but I'm about to give him his tea and bath.'

'In that fabulous outfit?'

Maeve flushed. 'It's all right, I'm very careful.' I laughed at that, but she ignored me and waved an arm. 'Oh, yeah, this is Hector.'

Hector tugged the photo off the fridge and said, 'Maeve's boyfriend.'

'Pleased to meet you,' said Jack.

'Likewise.' Hector ripped the picture in two and dropped it in the bin, then turned back and sniggered. 'I hear you're a private dick?'

With perfect timing, Alfie walked in dangling the cat.

'Hey,' said Jack, going over and bending down to toddler height. 'Are you Alfie? I'm Jack. Like in Jack and Jill? Is it right that you're really good at counting now?'

Alfie nodded. 'One, two, free, four, five, six, seven, eight, nine, ten, twelve, firtee–

'You missed out eleven!' said Hector.

'Excellent counting, Alfie,' said Jack. 'And is this Bidget? Isn't she lovely and cuddly? I can tell she really likes you. Do you know what cats really love you to do to them?'

Alfie shook his head.

'This.' He reached out and rubbed under Edie's chin. 'See, she's purring now.'

Alfie tried it for a while, then pointed at our large palm by the back door. 'Bidget pooed in the plant, cos Gan broaded up the cat flap when Rastus died.'

Jack looked my way. 'Would you like me to unbroad it?'

'Oh God, yes. Please. Don't move. Don't change your mind. I'll get the toolbox.'

Hector, who'd been studiously reading the Co-op's January food offers, tossed them to one side. 'I'm going out,' he said. That meant for a fag. When he opened the back door Bidget beat him to it.

* * *

We raved about Jack's Thai duck curry and he told us we were too kind.

'You could go on *MasterChef*,' Maeve said.

'Funny you should say that, I did apply a couple of years back. Got through the first audition, but my grandmother went into hospital and wasn't given a great prognosis. Just weeks, they said. We'd always been close and I didn't want to be pissing around with asparagus foam when I could have been with her.'

'Wow,' said Maeve.

'Plus, it would have meant missing an important gig.'

'Where?' I asked, washing the creamy coconutty curry down with the Singha beer Jack had brought along.

'At a uni. Nothing that impressive, I was just the support act.'

'Huh,' snorted Hector, who'd been very quiet.

'Who for?' asked Maeve.

'Morphic Resonance?' said Jack.

'Never heard of them,' Hector said.

Maeve gasped. 'I love Morphic Resonance. Harry Merritt's a genius.'

'I met him briefly,' Jack said, 'just before the gig. But Grandma was fading and I had to get to the hospice after my set.'

Maeve stared at Jack, her pupils like saucers in their M&M rings. 'And what else do you do for fun, Jack? Apart from music, cooking...'

'Let me think…' His eyes twinkled naughtily at her. 'Well, I like running.'

'Jogging, do you mean?'

'I dunno. Jogging somehow goes with cities and pavements and I avoid those.'

'Country lover?' asked Maeve.

He nodded. 'I do like the English countryside.'

'Me too,' she said, meaning in theory, I guessed. She'd been once, on a school trip to a farm.

'So,' said Hector, 'you obviously didn't reach dizzying heights as a singer, or you wouldn't be slumming it with us.'

Jack continued looking at Maeve. 'I can't think of a single place I'd rather be.'

'Did you ever make that CD for me?' I asked.

'I did.' He got up and took it from his jacket. 'Here.'

'Ooh, let's play it,' said Maeve. She stood and grabbed it from me, knocking over a glass with an, 'Oops,' then put the CD in our ancient system. We all listened quietly, as I mopped up beer.

'I love it,' said Maeve, more than once.

'Nice voice,' I told Jack. I wasn't sure about the song, which was a bit generic folky singer-songwritery. Pleasant, though.

'So,' said Hector, when the first track finished and Jack lowered the volume, 'why exactly are you doing what you're doing?'

'Oh, I don't know.' Jack got more beers from the fridge and topped up my glass, then Maeve's. 'It sounded exciting? But it isn't, is it, Edie? Not for ninety-five per cent of the time.'

'It isn't,' I said.

'I'm just messing around, I guess, waiting to find out what I really want to do.'

'What was your degree in?' asked Hector.

'Didn't do one.'

I caught a flash of relief in Hector's face. He'd dropped out of his degree course after one year. 'Political Bollocks at the University of the Middle of Nowhere,' according to Maeve, in one of her snobby moments.

'I didn't work at school,' said Jack. 'Well, not after we lost Mum… not in the sixth form. Got into music and had a band. We were called Bad Limes and did mainly stoner rock.'

'Wow,' said Maeve. Like Queens of the Stone Age?'

Jack laughed. 'We wished, but yeah.'

'Sorry about your mother,' I said.

'Thanks. Yeah, that was rough.'

Hector blew his nose into his serviette.

'Anyway, it was fun being in a band. We took drugs and hung out with wild girls and thought we were cool, then came the inevitable split and I looked around and everyone was gone. All at uni. I might do a degree now, though. Law or criminology, something along those lines.'

'Maeve's a musician,' I told him.

'Mum, please.'

'Grade 8 piano, no less.'

This time Jack said, 'Wow,' and their eyes locked for a while.

'I always find duck too fatty,' Hector said, skimming non-existent oil from his food and looking for somewhere to deposit it. 'Don't you?'

'No,' I said.

'No,' said Maeve.

'And this poor fucker,' said Hector, 'would never have seen water, you know. Farm-bred ducks aren't the waterfowl they're designed to be.'

'Maybe you could do something about it, Hector?' Maeve said. 'Start a campaign? You know, in all that spare time you have?'

'Or,' said Hector, 'the public could just not buy duck, or order it in restaurants.'

Meanwhile, Jack had left the table and was rummaging through the recycling. He came back with a leaflet and placed it on the table. "Paddleduck Farm" was written in a twee font. 'Free range,' he said, 'and organic.' He opened the leaflet and read to us. 'Our Barbary ducks are given the freedom to roam around extensive grounds that contain paddocks, hedgerows and several small ponds, because as we know, ducks love to swim. At night they are protected from predators in straw-filled rooms, where they're provided with free Wi-Fi, en suite facilities and a daily newspaper.'

'I'm going out,' said Hector.

During dessert, Maeve and I swooned over Jack's perfect chocolate fondants; still beautifully runny in the middle. Hector had declined one, saying he tended to avoid sugar on health grounds. I'd remember that next time he dug into our Ben and Jerry's.

'It's quite nauseating,' he said, watching us eat while shrouding the table in Marlboro smell, 'the amount of crap people consume on a daily basis.'

'You're not going to vomit?' I asked.

It was Maeve who giggled first, then I joined in and couldn't stop, and when we got to the tears stage, Jack found the two of us so funny that he joined in, and at some point Hector grabbed his jacket, his cigarettes and the greasy scarf he never washed and left.

* * *

Maeve and Jack retired to the front room, while I insisted on doing the coffees. It was something I could do, since it entailed spooning granules into mugs and adding water. At one point, Jack popped back to fetch Maeve's phone, so she could show him Alfie photos.

'Oh yeah,' he said. 'When I was in the shop earlier, Matt was there, asking Oscar if you were in.'

'Really? What did he say? I mean Matt?'

'I don't know. And I couldn't go up and ask him, because I don't want him to recognise me when I follow them to Middle Thing.'

'Perhaps I'll call him tomorrow. That was a fabulous meal, you know. Perfect in every way.'

'Like your daughter,' he whispered, picking up two hot mugs, vaguely curling a lip at their contents, and going back to her.

EIGHTEEN

Three days later, it being my turn to tail, I found myself approaching Middle Thing again, several cars behind Nadya's. This time only she and Shona were in it, and I guessed Matt was on a late shift. Jack had followed the three of them out here two nights previously, and it had been pretty much the same story. They'd stayed a while, then driven back to the services, where Shona and Matt had been dropped off by their car. That time, Nadya had driven off in hers, and not gone to the hotel. Jack had begun following Nadya, but lost her before even leaving the car park. We'd tried finding her address, with no luck, and I cursed myself for not getting it from Shona.

However, in an exciting development, when watching the house the following morning, Jack had seen an elderly man enter and a youngish dark-haired olive-skinned guy leave just minutes later. Curiouser and curiouser, we thought, and Jack had shot back to Oxford and my office, where we'd discovered online that the property belonged to an Alex Erskine. Nadya Erskine's brother or cousin, we'd guessed, as Shona hadn't mentioned a husband. We'd already decided against interviewing, or even contacting Nadya, since it might alert them all to the fact that we were suspicious. For now, we'd just watch.

I drove past the familiar landmarks: the water tower, the Norman church, the field where three horses huddled together against the cold. Had anyone worked out how much cold a horse felt? It wasn't like they could tell you. I remembered watching *Babe* and wondered if technology would one day allow animals to tell us their thoughts. 'Don't call me Bidget, Alfie. It makes your gran resent me.'

Light was fading fast as I entered Middle Thing and almost ran down a black-clad jogger, who clearly thought he had right of way. 'Idiot!' I said, slamming on the brakes as he disappeared into the woods. It shook me up, somewhat, and passing the Queen's Arms I had a hankering for a gin and tonic. Surely one would be OK? But I'd stand out, as a woman drinking alone. No, I couldn't risk it. So far, I felt sure both Jack and I had remained unnoticed. I found the same free spot and reversed into it, so that I had a good view of the house. Nadya's car was on the drive and lights were on in the house.

I'd heard my phone en route to the village, and checked it now. Jack. He'd left a voicemail message, saying he'd just driven past Shona and Matt's house and all lights there were off. He was heading home for an early night, he'd added with a noisy yawn. 'Let's catch up tomorrow.'

If Matt wasn't home, he was most likely working. If he wasn't already in the house opposite me, I thought… the house where the door suddenly flew open and two women ran out, Nadya with arms wrapped around her chest and Shona with a hand over her mouth. They seemed to be heading my way and I slowly sank down, but then there they were, banging on my window, opening my door.

'We thought you'd never get here!' cried Shona, her eyes red and tear-filled. That was when I noticed the blood on her hands.

She wailed loudly and Nadya hissed at her to, 'Shut. Up.' Then to me she whispered, 'We've called for an ambulance, but we don't know if she's still alive.'

'Who?' I asked.

'Bella, of course.'

Shona made the noise again. 'Would you be able to tell?'

What the…? Any minute, I'd be woken by my mobile. Maeve calling to pump me more about Jack, or because Alfie wanted to say goodnight.

'You were a teacher,' said Nadya. 'You must know first aid?'

She knew I was a teacher? 'A bit,' I said, surprised to hear myself sounding so normal in this strange dream. I got out of the car. 'But aren't you a nurse, Shona?'

'Quite!' said Nadya.

'I can't touch her,' Shona said. 'It's different when it's someone you know.'

'Where is she?' I asked.

We began walking towards the house, but then I stopped and ran back for my keys and phone, and to lock the car. I was never that pragmatic in dreams. This was really happening.

'In the kitchen,' Nadya said, when I caught up. 'We think we disturbed him, so we're worried about messing up the crime scene, like they're always going on about on the telly?'

'How did you know I was coming?' I asked.

In the midst of her distress, Shona managed a snort.

'Oh.'

'He seems to have come in and left via the back,' said Nadya. 'So, do you think it's OK for us to walk in the front way?'

I realised why she was asking me. I was a detective. 'You've already walked along the hall here,' I said, my eyes wandering to the kitchen and the sight of half a black-legging-clad leg. 'So, I'm sure the police won't mind. You have called the police?'

The two women looked at each other.

'Bella's not going to mind now,' said Nadya.

'I suppose not.' Shona took a mobile from her jacket, but on noticing her bloody hand, screamed and dropped it.

'Jesus,' Nadya said, picking it up and doing it herself. Her voice quivered as she explained the situation and that an ambulance had been called for.

The first thing I focused on, before even the woman on the floor, was the broken glass of the back-door window pane. There was a jagged-edged hole, just big enough to get a hand through. My eyes then lowered to the woman I'd spent weeks thinking about. The woman of those two photographs, lying still as a statue with globules of blood in her thick black hair. Thinner-looking blood was slowly spreading across the black-and-white tiled floor. Surely this couldn't be real. It was just some unfunny stunt with pretend blood. Any minute, Bella would sit up and say, 'Boo! Had you there!' and I'd get a grilling about why we'd been following them.

I went and knelt beside her, not caring about the blood and my boots and my coat, and checked her neck for a pulse, as taught on a first-aid course. What a striking face, I thought, my hand shaking, willing there to be a pulse, even a weak one. How strong and beautiful Bella was. She looked older than in the photos, but perhaps she hadn't an hour ago; half an hour. What had she done to deserve this? I shook my head at the appallingness of it and Shona screamed, thinking I was pronouncing her dead.

'Shut up!' said Nadya. 'You're no help at all. Never have been!' I heard the swish of tights and her black pumps were beside me. 'When we let ourselves in, we heard the back door bang and didn't think anything of it. Then we called out to Bella and there was no answer and when we brought these bags of food in, there she was. I opened the back door and looked out, but he'd gone. We should have got here sooner to take over from my brother, only–' she stopped and drew breath in short pants and I wanted to put my hand on her to calm her down, but there was the matter of the blood. '–only I had this difficult guest who wouldn't stop complaining… and my brother's shift here was over and he always leaves on the dot, because of his OCD, and oh, Christ.'

'Her eyes were open,' said Shona from the distance, 'and she was sort of gurgling. So we both rushed over and asked her who'd done this to her and she gurgled and gurgled, and so Nadya tilted her head a bit, and then Bella coughed up something, and then she sort of said something, really quietly, or she was trying to, and then her eyes closed and she went limp, and…' Shona unrolled kitchen paper and covered her face with it.

'How long ago?' I asked.

'About five minutes before you got here,' said Nadya. 'What took you so long? You or the other guy are usually right behind us.'

'I don't know.' I couldn't remember, it felt like an age ago I'd been driving along thinking of gin.

'To be honest,' said Nadya, 'we quite liked you watching over us, or out for us. Not that you'd have been able to help poor Bella today, unless you'd got here early. But even then, he came in and out the back way. I don't suppose you saw anyone suspicious-looking? Driving too fast, or running away?'

'I don't think so.' I recalled the jogger but would save that for the police.

'Is that a siren?' asked Shona.

She hurried to open the front door and we heard the ambulance approaching. It was distant but gradually grew louder. I pictured it passing the Norman church, the frozen horses, the Queen's Arms.

It was such a cold and stark scene in the kitchen. I wanted to turn the cruel strip light off, but knew I mustn't touch a thing. Out in the hallway, Shona's phone rang and we listened to her shouting.

'Why didn't you go to work, Matt? ... Liar! You never get migraines!'

Beside me, Nadya began crying. 'We were trying to protect her from him,' she said.

'Who?' I asked.

'We don't know. Neither did Bella.'

'Shona said she said something before she became unconscious?'

'Yeah, it was just the one word. Or, the beginning of a word, just sort of whispered.' Nadya took some of the same kitchen roll. 'She knew, you know. Knew he'd find her. Petrified, she was. Never told us why, though. Why he was after her, or what happened. She said that might put us in as much danger as she was in.'

'The ambulance is here!' called out Shona. 'Matt's on his way too.'

Nadya went to leave the kitchen, but I gently held her arm. 'Tell me what she said.'

Nadya sniffed and wiped her nose. 'It was just the one word. "Far". Then she said it again, but more quietly because she was slipping away.'

'Far? Any idea why she'd say that?'

'I wondered if she was trying to say father, or farmer, or if she was saying the guy's name, or trying to. Far-something?' Nadya shook her head. I saw blood on her sweeping fringe. 'I feel such a failure,' she said shakily. 'If only we'd told the police where she was hiding, and why, but she made us swear we wouldn't. So stupid not to.'

A rotating bright light filled the house and a male and female paramedic squeezed past us. 'If you'd like to wait in the hall for now,' said the woman. 'We'll just take a look at her.'

The man was soon down on his knees and doing what I'd done. He too shook his head and for a while the two paramedics, backs to us, attempted resuscitation as we watched from the hall. Shona was saying, 'Don't let her die. Don't let her die.' Nadya was saying, 'Shut up, Shona.' And I was holding my breath, every muscle in me tensed.

When a minute or so had passed and the female paramedic turned to us and said, 'I'm sorry,' it suddenly hit me. Not just the awful and tragic event, but the horrible realisation that Jack and I had led the killer to Bella; that it had been his plan, all along.

It was at that point that I chose to leave, before the police got there, before people with cameras arrived. I felt ill, I told Shona and Nadya, really ill. 'Tell the police I'll be happy to talk to them tomorrow.' I scribbled my address and number on a page of my pad and handed it to Nadya. Then I ran, very fast, to my car.

* * *

I expected police cars to whizz past me, but they must have been coming from a different direction. Banbury, perhaps. Somehow the sight of them would have been reassuring on the empty stretches of dark country road. Would he… the killer… Mike…? come up behind, then pull alongside and bump me into the hedgerow? Or would my crappy car conk out and make me a sitting duck? I just needed to get onto the M40, then I'd be safe. For the time being, at least. When a motorbike overtook me with a sudden and terrifying roar, I thought I might throw up. He'd be waiting around the next bend, for sure, straddling his bike, sideways on to me. Something would prevent me overtaking him. I'd slow to a halt, he'd remove his gloves, then his helmet. He'd unzip his leather jacket and reach inside. 'Hey, Edie.' There'd be a bright white smile and blood on his glass-cut hand. A hand with a knife in it. 'Long time no see. Got anything for me?'

NINETEEN

I pointed out Big Ben to Alfie. 'That's where our government meets and decides things.' The day was sunny and crisp and we could see for miles. I really wanted to be in bed, in a locked room, sedated, but here I was ascending on the London Eye, which was probably as safe as anywhere.

'Where the baddies are?' asked Alfie.

'Well...'

'The baddies what will send Bidget away?'

'Our cat?' I asked.

'No, Bidget at nursery.'

Terence looked on, mystified.

'Hector,' I mouthed.

'Ah.'

'Don't worry,' I told Alfie, 'that's never going to happen. Hector was just teasing you.' I pointed at a boat to distract him.

'Can we go on a boat, Gampy?' he said.

'I don't see why not.'

'Count me out,' shouted Maeve. She was sitting reading on the bench in the middle of our carriage, having claimed that when she stood up she felt 'totally wobbly'. I hadn't liked to suggest it was the mad shoes she was wearing, or that if poor Terence could manage it, surely she could, since five months back, she'd dangled and swung high above St Giles' Fair on a hideously sadistic ride and loved it. I remembered nervously jiggling Alfie, while watching, wondering if I'd automatically get him if Maeve didn't make it back.

Terence had insisted we all come to his place for a break, while he organised new door locks and window locks for us. Mike, or whoever, would have been crazy to come after me, or send someone after me, but we didn't want to take chances.

'You OK?' Terence asked quietly, while Alfie was distracted by a couple of older boys.

'Not really.'

It had been four days since finding Bella. I'd been interviewed, I'd given a full statement and I'd handed all my notes and computer documents over. I'd even described the jogger I'd seen, clad all in black and running into my path without looking.

Since the murder had taken place within Oxfordshire, Thames Valley Police were dealing with it. There was an incident room in Kidlington. Ten minutes earlier, while we'd been queuing for the Eye, I'd had a call from Detective Sergeant Ben Watson, saying some evidence that could be relevant had been discovered in the garden next door to the crime scene, and would I be able to drop in and see if I recognised it. I'd spoken to Ben a few times over the past couple of days, so felt able to ask what it was. 'A man's watch,' he'd said, lowering his voice. 'Looks as though it got caught on some fencing.'

I asked, also lowering my voice for some reason, if it was silver and gold, and he said it was. I told him Mike had one like that, and he said, yes, Emily in the shop had given them a full description. 'And I mean full,' he'd added. 'By the way, we confirmed that address was his house and we carried out a search, and found a lot of dressing-up gear. Fat suits and wigs and all sorts of paraphernalia.'

'Edie?' Terence was saying.

I shook away my thoughts, and looked at the view. 'Sorry, sorry. Am I OK? Well, I'm still waking in the night, palpitating. My first B.O.D.Y. and all that.' I gestured towards Alfie, not wanting to freak him out. 'I saw my dad, when he, you know, but that was different. I didn't feel responsible.'

'Oh, Edie, you must stop that. How on earth could you have been responsible? You see a lot of this in the army. Chaps ruining the rest of their lives by thinking if they'd only done this, or not done that, then their colleague wouldn't have–' he paused '–D.I.E.D. It's what a lot of the counselling deals with. Survivor's guilt, or plain guilt. It's so destructive but so unnecessary. Particularly in your case.'

'I suppose I was only doing my job. Something a client had asked me to do, originally at any rate. Before he disappeared. He hadn't disappeared, though, had he? He'd followed me. It all feels so twisted, that's what I hate.'

Alfie peered down at the Thames. 'Gan?'

'Yes, Alfie?'

'Will the man let me drive the boat?'

'I don't think so, love. You have to have a special certificate to do that.'

'And be over three,' said Maeve.

We got off the Eye and in shoes that were clearly too big, Maeve linked arms with Terence and the two of them clomped and limped along the South Bank, chatting away; Maeve occasionally tripping up on something, or veering and careering into oncomers. It was a case of being vigilant and jumping out the way when Maeve approached you.

I suppressed all jealousy, thinking instead how nice it was that Maeve had Terence to talk intellectually to, about the world, war, art. I felt sure I was capable of that; I read the papers, I had Tate membership. But after years of 'We're out of milk' and 'He needs a nappy change', it might have felt odd launching into the influence of the Quattrocento on the Pre-Raphaelite Brotherhood, which was what I caught bits of now.

Maeve left us after the Eye to go and 'work' in Terence's apartment. It may have been huge, but it was only three bedrooms, so she and Alfie had shared last night and he'd woken very early. She was really going back to nap, I knew, which was something she did well, and for hours.

Terence and I talked Alfie out of the boat trip and into the Aquarium, where Terence seemed to know a lot about fish as well as art movements. I'd never been before. It was impressive and enjoyable and occasionally I forgot that someone might be out to kill me to shut me up. But then I'd see a guy who was a little off… Is that a wig? Is his beard real? Or I'd catch someone who resembled Mike from the back. A black coat, square shoulders, too-blond hair.

I knew Terence was watching me carefully, perhaps as a juicy case study of post-traumatic shock. But I didn't mind. He was being protective, and I needed us to feel relatively safe while the police were hunting Mike. The papers had been having a field day, what with the suspect being an actor of sorts and what with him 'disappearing' – "A master of disguise, Mike Wilder could be the man standing next to you in the bus queue, or on the Underground".

Or the spotter with the ponytail, over by the piranhas? The one ticking things off in a book?

'Fishy,' I said, watching the oddball.

'Yes.' Terence did his smiley-eyed thing. 'Aquariums usually are.'

I found myself wondering if Bella had been there and seen these fish, photographed them. But then I doubted it, since her project had been a comparison of cultures, and aquariums were similar the world over. I'd been thinking about her a lot. Before leaving Oxford I'd met up with Shona and Nadya and been filled in on Bella a bit more, but not massively, since she really had, it turned out, been quite private.

'Bella came back from Northumbria a nervous wreck,' Shona had told me. 'But all she would say was, "If I tell anyone what I saw, he said he'll kill my family". That was all she gave away. He had her phone, she told us, but not how he'd got it. It was all on there, her life… emails, photos, photos of her family, texts, addresses, numbers. Bella never locked the phone with a passcode, she said, because sometimes she needed to quickly take a photo. Anyway, she made us swear we wouldn't tell a soul or go to the police, and we didn't. Now, obviously, we wish we had. We kept saying, Bella you can't go on hiding forever, but it was like she was stuck.'

'Why did you call me about the guy from the photography class?' I asked Shona.

'I was convinced he was the same bloke as in the photo you sent us, and we sort of wanted you to suspect Mike of not being who he said he was. I tell you, his Belfast accent wasn't right. Although we thought Mike was who she was hiding from, she wouldn't say if it was him in the picture. Didn't want us taking any risks, or getting too involved.'

When I saw them, both Shona and Nadya had still been upset, Shona especially so. Matt had been doing his shift at the factory, but I was hoping to get to talk to him soon. I wanted to ask why he'd called in the shop, the evening Jack cooked for us.

Bella had been stabbed with her own kitchen knife, found beneath her body. Knifing someone, who could do that? While I pondered on the act, the horrible physical act, a shark loomed up, baring its teeth. It reminded me of Mike and I jumped back and grabbed Terence's sleeve.

'Sorry,' I said, not letting go.

'Don't be.' He gave me a hug. He smelt good. No cologne or anything, just him and maybe soap powder, clothes liquid, whatever it's called. A twice-weekly cleaner did his washing.

That's what I should do, I thought. Be a domestic. Nice and safe, and with almost no chance of causing an innocent person's death. Unless they asked me to cook.

No mention had been made by the police, to the media, of either myself or Jack and our private investigation. At least for now, we were under the radar. That I was pleased about. One newspaper had run an interview with Mr and Mrs Rossoni, Bella's parents in Kentucky, where, apparently, she'd grown up. They said they'd received an email, purportedly from their daughter, in early December, telling them she'd be going to a remote part of Scotland for the purposes of her project and might be out of touch for a while. When, a month later, they still hadn't heard from her, they'd contacted "your Scotland Yard" and reported their concerns. The Oxford police claimed they were told at the time, but that the parents had been reassured by the Met. Reassured how? I wondered.

I'd made a quick call to Nadya, who'd said yes, Bella had emailed her parents that message, thinking it would prevent them worrying about her and at the same time let the guy who'd threatened her know she was doing as he'd wished. 'Her parents emailed her back, saying to take care, and he would have then read both messages on Bella's mobile. After that, she cancelled her phone contract, which was probably her biggest mistake. It meant he couldn't keep tabs on incoming messages from family and friends. That must have riled him, and maybe made him determined to find her.'

'If she hadn't cancelled,' I said, 'and he had hung onto her phone and used it, he could have been pinpointed, geographically, it having GPS. That is right, isn't it?'

'I don't know,' Nadya had said, laughing. I'd got the impression she thought I should.

* * *

Later, we were all mucking in, making dinner in a kitchen with huge sliding drawers full of interesting jars and packets. For someone who claimed to mostly eat out, Terence had a lot of food. By 'we' I mean myself, Terence and Alfie. Maeve was having a bath with a book.

'Is she always this L.A.Z.Y.?' Terence asked, darting his eyes Alfie's way.

'Her S.O.N. wears her out,' I said. 'And I think she's a bit sleep-deprived today. Plus there's a critical essay she needs to work on.'

'Does she do anything A.T. space A.L.L. around the house?' he persisted. I expected him to flash me a smile but he didn't.

'She washes her clothes because she doesn't trust me with them.'

Terence shook his head. 'It's none of my business, I suppose.'

No. It wasn't. I wanted Maeve to go places, and so I made allowances. 'She works hard,' I told him, tapping my head. 'Up here. And if she were my son with a child to look after, you'd take it for granted that I'd be supportive, while my brilliant boy forged an academic career.'

'Steady on,' said Terence, a hand on my shoulder.

Alfie had stopped stirring his saucepan of cold water and vegetable peelings. 'Where's Sniffy?' he asked.

'Sorry,' I said. 'Was I shouting?'

Terence grabbed his stick. 'A little. Your nerves are a bit jangled, that's all. I think Sniffy's on the sofa, Alfie. I'll go and get it.' He limped over, and before he got back his mobile rang on the counter. I managed to catch the name Chloe before he hurriedly picked it up and said, 'Hi, hi, how are you?' and walked off towards the living room. 'Is that so? Well, well … Indeed, indeed … Ha ha ha.' He was trying to sound bouncy and natural without achieving either. 'Slight problem, I'm afraid,' was the last I heard before he went into his study with no door.

Chloe, eh? That might explain a few things. I strained to hear, but what he was saying was unclear. From the tone it wasn't endearments. Before long, he was back, placing his stick against the island we were all working at and passing Sniffy over to Alfie, who'd forgotten all about it.

'A friend,' he said, settling on a high stool and shaking his head. 'Chloe. She's a nurse. It's… complicated.'

'It usually is,' I said, adding a chuckle to let him know I wasn't bothered. We peeled and chopped for a bit, passing all peelings to Alfie for his 'special stew'. 'Is she coming–'

'Here? No. No, she isn't. She's lovely, but not for me. I've put Chloe off so many times recently, but she still calls to see how I am. To be honest, I really like her, but… how can I put it… I, er, don't entirely fancy her?'

'Oh dear.' I crinkled my brow, hoping to look sympathetic.

'It's difficult to know what to do, how to deal with her. What do you think, Edie? You must be an expert, having been through dozens of relationships.'

'Dozens? Really?'

'Oh, Lord. Sorry, I shouldn't have–'

'I'll kill Maeve!' I said, waving my knife, then remembering Bella and feeling terrible. 'Not dozens, but a handful. That in itself tells you I'm no expert, surely?'

'Yes, get your drift.'

I'd have liked to know more about Chloe; how they'd met, what she looked like – he must have had a photo – whether they'd properly got together. Perhaps Astrid had been right and I was plain nosy, since I also wanted to know everything about Caroline. How often he saw his ex-wife. How friendly it was. But I didn't ask any of that because Alfie had stopped stirring and was sniffing noisily. Crying, I realised.

I jumped off my stool. 'Are you OK, love?' I asked. Had we been ignoring him? Was he missing Bidget? A tear trickled down his right cheek and I wiped it away. 'What's wrong, sweetie?'

He raised his sad and dirty little face. The potato peelings, I guessed. 'You said you're going to kill Mummy,' he sobbed.

'Oh, sweetie,' I said, giving him a hug and wiping away his tears with my fingers. 'Gran wasn't being serious. It was just a silly grown-ups' joke.' I kissed the top of his head and grimaced at Terence, who got off his stool and came over.

'What do you say we find one of your favourite programmes on my gigantic television?'

'Mr Tumble?' asked Alfie, tears all dried up and a big smile in their place.

'OK. Let's find him on catch-up, shall we?'

'I like ketchup,' Alfie was saying, as he was led by the hand across the expanse of white bamboo flooring.

'Yes, it's a splendid invention,' said Terence, while I squirmed and wished he'd shut up. Perhaps we could pretend only Terence's TV had the 'ketchup' facility.

'Thanks,' I said, when he got back and settled himself on the stool. 'You're good with him.'

'Really?'

I nodded. 'And how are your boys?'

'They're doing OK. Caroline says Theo's just cruising at school, but he's a happy little guy with lots of friends. She found some…' He glanced back at Alfie. 'D.R.U.G.S.

in his room. But that's par for the course these days. It was just a little pot, which he swears is all he and his chums do. He's quite a party animal, and we're fairly certain he's no longer a V.I.R.G.I.N. Terribly popular, I gather, and not just with the girls. I have to say I envy him, since I was the complete opposite at that age.'

I kept quiet. Terence still hadn't been much liked five years on, at Oxford. All those strong views and clever put-downs. He'd had a girlfriend for a while, the red-haired willowy Fiona, who'd walk three paces behind, carrying so many books that some had to have been his.

He gave me a lopsided grin. 'I know what you're thinking.'

I grinned back. 'Actually, I was thinking about Mike's watch.' I had been, earlier.

He started, slightly, at my change of subject. 'What about it?'

'OK, so, initially I was perplexed. Why didn't Mike go back for the watch? But of course that would have been foolhardy, with the police there and neighbours being extra vigilant. And who knows at what point he noticed it missing. What I'm thinking now is that Mike wouldn't have worn it in the first place. Not on a mission like that. If Bella had survived, it could have been the one thing to have identified him. After all, I'd noticed his watch. So had Emily. It's flashy. Memorable. No, it doesn't make sense.'

'But,' said Terence, 'even geniuses make errors. Remember, there was only a brief opportunity for him to get into the house and S.T.A.B. Bella – an opportunity that suddenly came up while he'd been routinely watching the place, presumably?'

'Yep. You could be right. He might not have been expecting to M.U.R.D.E.R. her that evening.'

Terence got up and started to gently rub my back. It felt nice.

'But, hey, Edie,' he said, 'don't forget you're supposed to be taking a break.'

'I know, I know.'

TWENTY

Maeve was back in the Bodleian Library, Alfie was back in nursery, and I was back in my office with, thanks to Terence, two new locks on my office door and a video-entry system below. 'Personally,' he'd said, 'I'd go down and meet a stranger in the safety of the shop before letting them up.' I'd promised to do just that but so far only Emily had buzzed, and she was now sitting opposite, listening to me pour out the entire grisly story.

'That's a bit weird,' she said, when I finished. 'Bella saying "Far", like that? Just before she…'

'Yes.'

'I reckon it was a longer word she was trying to say, like, I dunno…'

'Father?'

'Maybe.' She stood up. 'Thanks for the update. I'd better go, sorry. Oscar's put me on sell-by-date checking.'

'Sounds fun.'

'Well, I do get to take the old stuff home.'

'Careful what you eat, Emily. Multiplying bacteria and all that.'

She seemed to find that funny. 'I reckon my body's coped with a lot more than limp lettuce over the years.'

'Still…' I said as she left.

The person I really wanted to talk to was Jack. But Jack had, a day after telling the police all he knew, jumped on a plane for Portugal to hang out with an old girlfriend and play music. I'd emailed him twice and not heard back. So wrapped up had I been in the Bella business, that I hadn't made the link between Jack's running off to an ex and Maeve's mood swings, until Terence suggested it.

Jack had called me the day he left, saying he needed to have a long hard think about his future. 'Sounds like a good idea,' I'd said, mildly pissed off that he wasn't hanging around to be supportive. In fact, I hadn't seen him at all after finding Bella. I was beginning to view lovely Jack as something of a butterfly, hopping between things – music, detecting, maybe next a degree. Hopping between women, too. Hector may have been a dickhead, but at least he was a loyal one.

I tried calling Matt and got no answer. I left a message saying to phone me but by the evening I'd heard nothing. Why he'd dropped in to see me, the day Jack cooked for us, was all I wanted to know.

I sat back in my chair. What now? I wondered, eyes getting heavy. I hadn't been sleeping well, my nights being filled with images of Bella and crazy, muddled, guilt-riddled thoughts of what I could have done differently. Things I should have spotted, or might have spotted, if I'd been a proper investigator and not a teacher playing at being one. Horrible images. So much blood, and the way she'd lain so still. So dead. So utterly dead. And all my fault, for leading the killer to her. No matter how hard Terence, bless him, tried to convince me differently, I couldn't come to any other conclusion.

The more I saw of Terence, the more I liked him. He liked me too, I could tell. The looks, the tender hugs, the kiss on the cheek that lingered a bit too long. Best to take it slowly, though. I'd had too many disasters to rush into anything.

I shook my head awake. What did I used to do? Before Mike Smith/Wilder walked into my office? I stopped drumming and began twiddling again, then got iPlayer up on the laptop. There were three *Homes Under the Hammer* I hadn't seen. I opened the oldest, but instead of being compelled by the Nottingham semi with potential, I could only worry about its security. The buyers, two female friends, made no mention of window locks or burglar alarms. The back door had glass in it! Didn't they realise what could happen? I shivered and closed the laptop. Nothing was as it had been. Would it ever be as it had been again? Suddenly I understood why all cops and private eyes hit the bottle; in fiction, at any rate. I opened my drawer and took out the emergency brandy, or what was left of it.

TWENTY-ONE

Several practically sleep-free and very depressing days later – during which melancholic Maeve had dumped Hector, the *Oxford Mail* had switched its attention to the suspicious death of a college bursar, and I'd been asked to follow another wayward partner, but didn't have the heart for it – my buzzer went. It was half twelve and I'd been thinking about where to have lunch. I'd packed up my bag and laptop, ready to go, but there on my desk, on the video screen, was the face of DS Ben Watson.

'Hi,' I said, pressing the button. 'Come on up.'

'Have a seat,' I said, after he'd bounded up the stairs and I'd opened my office door. Once we were settled I asked how the investigation was going.

He smiled. 'Continuing with our enquiries, as they say.'

Although I'd been interviewed by Ben the day after the murder, I was only now registering him. Late thirties, six foot, and black, or mixed race. He was clean-shaven but bristly and had a bit of an accent that wasn't local.

'But,' he added, 'you can ask me questions. If you like?'

'Oh, Lord,' I said, 'where shall I begin?' I folded my arms and had a think. 'First off, do you have a prime suspect?'

'Not yet. We're still looking for Mike Wilder, but aren't ruling out others.'

'The others being…?'

Ben cleared his throat. 'Have you heard from Jack?'

'Not since he went to Portugal.'

'Let us know if you do.'

'Why?'

'We like to keep tabs on all persons involved, that's all.'

'Jack was pretty vague,' I said, 'about how long he'd be away. Said he was going to write some songs. Did he not tell you he was going?'

'We didn't know he was leaving the country, no. I suppose we might have suggested he didn't. His father only got a quick call telling him his plans, but he hasn't heard anything since, no emails or calls. Jack really needs to contact someone.'

'I'll try contacting him.'

'Cheers.'

'You know he called me, just before I found Bella? Said he was passing Shona and Matt's house and it was all in darkness.'

'That's what he told you, but…'

'Oh, surely not.'

Ben just shrugged. 'We can't rule him out.'

I suddenly felt unwell. Not Jack, please.

'Remember the jogger you saw? Slim build, you said.'

'I did. Slimmer than Mike, unless he wore a fat suit each time we met.'

'Also… and this is between you and me, right?'

'Of course.'

Ben leaned towards me, twiddling his thumbs on my new desk. 'There's Alex Erskine, Nadya's brother. Erskine claims to have left the house at seven on the dot, but since he didn't arrive home in Banbury until half eleven, he's got to be considered. Tells us he just drove around, psyching himself up before going back to his not-very-happy marriage. We've been checking traffic cameras and CCTV for both his car and the one Matt borrowed. Matt's was seen at several points on the motorway – eventually – but we've not identified Alex's car yet.'

'Interesting.'

'He couldn't tell us why he clocked off with Isabella exactly on time, when he knew his sister was delayed but would arrive soon. It wasn't like he had something pressing to do. He's not in work at the moment, no kids. Nadya said her brother likes order and routine, which might explain it.'

I thought about offering tea or coffee, but didn't want to stop the flow of information pouring out of Detective Sergeant Watson. And anyway, I didn't have any. 'I suppose,' I said, in an attempt to contribute intelligently, 'that whoever did it would have had to clean up somehow, somewhere. To get rid of blood-splattered clothes and shoes?'

'They would. And maybe clean up a car they'd driven. Easier for someone who lives alone, don't you think?'

Like Jack.

'We're particularly interested in a partial footprint, found on the back doorstep.'

'You mean a recent one?'

'Yeah. It had rained during the day, so previous prints should have washed away. We'll be going through everyone's shoes, as a process of elimination, then… well, it's incredible what can be identified these days, from the print of just a small section of a sole. Manufacturers are constantly changing patterns, especially with their trainers and casual shoes.'

'That's helpful.'

'Yeah, we might get lucky.'

'So, it's all still up in the air?'

* * *

'I'd love to know more about Bella,' I said. We'd moved to the café next door and were drinking teas.

'Shona and Nadya filled me in a bit, but I'm not sure they knew too much to begin with.'

Ben dunked a biscuit in his cup and quickly ate it. 'Well… Isabella's parents are here now and according to them she was always the perfect daughter. Said they didn't like the idea of her going to a retreat in the wilds of Scotland in winter, which fits in with what Shona and Nadya told us. Course now I've had to tell them Isabella didn't go to Scotland, but hid from the world in order to protect them. That was tough.'

'I bet.'

'Bella grew up in Kentucky and went to college there. Had a few part-time jobs, then finally moved away to teach in Pennsylvania.'

'Is Kentucky considered a Southern state?'

'Yeah, just.'

'So did she have an accent?'

'Isabella? Yeah. In fact, you can see for yourself.' Ben took a tablet from his bag and tapped the screen. 'Here,' he said, turning it my way when a video began.

It seemed to have been taken in a hall, and there behind the podium was Bella, beautiful and dressed in a pale blue suit. It was the face I'd seen on the floor, only it was moving and speaking. If not for my stupidity, it would still be doing those things. What I couldn't quite take in was the mismatch of face and voice. Was it really her speaking?

'Ayand so aah'd laahk to introdoose are spayker furr this evening…'

'No!' I said, handing it back. 'Why didn't the others mention her accent?'

'Well…' Ben dragged something else onto the screen. 'I think she toned it down quite a bit, once she was over here. Look at this.'

A more casually dressed Bella was with a group of people. 'Cheers,' she was saying, raising a wine glass. 'Thank you so much for letting me photograph you guys.

You've been awesome. Or jolly good sports, as you'd say.' There followed some laughter and hubbub, then the video ended.

'I see what you mean,' I said. 'Not much of a twang there.'

While Ben polished off another biscuit, I asked if there was anything I could help him with. 'I don't suppose you dropped in just to fill me in on the case?'

'Now you come to mention it,' he said, grinning. 'What I'd really appreciate is for you to tell us, me that is, anything you think of that might help. Anything you hear, or find suspicious, or something that suddenly occurs to you. I thought it best to have an informal chat, in the hope that you'd share any information that comes to light with... well, as I said, preferably me. You know, rather than the SIO.'

'Senior investigating officer?'

Ben nodded. 'Bit of a dick, to be honest. Does bugger all except create chaos, then takes credit for convictions.'

I thought perhaps DS Ben Watson shouldn't be telling me this. 'So, I'd be like your CI?' I asked.

'Been watching American detective series?'

'Reading mainly. So, what would I be, here in the UK – a grass? A snitch? Plain old informant?'

'Just helpful, I'm hoping. I don't want to report everything you tell me... just...'

'Use it to solve the case single-handedly?' I asked. 'No chance of money changing hands?'

'I might buy you lunch.'

'That'll do. OK, Ben. Can I call you that? Your full title's a mouthful, if you don't mind me saying.'

'You can. What we need is a code, to avoid phone calls between us. Maybe you could send me a text saying something like, have there been any developments, or you'd appreciate an update, something along those lines. Don't make it the same every time, OK?

'I won't.'

'And I'll come to your house, rather than your office, as soon as possible after hearing from you. Let's say within the hour, if I can. If not, it means I'm caught up in something. Luckily, as a detective sergeant, I don't have to work with a partner.' Ben reached for his bag and slipped the tablet in, then got up. He didn't look much like a cop, not in his black jeans, grey Gap-type jacket and battered old trainers. He pulled a striped hat down over his ears and stuck his hands in fingerless gloves. 'Cool,' he said. 'I'll leave you to get on. I expect you're busy.'

'Oh, yes.'

Once he'd left, I went into the shop and gave Emily a whispered update.

'Thanks, Edie. Can't believe that about Jack. He's so gorgeous.'

'I know.'

'Talking of gorgeous, Ben is so hot. Do you know if he's, like, with anyone?'

'I don't,' I said, laughing. 'But I'll try and find out.'

'Aw, cheers.' I turned to leave but she touched my arm to stop me. 'Kentucky, you say?'

'Yes. Kentucky.'

* * *

Around six, following a couple of naps at my desk, I finally heard back from Matt. I asked why he'd called into the shop, asking for me.

'Oh, that. Yeah. It was actually to tell you we were hiding Bella, and why.'

'No!'

'But then when we noticed you, and then the other guy driving behind us and watching outside the house, we thought it was probably too late; that Mike, or whoever, would have already discovered the place. Oh, and by the way, one of your headlights was only working on sidelight.'

'It does that sometimes, then corrects itself.'

'Still illegal. Anyway, I don't know if the girls told you, but we were on the verge of moving Bella elsewhere, to a place I'd found near Witney.'

'Oh, God. That's so tragic.'

'Isn't it? But please don't feel responsible. Bella should have gone to the police. It was ridiculous not to. Or we should have done. She just had this idea that British cops were a bit useless and nothing would happen, except the guy would go after her parents, her friends...'

'I heard you showed Bella the photo of Mike?'

'I did, but she barely looked at it and didn't say anything. No reaction at all, not even a no. She always clammed up at any mention of the man who'd scared her, or the incident itself. Poor thing was permanently traumatised, and unduly worried about us.'

'Why didn't she just fly home?'

'For a start, she didn't have her passport. It had been in her rucksack and everything in her rucksack had gone. She didn't tell us how. We couldn't try and get her a false passport because we were sworn to secrecy. Also, she'd have been terrified of going home, him finding out, and her parents getting caught up in some dangerous situation. Remember, Bella had no idea who he was, so it wasn't like she could give the authorities a name and have him barred from the States.'

'Right,' I said, finally realising how stuck she must have felt. 'But surely she wasn't planning on hiding like that forever?'

'I'm not sure she was capable of forming a long-term plan, and that was the main problem for us, the team. As much as we'd grown to like her, the whole thing was becoming tedious and time-consuming. For me, at any rate.'

'So,' I said, 'when you came to see me… that was, what, a unilateral act?'

'No, no. Bella didn't know, but the rest of us believed it was the best thing to do, at that point.'

We talked about that fateful evening and he told me the same thing he'd told the police. 'I went to a neighbour with the mother of all headaches and asked to borrow her car. But then it had refused to start. Ended up jump-starting it with another neighbour's car.'

'Oh dear,' I said. 'I'm guessing the police talked to both these neighbours?'

'Yes, Edie,' he said, now mildly pissed off. 'They did.'

After the call, I packed everything away and wandered home, where I took a bottle of white from the fridge, a glass from the cupboard, and a packet of Cheese and Onion from the stash I'd hidden from Hector.

TWENTY-TWO

At 6.03 a.m. Alfie landed on my shins and made me cry out, not so much in pain as in fear. I'd been having a bad dream, although immediately forgot what about.

'Here,' I said, reaching for him. 'Come and have a cuddle and try to sleep again. It's Saturday, so no nursery.'

But Alfie was having none of it, and I soon found myself making tea and feeding Bidget foul-smelling animal bits from a tin. I sprayed some revolting air freshener, washed and dried my hands and regretted the amount of wine I'd drunk in bed. Not the whole bottle, surely. I found the ibuprofen and took two and delivered a bowl of cereal to Alfie, who was watching TV. I went back to the kitchen, drank my tea, then returned to the front room and lay on the sofa watching *Horrid Henry*, before my eyes grew too heavy to stay open.

'There… you… are…' I heard a disembodied Terence say.

We were on the coast somewhere. I was lying on the sand and nearby were the sounds of seaside attractions…

terrible music and loud voices. 'Gan's… asleep,' a small child told us and Terence laughed and said, 'Yes… he could… hear… her… snoring.'

'It's not easy being me…' I heard sung… the *Horrid Henry* song…

I came round, closed my mouth and squinted out of one eye, in time to see Terence leave the room with Alfie's bowl. 'Want some more?' he asked.

'No,' said Alfie.

'No, thank you,' I whispered, before drifting off again.

* * *

Terence had come to Oxford the previous evening to see Barnaby in a school play and afterwards, around half nine, had called first me, then Maeve to see if we were in. I'd not heard the call because my phone had run out of charge, but Maeve had invited him to come and have a cup of tea. Instead of tea he'd had a couple of drinks, and unable to drive had slept in the cluttered box room. I'd given up being embarrassed about the house since Bella. There was nothing like a sudden and brutal murder to help get your hang-ups into perspective.

'You never said what the play was?' Maeve was asking Terence over lunch, a bacon and avocado salad produced entirely by her. Had Terence dropped a few hints?

'A Greek tragedy,' he said.

'Which one?'

Beside him, Alfie was quietly coughing in his toddler seat. 'Oh dear, Alfie, don't choke,' he said. 'Here, let me chop up your food. I remember the boys doing this when they were little. One forgets they have such tiny throats.'

Maeve gazed at him, her enormous blue eyes flickering briefly. It was a hurt look. Not, I sensed, because she felt criticised as a parent, but because she felt jealous.

Terence looked solemn. 'I was away from home so much that I missed almost all the boys' school events.'

'What a shame,' Maeve said, perking up.

'I'm trying to make up for it now.'

'That's nice.' Maeve was in a black polo-neck jumper and jeans tucked in long boots. Not wearing lipstick and fur took years off her. 'I was Sandy in *Grease*, wasn't I, Mum?'

'You were,' I confirmed, unable to add anything. Maeve had many talents, but singing wasn't one of them.

'How marvellous!' said Terence, beaming at her.

We were just about done when the doorbell went. 'I'll go,' I said.

It was DS Ben, hands tucked in his jeans, eyebrows raised.

'Oh, hello?' I said, surprised.

'You wanted to see me?'

'Did I?'

He got his phone out. 'I had a text from you?'

'You did?'

'At... 0.38 this morning... saying... "Git something impudent to tall yon." Here.'

I took a look. 'Autocorrect.'

'Of course. You didn't use the agreed code.'

'I'm sorry. I was probably a bit... tired.'

He was trying not to smile. 'I guessed you might have been, which was why I didn't rush round first thing.'

'It won't happen again. Listen, come in, won't you? It's cold out there.'

I led him through to the back room. 'Everyone, this is Detective Sergeant Ben Watson.'

'I'm sorry,' Ben said, 'am I interrupting your lunch?'

'No, no, we've just finished. This is Maeve, my daughter.'

'Hi,' she said with a little wave.

'Hi,' said Ben.

'And this is my grandson. This man's a policeman, Alfie.'

'Can I see your gun?' asked Alfie, and we all laughed and wondered what he'd been watching.

Ben gave him a big smile. 'Policemen and women don't carry guns in this country.'

'And,' I said loudly, before Alfie did his "Why?" thing. 'This is Maeve's father.'

Terence stood and stepped forward. They shook hands. 'Terence,' he said.

'Casal-ez,' added Maeve. 'Tell the policeman how it's spelt, Alfie.'

'Ka, ah,' said Alfie, nodding with each letter, 'sa, ah, la, eh, sa.'

'Hey,' said Ben, 'that's really clever of you.'

'Well, his mother's a genius,' said Terence, throwing Maeve a proud look.

She gave him her new Daddy's-little-girl smile. 'I taught Alfie how to spell it because I'm thinking of changing our names, aren't I, Dad?'

Terence shot me a look. 'I'm not sure…'

'Are you?' I asked Maeve.

'Maybe,' she said. 'I've never liked the *v* and the *f* being so close in my name. You know, Maeve Fox. It's either awkward to say, or it ends up sounding like May Fox. I love Maeve Casales, though. Ca-sa-lez… Exotic.'

Terence cleared his throat. 'Maeve Fox is a perfectly lovely name.'

'Yes,' I agreed, folding my arms.

Alfie gazed up at Policeman Ben. 'Gan's going to kill Mummy.'

'Oh, Alfie,' I said, stroking his hair. 'No, I'm not.' Maybe later.

Ben checked his watch. 'Is there somewhere we could…?'

'Yes, sorry. Let's go in the front room.'

'Good meeting you all,' he said at the door, then pretended to shoot a gun at Alfie. Maeve slapped a hand on her chest and keeled over, going 'Aargh,' and her father laughed heartily.

I led Ben through and sat on the sofa, while Ben moved a few things and settled in an armchair. 'Nice family,' he said.

'Thanks.'

'So.'

'So. Right.' I had no recollection of sending the text but I was pleased Ben was there. 'I finally heard back from Matt around six yesterday evening. I told you he'd been into the shop asking for me?'

'You did.'

'Did you know they were about to move Bella to somewhere near Witney?'

'Yes.'

'All my fault.'

'That she died? Don't be daft. If she'd contacted us in the first place…'

'Her parents did.'

'That's true. We could all feel responsible, if we allowed ourselves.'

'I know.'

Ben stood up. 'I'll let you get back to your family lunch.'

'OK.' I put a hand on my hungover brow. 'Listen, I'm sorry to have got you here under false pretences. Telling you something you already knew.'

'Not at all.'

I opened the door to find Alfie playing with Grampy in the hall.

'We have a budding striker here,' said Terence, as Alfie swung a foot and missed the enormous ball. 'Oh, bad luck!'

We wove around them and I waved Ben off with a 'Bye!'

He gave me a little salute. 'As I said, nice family!'

I went back in and closed the door. Alfie had gone and Terence was holding the ball in one hand, his stick in the other. 'Everything OK?' he asked.

'Yep. Fine. He just had a few more questions to ask.'

'Are you sure it's not getting to be too much for you?' Terence dropped the ball and gave me a hug. 'Why don't we all do something this afternoon? As a family?'

Sleep? I wanted to suggest. 'That sounds nice.'

'Or just the two of us?'

'That sounds nicer.'

* * *

We went to Blenheim Palace. Not into the palace itself, just the grounds, which are vast and impressive, even in winter. I worried about Terence walking so far, but he managed it, occasionally taking my arm, or sitting for a while on a bench. During one such rest he opened up a little more about the bomb blast that had left him injured. He could recall almost nothing of the event, but was told it had been an ambush. 'Lost two of my best men. I guess I got off lightly. A damaged pelvis, a few broken bones, including two toes, of all things. Tore a ligament in the same foot.'

'Ah,' I said, 'I noticed your left shoe isn't as snug a fit as the right.' When he'd been ahead, at one point, the wind blowing his trouser bottoms, I'd seen a gap behind his heel.

'Yes, I have to go for a bigger size on my left foot, as it's always a little swollen and a larger shoe does the trick.'

'Are you still sore in places?'

'A few, although it's variable.'

'You've really been through it.'

'Not compared to some, believe me. And I like to think I kept my sanity.'

'Oh, I don't know.'

He put his arm around my shoulder and kissed the top of my head. 'Cheeky, Edie.'

We stayed like that for a while, watching passers-by, until the wind got too much and we moved on.

The day was cold, blowy and cloudy but a least we were no longer wading through snow. It was almost possible to imagine spring arriving now, after the harsh past month.

At the end of a circular walk, around the lake and past the Duke of Marlborough, high on his plinth, we were back at the gift shop and café, where Terence bought a book on Churchill – born in the palace – and I bought us tea and carrot cake.

'Are you seeing Barnaby again?' I asked when we were seated. 'This weekend?'

'No.' Terence slowly stirred his tea. 'He's got some chess tournament.'

'He sounds very bright.'

'Barnaby does well academically. Straight A stars. He wants to study medicine, so he'll need those. He'll be fine. I don't worry about him.'

'Unlike his younger brother?'

'You mean Theo the skirt-chasing, weed-smoking slacker? Strangely, I don't worry too much about him either. He's got something about him that will see him sail through life, thoroughly enjoying it, I'm sure.'

'It's nice that you're quite chilled about Theo. If he has nothing to rebel against he'll probably knuckle down to study at some point.'

'It's a good theory, however Caroline can be something of a tyrant. She was always the strict one of the two of us. Because I was often away, I tended to spoil the boys rather.'

'That's understandable.'

'You're very good with Maeve,' he said. 'Not too interfering, or judgemental, as far as I can tell.'

'I learned early on that she knew her own mind and any input from me was generally ignored.'

'Maeve's strong-willed, that's for sure. However, she told me she never did the teenage, going-off-the-rails thing?'

'No, she left that until she was twenty-one, then did it big time.'

'You mean falling pregnant with a relative stranger and becoming a single mother?' He squeezed my shoulder and smiley-eyed me. 'How shocking.'

'I'd been hoping she wouldn't do that, as well. But, whatever. Things happen for a reason, don't you think?'

'Absolutely. And Alfie's a splendid little chap.'

'He is.'

Terence ran a finger around the rim of his cup, then looked up. 'You do understand, I hope, why I'm not telling the boys about Maeve yet. I'd hate to derail Barnaby when he's doing so well, or completely derail Theo. And as for Caroline, oh my goodness. She'd become fully lawyered up, being one herself, and find some spurious grounds for an injunction.'

'I completely understand, but I think Maeve finds it difficult. Mind you, she hasn't said anything lately, so perhaps she's got used to the idea. She also loves all the attention you give her, and perhaps she thinks that would get diluted in an expanded family group.'

'It's a damned shame it has to be this way. I think the boys would love her.'

We sat quietly for a while, eating cake, people watching. Then Terence said, 'So how would you say you're bearing up, generally?'

'Better. Although, I'm concerned about Jack.'

'Oh?'

'He hasn't returned the two calls I made to him in Portugal, and I've tried emailing too. Everyone's contactable when they're abroad these days, so it's beginning to feel deliberate.'

'Why does it worry you?'

'Because I thought I knew him, I suppose. And now I don't feel I do, or ever did. I'm also beginning to wonder if he's hiding something.'

'Surely you don't think he killed her?'

'Who knows? He could have been working for Mike all along. Did his dirty work for him, then disappeared. I know he called me that evening to say the lights weren't on at Matt's place, but he could have been… well, anywhere, I suppose.'

'I'm sure the police would have checked that, in order to eliminate him. They allowed him to leave the country, didn't they?'

'So it would seem,' I said.

'I'm certain they'd have checked that he did actually make that call to you from Oxford, just when Isabella was being attacked.' Terence shuddered. 'I have to say I find it disturbingly Big Brother, all this monitoring.'

'But if it makes criminals think twice before carrying out an act, then I'm glad the police have access to phone records, CCTV and so on.'

'I see your point… Do you think we're being watched now?'

We both scanned the room, top to bottom. 'No cameras anywhere.'

Terence nudged me. 'The guy on his own, in the corner?'

I looked over. 'Could be Mike, if he's managed to lose a stone and all his hair, and grow very long ears.'

'False ears,' whispered Terence, and I checked them out again. I thought about the paraphernalia found in Mike's house. The eyes behind the rimless glasses were brown, like Mike's. Suddenly it didn't feel quite so like a joke, or that far-fetched. Who knew what lengths he'd go to. I wanted to see the man smile, to completely rule him out, but he didn't look the jovial type.

'Mike?' I called out, like a madwoman.

The man continued sipping his drink, but the fair-haired guy to my right swung round and said, 'Yes?' and gave me such a bright and toothy smile, I jumped and knocked tea over the table.

I apologised to the Mike chap and mopped the table with serviettes.

'You can't take me anywhere,' I said to the laughing Terence.

He bent forward and kissed my burning cheek. 'Oh, I think I can.'

* * *

Terence had to get back to London, saying he had a fairly full weekend ahead. It was a blow, after our romantic stroll. I saw him at a candle-lit table for two with Chloe, and felt a jealous pang. I told him I too had lots on. It wasn't a lie, there were library books to return and a work email to reply to. A surveillance job I still didn't feel up to.

TWENTY-THREE

When I walked into the kitchen on Monday evening, Maeve stopped chopping and wiped her hands on a towel. 'Guess what!' she said. 'Dad's decided it's time for me to meet my half-brothers.'

'What?' I put my things down and unwound my scarf. 'He was saying, only on Saturday, that it wasn't possible yet. That it might derail the boys. I wonder what made him change his mind.'

'Could have been me putting pressure on him all the time.'

'Have you?'

'I think I have.' She pulled a face. 'Poor Dad. But I'm sure it's for the best that everything's out in the open.'

'I think Terence is worried about his ex getting angry and somehow stopping him seeing Barnaby and Theo.'

'They're old enough to decide if they want to hang out with their dad, surely?'

'You'd think so.' I went over to see what she was cooking.

'It's a chicken and veg doodah,' she said. 'All made up.'

'I'm sure it'll be delicious. You're becoming really good.'

'Maybe I should go on *MasterChef*,' Maeve said, then stared at the diced green pepper for a while. 'Nothing from Jack, I suppose?'

'Nope. Sorry.'

She shrugged. 'Men are so mysterious.'

'No, they're not,' I said. 'On the whole, they're very easy to read.'

Maeve went back to her prepping. 'Yeah, you're right. Not Jack, though.'

I began clearing things from the draining board and putting them in cupboards and drawers. 'So, if you're in London,' I said, 'does that mean I have Alfie here all weekend?'

'Oh, no, you're coming with us to London. I mean… if that's OK?'

'I guess so.'

'Then you'll be able to look after Alfie, while Dad and I go and meet my brothers. Barnaby's got permission to go home on Friday, and they'll both train in from Surrey, apparently.'

'That all sounds very organised. When did you and Terence discuss this?' It was weird how I couldn't refer to him as 'Dad' to Maeve. One day, perhaps.

'We talked for ages this morning, and he said, "OK, you've twisted my arm, I'll see what I can do." Then he rang back an hour ago.'

I got up and fetched my phone. Yes, I had missed a call from him, drowned out by traffic, no doubt, on my walk home. He'd left a voicemail message.

'Just don't go changing your name without warning me,' I told Maeve.

'I won't, Mum. Sorry, were you upset about that?'

'What do you think? I mean, it's all happened very quickly. All this with Terence.'

'I know. And I do like my name. Honest. It was actually Dad who triggered it.'

'Oh?'

'He said something like, just think you could have been Maeve Casales all these years. He liked the sound of that, and I said, yeah me too. That was all, but then I got a bit carried away.'

I knew Maeve and her father talked a lot on the phone, but never probed too much. This was good news, though. But I'd call Terence back and check he really did want me in London, and maybe suggest I stay here with Alfie.

'You could go on the Eye again,' said Maeve, 'as Alfie's been going on and on about it.'

'We'll see,' I told her.

While she stir-fried, I listened to Terence's message. He was, as I'd expected, apologetic about his change of heart and about not talking to me first.

'I had to contact Barnaby's school, and talk to Caroline, who was surprisingly fine with it. I think she's got a new man, which may explain it. And of course Maeve can be a tad pushy and wants everything done yesterday. I'm so sorry.'

He hoped I'd be OK about us all coming to his place for the weekend, and was very much looking forward to seeing me on Saturday. He said to call him, anytime. Tomorrow, I decided.

'I loved our afternoon at Blenheim,' he added. 'Hope you did, too. Bye-bye.'

Well that seemed very much sorted then. Terence had such a nice voice. A voice that tugged at my insides and released some lovely chemical that warmed and excited me at the same time. Mind you, Bloody Greg's voice had done that too.

'Oh yeah,' said Maeve, placing an aromatic work of art in front of me. 'Emily popped in earlier, wanting to talk to you. Said she'll try again tomorrow.'

I checked my phone for calls and texts from her, but there wasn't anything, so I guessed it hadn't been urgent.

TWENTY-FOUR

Emily had the day off, I was told the next morning, so I didn't get to see her until she dropped by the house at half five.

'Everything OK?' I asked, as she unhooked her bag and took her brightly patterned coat off. 'I've tried calling you.'

She rehung her cloth bag across her body, as though not wanting to lose contact with it. 'Phone got nicked at my place two days ago, by a mate of one of the other tenants.'

It had never occurred to me to ask Emily about her home life. I knew it was a shared house in Rectory Road, not far from me, but that was all. 'That's awful. Has anyone helped you find it?'

'Not really. They're all like, "Oh, I expect he just borrowed it and he'll bring it back," then he says no, he never even saw it. So now I've lost loads of pictures and phone numbers. I put the photos on my laptop before that got taken yesterday.'

'No! The one you brought to Astrid's that time?'

'I really loved that laptop. My mum and dad gave it to me for getting clean. There's no lock on my door, see, even though I asked the landlord like fifty times.'

'Emily, you can't live in a place like that.'

'It's not like I've got a choice, Edie. The rent's low, cos I've got this cupboard for my room, and I can just about cover my rent, so basically I'm like really stuck.'

'Can't you live at home with your parents?'

'No way. They downsized to a what do you call it, studio flat, four years ago. Said it was for, like, financial reasons on account of them both taking early retirement and running up hypnotherapy bills for themselves because of me. There isn't even a sofa bed where they live now. Well there is, only they sleep on it.'

'Gosh.' I remembered an earlier version of her parents, always fundraising and full of cheer.

I sat Emily down at the kitchen table and said, 'Wait there.' Then up in my bedroom I took four hundred pounds from my stash at the back of my knicker drawer, having moved it from the kitchen cupboard when Maeve took up cooking.

Back downstairs, I gave it to her. 'You've been incredibly helpful, Emily, so please buy yourself another phone and a laptop. You can keep the laptop in my office, if you want. Come and use it there anytime. I'll give you keys.'

'You sure, Edie?'

'Absolutely.'

'Think I'm gonna cry.'

'Just promise me you'll keep the cash somewhere safe.'

'I'll ask Oscar to look after it till I have time off?'

'Good idea.'

'You're really kind, you know.'

'Well, I do have a daughter your age…'

'Still, thanks ever so.' She put the money in her cloth bag and zipped it up.

'Anyway,' I said, 'you wanted to see me?'

'Yeah, I did. I was thinking about Bella and what you said she said, like right at the end?'

'You mean "Far"?'

'Yeah. And you know she was from Kentucky?'

'She was, yes.'

'Anyway, I went on YouTube, when I still could, and there's these films of people speaking in different American accents.'

'OK.'

'I dunno, it's like some project. So I went down the list and found Kentucky and the interviewer woman got people to say a list of words in the Kentucky way, which is like really Southern and a bit weird-sounding?'

'Not to them, perhaps, but go on.'

'Well… you're gonna think I'm a bit crazy, but the local people who had to read the list, when they got to the word "Fire" – guess what it sounded like?'

'Far, by any chance?'

'Exactly like "Far", I swear. And I bet she, Bella, said it dead quietly, on account of being nearly dead. So, that might have made it sound more like "Far"?' Emily did an impression. 'Fah… fah...'

'Mm.'

'If you want, I can show you the video?'

'That might be better.'

My head filled with images of Isabella's parents dying in a fire, but of course that had all been fabricated by Mike. Maybe I'd get in touch with Shona and Nadya and see if fire had any significance, or rang any bells.

I watched the interviews and Emily was right, the Kentuckians could all have been saying 'Far' when they were actually saying, 'Fire'. I looked up at an expectant Emily. 'I think it's worth mentioning to DS Ben Watson.'

Since Emily didn't have a phone, and Ben had asked me not to call him, I sent him a text asking if there'd been "any developments". I suggested to Emily that she stayed until he arrived, which she seemed more than happy to do.

* * *

It wasn't long before Alfie and Maeve were charging in with bags of groceries, boots, coats and crumpled paintings. I played with Alfie in the front room, while Maeve began preparing two dinners, one for Alfie and one for us. She really had become an enthusiastic cook, and even enjoyed shopping for ingredients. It dawned on me that I hadn't seen her with her face in a book for quite a while. She and Emily chatted while she cooked and it was lovely to watch them reconnect after twenty years, even if their lives had taken different courses.

Once again, we were eating when Ben rang the doorbell, only Alfie was in bed by then. When I let him in he said he'd have to be quick as something had come up.

'Hey, Emily,' he said in the back room. 'Hi, Maeve.' He took a seat and said no thanks to a drink, then turned to Maeve. 'Your father not here?'

'Uh-uh. Dad lives in London. You should see his place. It's this enormous riverside apartment on two floors that overlooks the Thames and Tower Bridge. It's seriously stunning, isn't it, Mum?'

'Oh, yes.'

I could see Ben looking around the room thinking how come dad's got that, while his family lives here?

'Terence has only recently come into our lives,' I explained. 'Well, again, in my case.'

'He didn't know I existed,' said Maeve. 'Not for sure. Or that he had a grandson.'

'Is that right?' Ben said. 'Nice happy ending, though.'

'We're going to his this weekend and I'm meeting my two half-brothers, finally.'

'Really?' asked Emily, frowning.

'Yep. The oldest, Barnaby, is at school in Oxford, or near Oxford, only Dad won't tell me which school, in case I go and stalk him.' She laughed. 'I'll find out this weekend.'

'That's brilliant,' said Ben. 'You must be excited?'

'Very,' she told him. 'It's not that great being an only child.'

Let it go, I told myself.

'You wanna try having a cleverer, much more loved older brother,' said Emily.

I really liked Emily, I decided.

'Anyway,' said Ben, and Maeve, taking the hint, went to check on Alfie.

We sat at the table and Emily told Ben her 'fire' theory, then showed him the video. He thanked her, told her how useful that was, and after writing down his email address, asked her to send him the YouTube link. He then leapt up and was off before Emily could tell him she couldn't email anyone at the moment, and before I got to ask any of the questions that had been swirling around my head, mainly when trying to get to sleep.

Each night I prayed that the police knew what they were doing. Mike had to be somewhere, maybe dead, maybe not. I just wanted him caught, but how would they ever find someone so cunning with disguises? Mike could be anyone. At least anyone on the periphery. A vagrant, a hill walker, a potato picker. But not, as I'd briefly and paranoidly wondered the other day, Alfie's new nursery assistant, Michele.

I gave Emily a hug on the doorstep and told her to take care, then rang Astrid to see if she fancied a drink.

'Jonathan is away,' she said, 'so if you have anything illegal we could partake of, why not come here?'

I did, and so I did.

* * *

'But have you shagged yet?' she asked. 'Or even snogged?'

Such ugly words. 'No. Lots of hugs, though.'

'How polite.'

'I'm wondering if Terence has… problems.'

'So you said. Well, there are strategies, Edie. Ways and means.'

'Ways and means? Like those committees? We're talking about intimacy, here, not government funding. Raising Terence's doo-dah, not raising taxes.' I laughed again, thinking that was quite funny. Then I couldn't stop. 'Get it?'

'Hilarious,' she said, sounding half strangled while she held the smoke in.

'Anyway, what's the hurry? He's a lovely guy and I don't want to charge in and fall heavily and then find he's another commitment-phobe.'

'You know your trouble?' she said.

I didn't. 'What?'

'Plural, actually.'

'My troubles?'

'I'm basing this predominantly on what you've told me.'

'OK, fire away.'

'One, you're drawn to arseholes. Two, you always have to fall in love. And, three, you're too quick to forgive and so the relationship loses its usefulness and drags on.'

'Usefulness? That makes it sound as though people, couples, use one another.'

'Oh, Edie. Of course, that's what it's all about.'

She was probably right. 'So,' I said, 'how are things between you and Jonathan?'

'Fine. Excellent, in fact.'

'Really?' If I'd been next to her, I'd have given her a nudge. Go on, you can tell me... Instead, I smiled and bounced my eyes around. She just stared at me, impassively. 'So,' I said, 'you're not seeing someone on the side?'

'Yes, I am. But that wasn't what you asked me.'

'You are? Actually, I thought you were.'

'You only had to ask.'

'What if Jonathan asks you?'

'He won't.'

'How do you know?'

She reached for the wine and topped up her glass, then handed the bottle to me. 'Because we have an understanding. An arrangement.'

'What? Are you saying you and Jonathan have an open relationship?'

'We do.'

'I had no idea. And neither of you gets jealous?'

'I can't speak for Jonathan, but no, I don't. We've been married for eight years. That's a long time to sustain lust.'

'I wouldn't know that either. But I'd imagine it would depend on how important exciting sex is to a person, both persons. Perhaps most couples move on to something very loving… and still a bit romantic, but really more companionable.'

Astrid was giving me the stare again. Was I boring her, or was she just not getting it? Poor Jonathan, I thought, but hopefully he'd found someone gloriously normal. Was that where he was tonight?

'Tell me about the case,' Astrid said. 'Are the police getting anywhere?'

'I've heard one or two things,' I said, and I told her about Mike's watch being found, and Emily's 'fire' theory. 'The police aren't focusing solely on Mike, though. They have concerns about Jack.'

'Oh?'

'He has been gone a suspiciously long time now, and nobody's heard from him. And who knows, maybe my jokey notion that he and Mike had been working together wasn't that stupid.'

We both went quiet for a while, then Astrid stretched her arms in the air and rotated her wrists. It was one of the many signs that I was too uninteresting to talk to any longer.

'You could go on speculating forever,' she said, 'but really, what would be the point?'

'True,' I said, getting up to leave. 'I'd better be off. Lots to do tomorrow.'

'Me too.'

'How's business?' I asked, a little late, I realised.

'Busy. Oxfordshire Artweeks are coming up in the spring. I'll be opening the workshop and house to visitors.' She folded her arms and went, 'Ugh.'

'What?' I asked.

'People,' she said.

TWENTY-FIVE

The buzzer made me jump, since I still wasn't used to it, and there were the big brown eyes of DS Ben on screen.

'Hi!' I said, pressing him in and chucking my lunch wrapper in the bin. Once again he bounded up the stairs, then sat down opposite me, not even breathless. 'How's it going?' I asked. 'Continuing with your enquiries?'

'Pretty much,' he said. 'However, there have been developments.'

'What developments?'

'Jack.'

'Oh?'

'We've been checking his mobile records with his phone company.'

I felt my heart speed up. 'You're going to say he didn't call me from the Florence Park area that night.'

'I'm going to say he almost certainly didn't call you from the Florence Park area that night.'

'Where was he when he rang, then? Probably? Not Middle Thing? Please don't tell me it was Middle Thing?' I hoped I wasn't sounding hysterical. I was feeling it.

Ben nodded. 'Triangulation has it in the area.'

'Christ, the jogger.'

'I'm afraid there's more.'

'I feel dizzy,' I said. I really did. And my throat had filled with bile. Mexican-bean-wrap bile.

'Do you want me to fetch you some water?'

'Please. Yes. Sorry. You could grab a bottle from the shop? I'll pay them later.'

'Still or sparkling?'

'Still. Thank you.'

I listened to him run down the stairs, completely stunned. Jack? Why? He had to have been working for Mike all along. But he was so lovely. Great with Alfie. He'd cooked us that meal. What was I going to tell Maeve, that I'd invited a killer to feed us and play with Alfie? Oh, Jesus. Jack? But what about the watch they found?

Ben was back and handing me a bottle. 'What about Mike's watch?' I asked. I was trying to open the bottle but my hands were shaking.

'Here, let me,' said Ben. 'We don't know about the watch, but when we find Jack Bevington and get him back here for questioning, I'm sure he'll fill us in. The Portuguese police are onto it, and Interpol have come in and they'll check all border crossings and airports. Jack's father has heard nothing from him, and he's not been emailing. So, well, suspicious behaviour, to say the least.'

I sipped the water. 'You said there's more?'

'The partial footprint. We've identified the brand and style of shoe. A brown casual lace-up type. Ring a bell?'

I could only nod.

'We found a payment made by Jack for that particular shoe, four months ago. It's looking pretty bad for him, I'm afraid.'

'I guess you've searched his house in Botley now?'

'We have. Nothing incriminating there and nothing to give us a motive. My guess is he was working for Mike Wilder. So far that shoe print and the call to you, probably from the vicinity of the crime, is all we have. We've got some of his DNA now, to try and find a match at the house and on Isabella.'

'How did you get the DNA? From a hairbrush?'

Ben laughed. 'Been reading those novels again? Hairs aren't much use, but don't ask me to get technical. A recently used toothbrush is better, or a shaver. Fresh saliva's best, but not possible in this case.'

'Oh really?' I said. 'Interesting.'

Ben's face became serious again. 'I've had to go and speak to his father. That wasn't easy, particularly as Jack hasn't been in touch since taking off.'

'Where did he fly to?'

'Porto. The Portuguese police are checking trains, car hire, buses, but haven't come back to us yet. He withdrew a lot of cash before leaving the UK… so… anyway, I don't suppose, by some miraculous chance, he told you where he was headed? Or did he mention to you, or your daughter, any studio in Portugal, or where this supposed ex-girlfriend lives?'

'Sorry, no. I'll ask Maeve, though.' That was going to be a fun conversation. I looked up at Ben, chewing the inside of his mouth and imagined how cross they must all have been feeling in the incident room. 'I still can't believe it. We really liked him.'

'Sorry for delivering bad news. And, obviously, if you hear from him…'

'Don't worry, you'll be the first to know.' Something horrible occurred to me. 'He is definitely still abroad?'

'As far as we know. No one's entered the UK with his passport since he left, but that's not to say he's not used another. I mean, I don't want to get you unduly worried or nervous, it's best to be upfront. We are working as a team, after all.'

Jack and I had been working as a team, so I wasn't currently convinced they were good things.

He zipped up his jacket. 'I'm gonna have to…' He cocked his head towards the door. 'You OK now? Would you like me to walk you home?'

I laughed in a strange-sounding way. 'I haven't been asked that since I was sixteen.'

'Back when guys had manners, eh?'

'No, just ulterior motives.'

'Ah.'

I went home and tidied and cleaned in a frenetic manner. It was supposed to stop me fretting, but it didn't.

I rehearsed over and over what I'd say to Maeve – how sorry I was to have subjected her and Alfie to a potentially harmful person and situation, and how, if she wanted me to, I'd give up the agency and find something safe to do. Go back to teaching, even.

* * *

Maeve was naturally shocked and shaken but didn't appear angry with me.

'Jack was just a bit too charming,' she said, arms wrapped round her middle. 'Didn't you think?'

'He was around you, but to me he seemed very ordinary. Nice.'

'Narcissists, they can do that. They read people, and they're able to feed them what they want, and all without feeling anything. But why? Why would he have done that to Bella?'

'I don't know,' I said. 'He could have been working for someone else. Perhaps the financial inducement was large.'

'You mean the Mike guy?'

'I mean the Mike guy.'

Maeve was still hugging herself. 'I can't believe he was here, and flirting and asking me out and making me almost fall for him. Christ, he's not likely to come back here, is he?'

'Of course not, love. He's in hiding abroad, remember. I don't suppose he'll ever return to Oxford, let alone to a house where the police would immediately be called. And don't forget, we've got very good locks.'

Although we were both upset, Maeve and I kept up jollities for Alfie, then after he went to bed, Maeve tried on the different outfits she'd been thinking of wearing to meet her brothers. I approved of the casual jeans and jumpers and gave the thumbs down to the Greta Garbo get-ups, but knew, in the end, she'd please herself and be herself. She'd roll up, cool as anything, with a fake mole on her chin and a baby fox around her neck and they'd love her, because somehow Maeve got away with these things.

In spite of what I told her, I double-checked every door and window lock before going to bed. I also slept with the light on. Or, truth be told, didn't sleep.

TWENTY-SIX

On Thursday Naz called, offering us a lift to London. He was delivering a cab to some family member.

'Maeve said you were all going this weekend, and I'll be driving a people carrier. It would have to be tomorrow, though, not Saturday.'

The idea of heading off the next day was appealing. Maeve wouldn't be meeting her brothers until Saturday afternoon but at least we wouldn't have to rush down Saturday morning. 'That's a kind offer,' I said, 'but I'll have to check with Maeve and Terence. What will the fare be?'

'Nothing, since I'm going anyway. And my boss is paying me a bit extra.'

'Well, if you're sure.'

I told Naz I'd get back to him and then I phoned Terence, who I thought would be fine with us coming a day early, only he seemed thrown by it.

'Is this definite?' he said flatly. 'Only I'll have to cancel something.'

Chloe? I thought I heard his stick tapping. 'Don't worry,' I said. 'We'll come on Saturday, as planned.'

He went silent and the tapping stopped. 'No, no,' he said. 'It would be super if you all came tomorrow.' Now he sounded like Terence again. 'Lovely. I'll book a table for dinner somewhere, suitably early for Alfie.'

‘Are you sure?’ I asked, wanting more than anything to know what he’d be cancelling. ‘I hope we won’t be keeping you from something important?’

‘Not at all. You will all be safe,’ he said, ‘with Naz driving?’

‘We’ll find out, ha ha. But listen, big news.’

‘What’s that?’

‘The new prime suspect is Jack Bevington.’

‘Goodness.’

I told him everything I knew, then Terence said, ‘I do hope you’re not feeling too upset, or foolish, or unnecessarily guilt-ridden?’

‘Thanks, Terence,’ I snorted. ‘I wasn’t but I am now.’

‘Oh, sorry. And poor old Maeve, too.’

‘She’ll be fine.’ Tough as old boots, I didn’t add.

I told Terence I ought to call Maeve about the change of plan, and he said again how very much he was looking forward to seeing me, and I said, ‘Ditto.’

* * *

It was a relief to be packing our bags, mine and Alfie’s. Only Maeve was capable of packing for Maeve. How great it felt to be leaving Oxford and its tensions for a while. All I had to worry about was Maeve hitting it off with her brothers and not rubbing them up the wrong way by being overly attention-seeking. She’d probably benefit from having Alfie with her to share the limelight, but he hadn’t been invited along.

I finished packing but wasn’t happy. None of it was stylish enough for Terence’s beautiful apartment, or for him. I folded my one little black dress into the case, together with barely black tights and classy grey heeled shoes. Just in case. I hoped the dress would still fit and recalled the last time I’d worn it, to a chick-lit book launch in Soho. The author, Greg had claimed, was someone he ‘vaguely’ knew. Poppy turned out to be mid-twenties, drop-dead, and overly tactile with my partner, as he’d also been with her. They'd done lots of whispering and chuckling, forcing me to the ladies to shred toilet paper.

I took the dress and shoes out of the case and made a note to charity-shop them.

TWENTY-SEVEN

The following day, after I'd dashed into town to buy clothes, we were picked up by Naz and made it to Terence's by four, missing the rush hour. Naz had driven well and after he helped unload our bags I gave him thirty pounds, which was all he'd take. He'd be staying with his cousin all weekend, he said, if we needed anything. He gave me a card and told us all to have a great time before driving off.

'Here goes,' I said, and I took a deep breath and pressed the buzzer.

* * *

'Ah, yes,' Terence was saying, casually swilling wine in an over-sized glass. We were in a posh burger place that didn't do chicken nuggets for Alfie. 'The boys say they'd very much like Alfie to join us tomorrow. What do you think, Alfie? Would you like to meet your uncles?' He chuckled. 'How very odd that feels. My Barnaby and Theo being uncles.'

'Hey, brilliant!' said Maeve.

While I waited to be invited along, Alfie stopped eating fries and pouted. 'But Gan's taking me to the big wheel.'

'Why don't you and Gran do that in the morning?' Terence said. 'Or we could all go on it again?'

'Good idea,' said Maeve. 'I was in a bit of a mood last time.'

'Excellent!' said Terence, with a clap of his hands.

'Essallent!' said Alfie, clapping like Grampy.

I caught the look Maeve shot her father, and the one he gave her back. Why I was worried about Chloe, I didn't know, since Maeve was clearly the love of Terence's life?

'So,' she asked him, 'where are we meeting them, and what are we going to do?'

'The boys are going to come up with some ideas and call in the morning. We may as well make an outing of it, since they're coming all this way.'

'Cool,' said Maeve.

No, I wasn't going to be included. Understandably. Barnaby, Theo, meet the woman I didn't know but managed to impregnate at Oxford.

* * *

My head raced as I lay in bed in the white room. Jumbled images whizzed around and tripped over one another. Jack and the service station, and dead Bella's body, and Maeve flirting with Jack, and Chloe having sex with Terence, and the bastard stealing Emily's things… I took deep breaths and tried to clear my mind, but more things popped up. Jack stabbing Bella being the worst.

I gave up trying to sleep and sat upright. With hands loosely clasped I began silently repeating my mantra. I released each thought, letting it drift away, and after a while, found myself surrounded by white… white walls… no, a white marquee, with fairy lights. It's pretty… and *Tainted Love* is playing... a band, or a DJ. I'm dancing, we all are, then someone touches my arm. I turn and it's Terence and he hands me a drink… a shot. 'My favourite song,' he shouts. 'Dance with me.' I knock it back and we dance, and while we dance, I feel the glass fall from my hand and while I wait for it to smash, my eyes have popped open and I'm sitting upright in bed, in his apartment, heart thumping wildly.

TWENTY-EIGHT

I looked out at Tower Bridge and the City skyline beyond, feeling relatively calm. This time my tea had been made by Maeve, who said Alfie was asleep but she'd been up for hours.

'That's not like you,' I told her.

'No,' she said heavily, padding off on bare feet. Was she nervous? Even Maeve got jittery about some things.

I messed about on the laptop for a while, reading the online papers and checking the weather forecast for London. No rain, occasional sun. That would do. I googled Isabella Rossoni, as I did daily, and found nothing about the hunt for Jack. But perhaps the police hadn't wanted to alert him to the fact he was now their prime suspect.

Downstairs, we produced a full English breakfast and all dug in, with the exception of Terence, who excused himself to go and catch up on things in his study.

'Not big on breakfast these days,' he told us. 'The army encourages soldiers to fuel up with calories first thing and officers are expected to set an example. Good advice, I'm sure, if you're spending the day in combat.' He limped to his office, stick in hand, while Maeve gazed on adoringly.

'Your egg's going cold,' I told her.

* * *

'I feel sick,' she said, once we'd ploughed through it all. She sat on the kitchen stool, her face definitely wan above the Bette Davis robe, her arms tightly folded. 'I don't know why I'm so worried about this meeting. Nothing fazes me normally.'

'It's quite a big thing, love.'

'God, I wish I hadn't eaten so much. A fry-up always sounds like a good idea, but then afterwards… yuck.' She rocked on her high stool and closed her eyes. 'I was up at, like, five.' She yawned a big yawn and I got the hint.

'Do you want to go and have a rest, while I clear up and get Alfie dressed?'

'Do you mind?'

'Of course not. I'll wake you in, what, an hour?'

'Yeah, OK. Don't go without me!'

'We won't.'

As it turned out, she was impossible to rouse and we left her to recover in time for the 2.30 get-together.

Terence had suggested we walk to the Eye, so beneath the pricey but gorgeous leather jacket I'd dashed into town for on Friday morning, I'd added a long, chunky, bottom-covering cream jumper; the kind young blonde women in the Cotswolds wear. On my feet, skinny jeans tucked in, were the eye-wateringly expensive, short suede boots I'd also picked up. All bought with Mike's cash.

We strapped Alfie in his pushchair, promising him an ice cream if he stayed in it. Along the way I talked about the Bella case, going over the same old details, incidents and conversations, and coming up with the same theories. I hoped I wasn't boring Terence as much as I was myself.

'I wonder if we'll ever know,' he said after a while. 'If neither Mike nor Jack are ever found.'

'That would be the worst outcome of all. Never knowing, and always wondering if they'll turn up.'

Terence tried putting his free arm around me, as we walked, but I was pushing the buggy and he had his stick, and my diagonally slung bag hung between us, so we stopped and cuddled instead. 'You look lovely,' he said.

'Thanks.'

'Pretty earrings.'

'They're new.' I wouldn't tell him everything was. I kissed his cheek, then pulled back and looked at his very nice face. 'How are you feeling about the kids all meeting?'

'A little anxious, just as Maeve is. Let's hope she catches up on sleep and recovers her natural exuberance.'

'She will,' I said, suddenly stiffening, because there over Terence's shoulder was Mike. His hair, his build and stance.

'What?' asked Terence.

'Mike.' I whispered. 'At two o'clock.'

He laughed. 'Is that your two o'clock, or mine?'

'Mine. It's your… let me think… eight o'clock.'

Terence took a look. 'Edie,' he said, 'he's nothing like him.' He hugged me again, rubbed my back and kissed my nose. 'Silly.'

'I know.'

'Come on,' he said, 'let's get this little man to the Eye before he falls asleep.'

I bent over the pushchair and peered inside. 'Too late.'

* * *

Alfie woke just in time, refreshed and excited. Maeve kept a number-combo bike lock in the bottom tray and Terence used it to attach the buggy to railings.

'I take it you know the four digits?' he asked, still hunkered down, the lock firmly locked.

I slapped my forehead, dramatically. 'Damn!'

Terence grinned. 'Maeve's year of birth?'

'How did you guess?'

'She and I took Alfie to the park, the first time I came to your house. You remember, you drove off in a huff?'

'It was an urgent work matter.'

He stood upright and kissed my brow. 'Yeah right, as my sons would say.'

While Terence went for the prepaid tickets and I helped Alfie with his hat and gloves, I heard the phone ring in my bag. I got to it too late and saw an unknown number. Another adultery job I didn't want to do? Whoever it was had left a message, and I was about to listen when Alfie spotted an ice-cream van.

He opted for a cornet, as I knew he would. 'Careful,' I said, as ice cream flopped over the side of the cone. 'Quick, quick, give that bit a lick. That's it.' There was a cute blob on his nose and I snapped him twice with my phone.

'Ready, guys?' said Terence, beaming and waving tickets.

It was Saturday, so the line was longer than last time we'd been, although nothing like the queues I'd seen there mid-summer. But it was still early in the day. After ten minutes, the cone all gone, we stepped gingerly into our capsule while it continued to move along. I heard the people behind us laughing nervously as they jumped in.

Then, there we all were. Me, Terence, Alfie and a group of middle-aged-to-elderly Japanese people.

'Let's find you a good spot,' Terence said to Alfie, as we slowly ascended. 'And maybe we'll take pictures on Gran's phone to show your mum?'

I nodded. 'I've just got a message to listen to first.'

'Big Ben!' shouted Alfie, spotting it.

The Japanese tourists laughed and started saying, 'Ah, Big Ben!'

The day was clear and bright, better than the forecast, and I slowly circled the car for a while, taking in the views in all directions and trying to feel Alfie's excitement. For an adult, once on the Eye was probably enough. I made out roughly where Maeve was, spreadeagled on her front, plugged into music while she slept. She'd be over there, beyond the bend in the river, not far from the Shard. The boats grew smaller as we rose, and I was puzzled again by why there was so little marine activity on the Thames in London. The tide, perhaps.

The message. I sat on the central bench beside a thin elderly man, who had his eyes on the floor and talked to himself in Japanese. Vertigo, I guessed, or dementia.

'Gan, look!' I heard. 'Plane!'

'Oh, yes!' I pressed keys to get to the message.

'Hey, Edie,' said Emily. 'I thought I'd let you have my new mobile number. Thanks a lot for the money again. I found, like, this really nice second-hand laptop that I want to get. I'm gonna go to see it with Oscar, who knows about computers. And, yeah, maybe I could, like, keep it in the office, like you said–'

'Gan!' Alfie, now in Terence's arms, was waving at me. 'We're really high!'

'I know!' I said. 'Isn't it fun?'

'I can see Oxford,' he shouted, pointing in the direction of France.

'Ah, Oxford,' a woman said, and they all turned to France.

'Give Bidget a wave!' I told Alfie, and he did.

I hadn't heard the end of Emily's message, so listened again from the beginning.

'...in the office, like you said. Um,' she went on, 'I sort of wanted to talk to you about something that has been like bothering me? Only it seems silly... I dunno, anyway, when Maeve said she was going to like meet her brothers, or like half-brothers, I thought about when Terence gave me the money when I was begging? And I was talking to him about my parents and how, like, we didn't hit it off, seeing as how they were crap and I'm like carrying loads of resentment–'

Alfie shouted again, and I watched him pointing and talking animatedly. I hoped it wasn't a strain for Terence, holding him. They looked lovely together with their dark good looks. Terence, in his brown suede jacket, with that scarf I loved so much. Nice grey jeans. His shoes I liked too, even if they were odd sizes. I wondered what his swollen foot looked like, whether it was ugly and twisted. He lifted Alfie even higher to see something and his trouser bottoms rose. The left shoe was a snug fit and the right had the gap at the back. Strange that that seemed to work for him; the extra width, as he said.

'Come here, Gan!'

'Just coming,' I said. I went over and stroked his hair. 'What have you seen, Alfie?'

'We sawed Big Ben, and long way away we sawed the football stay… stay…'

'Stadium? It's called Wembley Stadium. Did you see its arc?'

'Like a rainbow.'

'Yes, it is. You know, lots of famous teams play there.'

'Indeed,' said Terence, his eyes lighting up. 'The crème de la crème being Man U.'

I laughed. 'I didn't have you down as a football fan.'

'My darkest secret,' he said, with that smile. 'We all got into it at Eton, the chaps in my year. As a kind of rebellion, I suppose, against the enforced rugby.'

I had an image of him in a scrum, all dishevelled and mud-covered. I blinked it away and said, 'There's only one thing I've ever liked about football. Thierry Henry.'

'Great player,' Terence said.

'Was he?' I asked, smiling.

'It was Beckham for me, back in the day.'

'Also gorgeous,' I said.

'Are you trying to make me jealous, Edie?'

I blushed and stroked my grandson's hair. 'Enjoying the ride?' I asked Alfie, but he was busy waving at the next carriage.

'Enormously,' said Terence. 'We both are.'

I moved my hand across to Terence and patted his shoulder. 'You really are very good with him.'

'Thanks.'

'Sorry. Listen, I just need to replay this strange message from Emily, then I'll take some photos. Are you OK with Alfie?'

'We're fine, aren't we?'

Alfie agreed and gave him a big noisy kiss on the cheek. I was being usurped but didn't mind, not too much.

I'd missed the end of Emily's lengthy message, and listened again until the bit about her parents…

'...carrying loads of resentment... And how they disapproved of my lifestyle when I was a teenager and how they shut me out their lives?' I thought about listening another time, but found the stamina to persist. 'And Terence said that he'd experienced that too, only from, like, the other side? And I said what do you mean, and suddenly he looked dead sad and said he never saw his sons and they haven't spoken to him for years, and then the sad look turned into like an angry look? And then he gave me the cash and said to take care and stuff. Like I told you, I've been avoiding him since. Don't want him knowing I was Millie the, like, pretend homeless girl? So, when I heard from you guys about his son being near Oxford and him visiting and how Maeve's gonna meet the two boys, I dunno... I just didn't understand why he'd tell me they never saw him or spoke to him?'

Because he'd wanted her to feel better, of course; to think she wasn't alone in feeling cut off from her family. It had been sweet of him, trying to cheer up a homeless girl and being generous too. I saved Emily's new number and kept the message to listen to again.

Terence, with his back to me, twisted to point out something to Alfie, and again I found myself looking at his shoes. The right bigger than the left. I thought back to sitting on the bench at Blenheim Palace. Hadn't he said the left was the bigger size? I'd been walking behind him that day, the breeze blowing at his ankles, the left shoe looking slightly too big, with the gap at the back. Had it been the left?

I heard a bizarre noise beside me and turned to see the Japanese man throwing up into a bag. It was a Harrods bag, so I felt doubly sorry for him. I didn't know if I should help, or move away and save my new clothes. After Hector's eruption, I knew the smell hung around for days. As I slowly rose, a woman came over and produced a pack of wipes. His wife, I assumed. She whispered in Japanese to him and did a kind of half bow of apology to me.

'*Sumimasen*,' she said as she dabbed a bit of puke off my leather sleeve. '*Sumimasen*.'

'Oh, please don't worry,' I told her, overly enunciating. 'Very old jacket!'

Now Terence and Alfie were holding their noses and giggling. I edged away and found myself leaning against the doors that told me not to lean against them, and once again studied Terence's shoes, thinking, remembering… or trying to. I closed my eyes. Yes. Yes, it had been the other shoe, at Blenheim. Why would he be able to switch that way, if one foot was badly damaged and needed more width and length… 'He never saw his sons and they haven't spoken to him for years...' I raised my eyes and caught Terence looking over his shoulder at me. He'd been busy in his office just before we'd left the flat, and at the last minute had gone upstairs to get ready, while Alfie and I waited, already in our jackets and boots, Alfie calling out, 'Hurry up, Gampy!' and me telling him not to because Grampy couldn't walk properly. It must have been accidental. In haste, Terence had put the wrong odd pair on. The other halves, as it were. Was it causing him pain, having the small shoe on the wrong foot?

I took in the view for a while to distract myself from silly thoughts. Just as it was working, the phone flew from my hand.

'Time for photos,' said Terence, plonking Alfie beside me. 'Let me take some.'

I bent down and put an arm around Alfie, and Terence leaned towards us, holding my phone out. 'Say cheese!'

Alfie said it loudly enough for the both of us, while I squeezed him and did a daft smile. Since turning forty, I'd loathed all photos of myself. Terence showed us the picture. Alfie looked cute, I looked ninety.

'Couple more?' he suggested. 'And Gran, do try and smile.' I thought I had, but this time I beamed toothily. Now I'd look like a batty ninety-year-old. 'And another!' said Terence. 'Big smile, Alfie! Lovely!'

He took a couple more photos, then hobbled over to the glass and looked down as we descended, slipping my phone into his coat pocket. I noticed a cheek muscle flexing, once, twice, three times, then he turned his back to us. I got distracted by Alfie for a while, and when I looked again Terence was on the phone. His or mine, I couldn't tell. We both had white iPhones. Still with his back to me, he appeared to lower the phone, tap it twice, then put it back to his ear. Oh, Jesus, Emily's message… 'He never saw his sons and they haven't spoken to him for years…' I went completely cold, then told myself it was ridiculous; I was being ridiculous. Of course he wouldn't do that, not with my phone, my private message. He listened for quite a while, and I was pretty sure he wasn't speaking. Finally, he spun round to face us, tucking the phone in the inside pocket of his coat. It must have been his, then, since mine had gone into his outside pocket. I relaxed. Stupid me.

'Can we go round twice?' asked Alfie.

'No, sweetie.'

'Pleeese, Gan.'

'No, we're not allowed.'

'Gampy?' said Alfie, reaching for Terence, who hung his stick on an arm and picked him up. 'Can we pay the lady again and go round again?'

Terence laughed. 'Do you know how much it costs, young man?'

'But Mummy said you got lots of money.'

Terence shushed him. 'Don't tell everyone. Hey, look, we're almost at the bottom. We'll have to jump off quickly, Alfie. The way we got on.'

All felt well again. Terence had told Emily a tale, and he'd put on the wrong odd pair of shoes. That was all.

'Can I have Coke in a café?' Alfie asked Terence.

'Certainly not!' he told him, ruffling his hair. 'But it might be nice to go to a café. We've got plenty of time before meeting the boys. What do you think, Gran?'

'Good idea,' I said. 'But no Coke.'

Alfie buried his head in Terence's neck, saying, 'You always let me have Coke, Gan.' That wasn't entirely true, he sometimes had a sip of mine.

'How about orange juice?' asked Terence. 'I love orange juice. It's my favourite drink in the whole world.'

'Yeah!' said Alfie. 'Orange juice!'

While I was wondering how Terence had done that, we moved towards the exit. The Japanese group had got there first, milling quietly, cameras packed away. We stood behind them, me at the very rear.

Terence bounced Alfie up and down. 'Ready to jump off?'

'Yes!' said Alfie.

It occurred to me that a mildly disabled person, wearing the wrong shoes, might find it tricky to step off a moving vehicle with a stick in one hand and a child in the other, so I suggested to Alfie that he let Grampy put him down. 'Then you can jump off all by yourself?'

'No,' he said firmly, and I knew there'd be no swaying him.

'OK, but no wriggling.'

'We're fine,' Terence said.

I was right behind him, and his coat, and his coat pockets, so, smooth as anything, I slipped my hand first into one, saying, 'I think you've still got my phone, Terence,' – then the other. Both pockets had one glove in, neither contained my phone.

The doors slid open and before the Japanese group could disembark, Terence clumsily moved his way through, inadvertently sending the chap who'd thrown up flying backwards, past his wife and towards me. I managed to catch him, or at least break his fall, and again the smell of vomit wafted my way. Within seconds, the Eye stopped moving and two large men stepped into the carriage. With one either side, the frail old guy was helped out and onto the platform, with a, 'Hold on to us, sir.'

'Is he OK?' I asked, following them out.

The Japanese man, now completely upright and regaining his dignity, bowed and said, '*Arigato.*'

'I'm so sorry,' I said, looking for Terence so he could apologise too. But I couldn't see him. I stood on tiptoe to look over the group approaching the carriages, and the long zig-zagging line of people queuing. No Terence, no Alfie. I thanked the security guys, then hurried down the walkway exit and over to the railings where we'd left the buggy.

It wasn't there.

TWENTY-NINE

With no phone, I couldn't call Terence to find out where he and Alfie were, so I darted here and there through the growing late-morning crowd, frantically scanning the faces and backs of heads. I stepped onto a small wall for added height and looked from my left, slowly around to the right. Then I turned around and did the same thing again. Why hadn't Terence waited by the buggy? That was what I would have done. I automatically dug into my jacket pockets to check for my phone. All I found was Naz's card... 'He never saw his sons and they haven't spoken to him for years...' I began to feel panicky. What to do, what to do...

A pale couple in their fifties were close by, huddled over something. Ice creams, 50p, five-pound note were mentioned. I approached them with a wobbly, 'Excuse me. I wonder if you can help me?'

The woman snapped her handbag shut and hugged it. 'Yes?' she said, looking me up and down. Her nose twitched, as though she could smell sick.

'I'm sorry to bother you but I've lost my mobile and need to call for a taxi.' I showed them Naz's card. 'I wonder if you might have a phone I could use?'

'I'm not sure…' said the man, slapping a hand against his top pocket.

'I need to be somewhere urgently, you see, to pick up my grandson. I'll pay you for the call.'

The man held out his other hand. 'Tell you what, love. Give me the card and I'll ring the number for you.' He had a Yorkshire accent and clearly didn't trust leather-clad southern women. Or else I was coming across as mad as fuck and desperate with it.

'Thank you, thank you,' I said, dropping it in his palm. 'Ask for Naz from Oxford to come to the Eye. Or maybe to the hotel over there. The Premier Inn?'

'OK. And your name?'

'Edie. Edie Fox.'

I continued to search amongst the heads and faces, approaching, retreating and swirling, while the man stepped a few paces away and his wife followed him. The call was brief and then they were back and returning the card.

'Naz will see you at the entrance to the hotel in a few minutes. Apparently, he's quite close.' The woman gave me a friendly smile and asked if I was going to be all right.

'Yes,' I said. 'And thank you so much.' If I'd had any idea of Maeve's number, I'd have asked them to ring her too.

The couple disappeared into the crowd, and after one last scan I walked on shaky legs to the hotel.

* * *

'You OK, miss?' Naz kept checking me out in his rear-view mirror. 'You seem a bit anxious.'

'I'm fine,' I insisted, not wanting to say anything. I couldn't be sure Terence hadn't searched for me, the way I had for him. 'I'm just tired.'

'That's London for you, miss.'

In heavy traffic, we headed for the apartment in stops and starts. I pretended to sleep to avoid conversation, then when I pretended to wake up, outside Terence's block, I said, 'Naz, I don't suppose you could hang around for five minutes?'

'Is something amiss, miss?'

I would have laughed, if it hadn't been for the terror and the horrible dread inside that told me Terence had stolen Alfie. 'No, no.' I took a tenner from my purse and gave it to him. 'I'll pop back out in five minutes, or less, then you can go... if I don't… then… well…'

'Er, OK.'

'I'll definitely be back,' I said firmly. 'I think.'

Terence had given me a set of two keys, and once through the entrance I took the stairs to the first floor and with a trembling hand opened up the door to the flat.

'Maeve?' I called out. There was a faint echo. 'Hello?' I tried again.

Please God, let her be asleep, headphones on. I ran across the expanse of living room and up the wooden stairs. The door to Maeve's bedroom was ajar and I pushed it wide open. No Maeve. A messy bed but no Maeve. I stood still and heard water running, just before it stopped. The bathroom. Thank God, I thought, turning and walking across the landing. I was about to knock and call out when the wet-room door swung inwards, and out stepped Terence in a brown towelling robe. I swallowed a scream and put a hand on the wall to steady myself.

'Hi, Edie,' he said, 'where did you get to?' He came over and kissed me wetly on the forehead. 'Alfie and I looked all over.'

I shook, inside and out. 'Where is he now? And where's Maeve?'

'Hey, hey,' he said, holding me by the tops of my arms. 'I'm sorry we left, but I assumed you'd just come back here. Which you have.' He smiled, warmly. 'Maeve's taken Alfie out for lunch. She left you a note in the kitchen.'

I shook Terence off and ran downstairs, where I found Maeve's distinctive handwriting on an envelope.

Mum, sorry not to make it to the Eye. Feeling better and starving, so taking Alfie for a HEALTHY sandwich to make up for the ice cream!!! See you later X

Relief flooded through me. Alfie was fine. They were both fine. They'd soon be back in the apartment and all would be well. And perhaps I could talk Terence into letting me come along to the meeting with his boys, even if only to say a quick hello, then leave them to it. I suddenly remembered Naz, and leaving both doors on the latch, went back to the taxi and thanked him.

'I thought I might need another lift, that was all. Do I owe you any more fare?'

'Not necessary.' Naz's expression was serious, which wasn't unusual, but quizzical too. 'Are you sure you're all right?' he asked.

'Yes, I just… No, I'm fine.'

'If you say so, miss.'

* * *

After a quick search of the kitchen for my phone, I was filling the kettle when Terence appeared, beautifully turned out for his big afternoon. He even wore a loosely knotted tie over his dark grey shirt. I took the kettle to the counter and as I stood it on its base and flicked the switch, I felt his arms encircle me. I flinched.

'Ooh, you gave me a fright,' I said.

He nuzzled my neck and I went along with it, quietly moaning. 'Why don't I rustle us up an omelette?' he whispered.

'Sounds lovely.' I was still full from breakfast, but he'd missed that meal.

'Cheese? Mushroom?'

I lifted a heavy arm and stroked his hair. 'Both?'

'OK.'

Terence detached himself and crossed the kitchen to the built-in fridge. He gathered eggs, cheese, milk and butter and placed them on the island counter, and from a base cupboard took a bowl and a cast-iron pan. He cracked a large egg, then one, two, three more. Grabbing a hand whisk from the metal rack above, he began beating the eggs, grinding black pepper, whisking again. The kettle was bubbling and hissing now, and it was altogether too noisy for me to ask where my phone was. I decided I'd look for it myself.

'Just popping to the loo!' I shouted, gesturing towards the cloakroom at the far end of the flat, past the living area and between the study and the lobby. The lobby where Terence's coat hung. I walked briskly, but not obviously so, and once there checked his coat pockets, outside and inside. I found only the two gloves. Could he have taken my phone and attached it to a charger, and if so, where? My bedroom? Maeve's? We all had the same chargers.

The study? It was tucked out of sight of the kitchen and I slipped in there, heart thumping. There were no mobiles, just the landline, which was of no use to me. I made a resolution, there and then, to write everyone's mobile number in my address book. But to do that, I had to first find my phone.

'Looking for something?' he said, filling the doorless doorway, rubbing omelette mix off his shirt.

'Oh, just my mobile,' I said, casually, pleasantly.

He smiled his beautiful smile and his eyes joined in, and he just seemed like Terence again. 'It was out of battery, so I plugged it into Maeve's charger upstairs. Five minutes ago? I'd give it a while before using it.'

'OK.'

'Sorry, I should have told you.' He took a step forward and leaned on his stick. 'And I'm sorry, too, for accidentally keeping it. It was distressing when we were looking for you, not to be able to call. We even went back to the platform by the carriages. They let me through when I said I'd lost Alfie's grandmother. Alfie was… well, a little upset.'

'Poor love.'

'But just briefly. I said you were probably racing us back to the flat, so we should hurry and get there first. That cheered him up.'

'Clever.' How could I have not seen them? Just bad luck.

'We got a cab, which we decided wasn't cheating.'

'So did I.'

'Come on,' Terence said with a smile, offering me his hand. 'Let's eat.'

I complimented him on the omelette, although I couldn't eat much of it, and while I made a tea for me and a coffee for him, we listened to *The News Quiz* repeat on Radio 4, laughing at the same things and agreeing on which panellists were the funniest. Finally, finally, I began to relax. We threw everything in the dishwasher and when Terence hobbled off to change his shirt, I thought I'd go and check my phone and give Maeve a ring. They were cutting it a bit fine, if they were to meet the boys at half two.

Upstairs, I straightened out Maeve's bedding and opened the blinds, then went over to the bedside table and picked up my plugged-in phone, which for some reason wouldn't switch on. I swore and tried again, and again, then followed the lead to a socket behind the table. The switch was up. I growled and cursed Maeve and when I flicked the socket on, the phone came to life and told me it was at rock bottom and charging. Strange. I'd charged it overnight, but perhaps Alfie had been watching videos on it in the taxi.

I sat on the bed and took in Theo's room. Apart from the view and Maeve and Alfie's clothes, spewing from bags and hanging off the one canvas chair, there wasn't much to see. Just Theo's guitar on the wall, basically. I pictured the boys coming to stay and filling the pristine rooms with noise and activity. Guitar strumming, Xbox games…

I heard Terence showering again, which seemed a bit over the top for a few splashes of egg. He'd be a while, so I got up and went over to the fitted white wardrobes, and in the corner furthest from the door and window, I slid one open. As in his brother's room, the one I was using, the cupboard was packed full of games, clothes, tennis rackets and cricket bats. There were ice skates, too. I used to love ice skating as a kid, but remembered the discomfort of the hard boots, tied extra tightly for ankle support. I picked one up and noticed the blades were completely scratch-free, and that the long laces were threaded only through the first couple of holes, then tied in a looped bunch. They were clearly brand new and never worn.

I put the skate back and bent down to examine the cricket bat. No dents, no scratches, not even a scuff. Maybe Terence had encouraged Theo to be sporty, and bought him all this equipment, but he'd been more into music, girls and bongs. If I delved deeply, would I find condoms and drugs?

Level with the top of my head was a shelf containing piles of T-shirts, hoodies and rugby shirts, along with some books. I pulled down a book to see what Theo read, and with it came a rugby shirt, which flopped open to reveal a small price tag dangling from the sleeve. The book was *Animal Farm*, and again it looked brand new, unopened and unread. Emily's words filled my head, and while I refolded the shirt, my stomach squeezed tight. In order to lay it flat, I stood on the wardrobe frame and held on to the top shelf, and as I did so a fragrance hit me. I breathed in deeply, hanging on to the shelf. It was familiar, so familiar, but I couldn't place it. I shoved a pile of T-shirts aside and stretched into the darkness until my hand hit something soft. I managed to grab it, and as it came into the light and I stepped down off the frame, I was shrouded in Mike's cologne. In my hand was a black felt hat, and inside the black felt hat was a short blond hair.

‘What the heck?’ I whispered, then noticed the shower had stopped and quickly lobbed the hat back on the shelf. This was too weird. Terence didn’t wear cologne, or any noticeable aftershave. And there was the hair. It had to be Mike’s hat, but it made no sense that they knew each other. Maybe they didn’t. Maybe Mike had left his hat behind in my office, and I hadn’t noticed. And Terence had picked it up and… what? Brought it to his apartment and kept it at the back of a wardrobe?

I couldn’t get my head around any of it, not the unused sports gear and unworn clothes, not Mike’s hat. All I knew was that I should really get away from Terence. But I couldn’t, not without Maeve and Alfie. My heart thumped and I was breathing rapidly. I should have asked him where they were. Which café. I’d have to act normally until I either found out where they were, or they returned to the flat. Then, and only then, could I take action. My phone would be charged and I could call Naz to come back. Or use the landline, since I had the business card. Although shaky and petrified, I almost felt better for having a plan. Almost.

‘There you are!’ Terence said, fully dressed and rubbing his head with a towel.

A strange, shocked noise came out of my mouth and he stopped rubbing.

I smiled, but it was hard. ‘I guess Maeve and Alfie will be back soon?’ I asked.

He didn’t respond straight away, but threw the towel on the bed and with hands on his hips stared at me. ‘I’m going to meet them at the café at two, didn’t I say? We’ll head off from there to meet Barnaby and Theo.’

‘I’ll come along with you, to the café.’

‘No need.’

‘I’d like to see Alfie,’ I said, ‘and for him to see me, since he was so upset earlier.’ I couldn’t keep the desperation from my voice. ‘Where are you meeting them?’

Terence walked over, around the bed until he was beside me. Something was different. His gait. And where was his stick? He put his arms around me, and with a finger under my chin, pulled my face up to his. 'Edie, Edie,' he said. He kissed me, passionately, and I tried hard not to shake. It made me feel ill, but I kissed him back. I knew I had to go along with this, whatever it was that was going to happen. Sex, I guessed, or an attempt at it. 'Too bright,' he said, after the kiss, and he let go of me. 'I'll adjust the blinds.'

'Good idea,' I said, running a hand down his arm. When he turned and walked perfectly normally over to the window, I sat on the bed and reached for my plugged-in phone. With fumbling fingers I switched it to video and tapped to start record, then quietly put it back on the table and covered it with Sniffy.

Terence stretched out on the other side of the bed and began stroking my hair, shoulders and arms. I lay down and he put an arm around me and continued to caress me through my chunky jumper.

'I've wanted to do this for so long,' he whispered.

'Me too,' I said.

He kissed me again, lovingly. Just the previous evening, following our family meal out, I'd have been so happy that this was happening. Now it felt like some sadistic game I was compelled to go along with. Or perhaps I was wrong, and this was genuine and all was well, and having two showers helped Terence walk unaided. It was the not knowing that made me tense; that made the situation feel awkward and bizarre. The last thing I wanted was sex. I just wanted my family back.

'Why don't you take this off?' he asked, tugging at my jumper. I sat up and did so. 'This too,' he suggested, running a finger down my cotton top.

'OK,' I said, smiling at him before stripping down to my bra and dropping both items on the floor. I tugged at

Terence's shirt, playfully. 'You too,' I said, with no idea how I was able to do this.

He used his free hand to wriggle his tie loose and pull it off, over his head. I undid a shirt button, then another, and he did the rest. His chest was hairy. Dark hair, with bits of grey. I stroked it with the back of my hand, disgusted by it and by the smiling face above it. All I wanted was for this to be over, quickly, so that I could either talk Terence into letting me come with him, or follow him. He was undoing his belt, unzipping his flies and tugging his trousers down and off, taking socks with them.

I propped myself up and saw his two perfectly normal feet, then just as he was noticing me noticing them, there was a quiet thud and we both turned to where Mike's hat had fallen off its shelf and onto the floor. I hadn't closed the wardrobe door properly.

I shot Terence a guilty look and saw his expression turn from friendly and playful to cold. 'Oh dear,' he said, and a nanosecond later I was lying beneath him, my left arm being lifted up above my head. He held it there, and with his other hand yanked my right arm up and made me yelp with the sharp pain in my shoulder. I feared then, with that sudden act of violence, that I wasn't going to survive. Although I'd known from the moment he'd walked in the room, or even before, that he'd be in control, I hadn't expected this, and couldn't, in my panic, work out how to behave. Neither fear nor anger would work; I knew that. I had a flash of Connor ruling the playground and my advice to his victims. Don't let bullies know you're afraid. They like to see you're scared. Terence's entire weight was on me now and I knew no amount of effort on my part would free me. My mouth was right by his Adam's apple. I could have taken a bite, so easily.

'You employed Mike,' I said, for the benefit of my phone.

'Fucking useless Mike, you mean.' One of his hands held both my wrists, the other was wrapping his tie around them. I could smell toothpaste, all trace of lunch scrubbed away. 'Let's just say he mis-sold himself. I needed someone found, he claimed he was a good character actor. I hired him, he fucked up, I fired him.'

'Lucky you had me, then? To lead you to Isabella.' I tried not to shout and raise his suspicions. Did he have a knife, I wondered, brought up from the kitchen?

'Very lucky. Don't move your arms,' he said, sitting up.

'I won't.' My wrists were tightly bound and they hurt. Would he use the tie to strangle me, afterwards?

'Why did you kill Isabella?' I asked, this time I did shout because hysteria was kicking in, as he pulled my boots off, then undid my jeans and jerked at each leg until they too were off. Uppermost in my mind were Maeve and Alfie, and what he'd do if they turned up now, or if I didn't survive this. Don't cry, don't protest. Did Maeve have keys? I thought not. Terence flopped back on top, knocking all air and strength from me. He wore only his shirt now and I could feel his erection.

'Because she poked that camera of hers into one place too many.'

'But she didn't tell anyone anything,' I wheezed, struggling to breathe in.

'Oh, she'd have said something one day. About what she saw. To someone.' He kissed me again, hard, so that my teeth dug into my skin.

'I suppose she would,' I panted, when he stopped. I thought I could taste blood. 'You had no choice but to kill her, Terence.'

He pushed himself up and looked down, assessing me, I felt. He was surprisingly jowly in that position and his eyes were tired-looking and puffy. 'I didn't, did I?'

'She saw something she wasn't supposed to.'

'Unfortunately, yes.'

I was about to ask what it was Bella had seen, but my phone chimed a text tone and made us both start.

Terence rolled off me and reached down to the floor. He lay with his back to me and read the message. 'Oh dear, Edie. Shame you didn't press record properly.'

We were still touching, so I couldn't safely move without his knowing and he'd soon catch me if I tried. I was cold now, so exposed, and I felt myself shaking. I didn't want my dad seeing me like this, trussed up and almost naked, but, with eyes tightly closed, as if that might help, I pleaded with him to save me.

Terence sniggered. 'I'm just texting your daughter, pretending to be you… "Hi, love… I'm… having to return to Oxford. Sorry. Something's… come up to do with the… case. Have a lovely time with your brothers…"'

My eyes filled up and I let out a series of choked sobs.

'Now, now, Edie. Just when you were being so brave. Gutsy, even. "Love… Mum".'

Something was happening with my wrists. The tie was loosening itself, or Terence was using his spare hand again. Was he freeing me? No, he wouldn't let me go, not now. How had I got myself trapped this way, when I'd known, even back on the Eye, that things weren't right. The shoes, the message, my appropriated phone. But now my hands were loose, and I guessed I was about to either be strangled with the tie, or moved somewhere; the boot of his car, the bottom of the Thames. I heard myself wailing and sniffing pathetically, while Terence managed, somehow, to still be texting.

'Two kisses, isn't it?'

I flexed my freed wrists before opening my water-filled eyes to see, through the bleariness, a figure silhouetted above me, on my side of the bed – the window side, the door side. The door I could run through and escape. It was a man with a beard, who had a finger to his lips, telling me to keep quiet. I tried blinking away the tears but more kept forming, and then I heard a thump and a crash and Terence crying out savagely.

I flung myself onto the floor, where I used the duvet cover to wipe my face and eyes, then stood up on weak legs and, unable to see my clothes, grabbed some of Maeve's and pulled them on while the two men crashed around on the far side of the bed.

'You bastard!' hissed a voice that wasn't Terence's but was vaguely familiar.

Terence, in only his shirt, had the bearded guy pinned against the wall. I heard another thump, and a groan from the bearded man, and frantically looked around the room for a weapon. The guitar. I pulled it from the wall and climbed on the bed, then aiming at Terence's head thrust it down with all my might. It struck his back, making him howl and keel over, and I was about to go in for a second hit when he leapt up, grabbed his clothes and staggered from the bedroom.

'Fuck!' said the stranger, as my knees gave way and I fell into a sitting position on the bed. He heaved himself away from the wall and rubbed at his middle, then lifted his head and looked me in the face. 'Think he cracked me ribs,' he said, breaking into a very toothy smile. 'You OK, Edie? Edie?'

Mike? A kind of wail came out of my mouth. Mike's hat was here; he and Terence were obviously in cahoots. Was Mike going to finish me off?

'Come on, old girl,' he said, holding out a hand. 'No time for that. Let's get to Maeve and Alfie before that fucker does.'

THIRTY

'Where the hell's Naz?' Mike yelled.

We'd run, quite fast, down the stairs and across the living room. I'd stopped to put shoes on, then down more stairs we'd run, out the building and to the end of the side street. Mike was scanning the area, scratching his head.

'What do you mean?' I puffed, searching nervously for Terence. 'And, just out of interest, how did you get in there?'

'When you were talking to Naz outside.' He flagged down a black cab and we piled in. 'You left the doors open.'

'Thank God I did.'

'He was supposed to wait for me.'

'Oh, I see.' But did I?

'Organical, please,' Mike told the driver. 'It's a café in–'

'Yes, I know it, sir.'

'Fast as you can.'

We did a three-point turn and sped off.

'How do you know they're there?' I asked. I did up my seat belt and stared at new Mike. Slimmer. Bearded. English.

'I followed them earlier.'

'What?'

I could tell Mike was still pumped up from his encounter with Terence. His eyes were darting here and there, checking out pedestrians.

'Are you OK?' I asked.

'Yeah, yeah. Well, apart from the ribs.'

'Oh God, I'm so sorry.'

'Hardly your fault.' It was unsettling hearing the northern accent, seeing the longish brown hair, but then everything about the day was strange and horrifying. Mike briefly squeezed my hand. 'Sorry, Edie, there's just too much to explain.'

'You're not kidding,' I said. I too looked at passing faces, both wanting and not wanting to see Terence.

'As long as you're all right?' Mike asked.

'I will be once I've got my family back.' I felt myself welling up again. Shock and disbelief flooded through me, along with images of what Terence might do to my daughter and grandson. 'But no, I'm fine physically, thanks to you.'

'I could say the same.' The traffic had come to a standstill, and after three or four heavy sighs, he got a ten-pound note out of his wallet and told the driver to stop. 'It'll be quicker to walk from here,' he said, and before I knew it, we were out and haring along a pavement, hand in hand, as we wove through startled people.

It was hard running in my wedge-heeled pumps, but they'd been the only shoes downstairs by the door; my boots being up in the bedroom. Around a bend we went, across a street of more stuck cars, down an alley, along another street, then left into a very busy Southwark road.

'It's not far,' Mike shouted.

'Good,' I puffed, impressed by his knowledge of London shortcuts.

He let go of me at a pedestrian crossing and pointed. 'There,' he said, out of breath but not as badly as me. The other hand was on his ribs.

Over the road was a café with "Organical" spelled out intricately in vegetables above the door. I remembered spiritual Tanya explaining cosmic ordering to me once, and as I stood there, cars shooting past, I focused on the café and imagined little Alfie in there, wading through broccoli. I imagined hard, then harder, and when the green man lit up and we crossed the road, I imagined harder still.

THIRTY-ONE

'Oh, Mum, that's hilarious!'

I looked down at myself. Cream just-below-the-knee culottes; very Wallis Simpson on a yacht. My calves were bare but my feet still sported the short black socks I'd worn under my jeans. Then there were the cerise wedgie pumps. Under my leather jacket was a lilac tasselled scoop-necked flapper top of Maeve's. I zipped up my new leather jacket, then bent and squeezed Alfie in his chair, kissing his head over and over. He wriggled and clearly hated it, but not as much, I guessed, as the untouched items on his plate.

'Your mum left home in a hurry,' explained Mike at the rear.

'This is Mike,' I said to Maeve, who'd never met him, only heard and read about him. 'You know, my client.'

She let out a gasp, stood up and tugged Alfie from both me and his seat. 'The murder suspect?' she asked. 'Or is that Jack now? I can't keep up. And why are you speaking Manchester, not American?'

'Lincolnshire,' he told her.

'Same difference.'

'Not really. Lincolnshire is a large county on the east coast and very agricultural.'

She put Alfie back in his seat and half-grinned at Mike. 'Is that right?'

He did his toothy smile back through his beard. Remembering the disguises found in his house, I wanted to tug at it, see if it was real. 'Lots of pigs,' he added.

'Right,' Maeve said, not moving her eyes off him. 'And I take it you're not a murderer?'

'He's not,' I told her. 'Listen, guys, we have to get you out of here.'

'But we're meeting Dad?'

I looked at Mike for help.

'That,' he said, scooping up their coats and Maeve's pearl-covered clutch bag, 'is why we have to get you out of here.'

THIRTY-TWO

'So let me get this right,' said Astrid, up on her stool, holding something shiny with tweezers. We were having a drink and a sneaky puff in her shed, while the latest au pair watched the boys. Well, I was. I gulped down red wine and balanced the glass on the arm of the recliner. Astrid was sticking to hot water and lemon, as not even my almost being killed derailed her Tuesday detox. 'Mike was employed by Terence to find Terence's ex-girlfriend, Isabella. Only she wasn't his old girlfriend, and she certainly wasn't Mike's cousin, and neither of them had actually met her, not properly.'

'Correct.'

'Isabella had, in fact, witnessed something bad Terence had done, but we don't know what. And it was something so bad that he had to find her and kill her.'

'Yep.'

'Terence instructed Mike to use your investigation agency, then got himself close to you, by pretending he gave a shit about his illegitimate daughter.'

'Well, I wouldn't–'

'And through you, Terence discovered that Mike was blowing his, Mike's, cover. He sacked Mike and threatened to do evil things to his sisters if he didn't do a good job of disappearing. But first, he got him to bring Jack in on the case.'

'Correct.'

'Mike put a label on his cat, then legged it to a silent retreat in Bedfordshire, of all places, away from all communication and media. When he finally emerged, he saw the newspapers, googled, whatever, and after sounding out Emily, rushed to London to save your life.'

I nodded.

'Meanwhile,' continued Astrid, 'Terence decided he rather liked his new family and wanted to keep them. But not you.'

'Ouch, but yes.'

'Going back to the Eye incident. Naz sensed you were upset about something when he picked you up, so once at Terence's apartment block, didn't leave immediately after you told him you didn't need another lift. He and Mike had spotted each other there, when you first went in, and had a quick conflab, then Naz was supposed to hang around in case a getaway driver was needed.'

Astrid's ability to listen and retain information was impressive. She should give up the pots, I thought, and become a barrister. 'Correct,' I said.

'But he didn't hang around. Instead, when the opportunity presented itself, he inadvertently abducted Terence.'

I thought back to Naz's shakey-voiced phone call. 'I just dropped the posh bloke off,' he'd said. 'As far north of the river as I could get before he jumped in the front and strangled me with his bare hands, which was what he kept threatening to do. Said he'd done it in combat. Only when he tried, I elbowed him in the gut, and then I stopped and dragged him out the cab and left him in a heap on Holloway Road.'

'Something of a hero,' said Astrid.

'Indeed. Argh, must stop using that word. Naz might well have thought twice about letting Terence in the car, if he'd known the whole story.' I shuddered at the thought of what could have happened, and me having to tell Naz's parents.

'And Terence is still on the loose, three days later.'

'Thanks for the reminder,' I said with a titter. I hadn't tittered for days, and thought I might never ever titter again, but, owing to the weed, the terror I'd felt since arriving home on Sunday had dissipated. For two nights

I'd lain awake, waiting for Terence to jab a leg through my bedroom ceiling, having parachuted onto our roof and prised slate tiles off. I'd had it all worked out, the ways he could have got to us again. But now... now I felt a lot safer. The police had every eventuality covered and, as a family, we were being protected to death. Maybe not death. Hopefully not.

'It's a funny word, isn't it?' I said.

'What?'

'Titter.'

She did her sigh-slow-blink thing. 'Only because it's got tit in it.'

'Oh yeah. Go on, Astrid, have a drink. I'm alive!'

'But it's Tuesday. Tomorrow, perhaps.'

'I can't do tomorrow,' I lied.

Astrid tapped her red nails together as she thought. 'I guess you were too blinded by foolish romantic fantasy to see what was going on. I mean, the timing, for one. Terence just happens to show up when your first big case comes in? He involves himself, asks questions, gets you to use him as a sounding board. I mean, Edie. Come on.'

I grinned at Astrid. How fantastic it was to be here, in her shed-studio, being judged and berated.

'What?' she asked.

Somehow, I was nowhere near as afraid of her as I used to be. 'You know Jonathan's birthday dinner party?' I said. 'Last... what was it, September?'

'The twenty-fourth, yes. What about it?'

'Why wasn't I invited?'

'Goodness,' she said, a hand flying to her chest. 'Talk about bearing a grudge for a long time.'

'I'm suddenly feeling brave enough to bring it, and all the other dinner parties, up.'

Astrid looked uncomfortable, which was pleasing. 'To be honest,' she said, 'it's the wives. Partners, whatever. The women. I know you'll find this hard to believe, Edie, and I certainly do...'

Here goes, I thought, bracing myself and thankful I was stoned. 'Go on.'

'They feel threatened by you.' She laughed heartily. 'I know, ridiculous, isn't it? You're a single, moderately attractive woman.'

I squinted at her. 'I think you're bullshitting me, Astrid. You don't want me at your fine-dining parties because I'd make the numbers odd, and because you don't know any single men who are dysfunctional enough for me.'

'Yes,' she said, shaking her pretty blonde head, then nodding it. 'You're right.'

Somewhere, in the deep and muddled past, I recalled a man talking about contradictory body language, but I was far too fuzzy to work out which were Astrid's fibs and which weren't. And what did it matter? What would I want with another man? They cheat, they lock your cat in the shed and they try to steal your family.

THIRTY-THREE

'This,' said DS Ben Watson from across my desk, 'was amongst the things we found yesterday in the chimney breast of Isabella's room in Florence Park. It was Emily and her fire theory that led us to it. There are also photos of Terence Casales, which I'll show you in a while.'

I stared at the crumpled sheets of paper. 'But why didn't you check the fireplace when you first searched her room?'

Ben looked put out. 'We did. It was boarded up pretty solidly, so we had no reason to suspect there'd be anything higher up the chimney breast.'

'I didn't mean to sound critical.'

'That's OK.'

'Shall I just read this? Now?'

'Well, it's written by Isabella and rather harrowing. So if you'd rather not?'

'No, it's OK. I want to know everything.' There were three pages altogether, beautifully handwritten with the loops and other tell-tale flourishes of an artist. I took a deep breath and began.

> *November, Northumberland*
> *I pulled over and parked, tilted half up on the rough grass verge, like the black car in front. Glorious, I thought, lowering the window. These UK colors were as stunning as any Fall in New England. In addition, the rolling hills created a whole other palette of shades. This, I had to capture. I opened the map and examined it. Better and better, I thought, noticing a small lake, roughly two miles away.*
> *From the trunk I took out my large backpack and pushed my camera into one outer pocket and the map into another. Rather than leave my purse in the car, I tipped its contents, which were wallet, passport, address book and makeup, into the larger bag. Already in there were water, a banana, two sandwiches, trail mix, an extra sweater, a compass, three lenses and a collapsed mini-tripod. I was about to drop my iPhone in, but for easy access to take impulsive photographs, tucked it in my jeans pocket. As I tightened and buckled the full round backpack, I was pleased I'd left the MacBook in my room.*
> *There seemed not to be any official trails, but that has never stopped me in the past, particularly in the UK. There's literally no areas of wilderness left here. All land is managed, to one degree or another, which means nothing is truly impenetrable.*
> *The day was fabulously bright, but it was also chilly. There'd been no rain predicted, so when choosing which jacket to wear I went for wool, in a rust shade that both matched the vivid scenery and complemented*

my hair. It wasn't vanity, since I'd likely see nobody. But, rather, I felt it respectful to blend in with nature. There were no Day-Glo anoraks in my trunk.

I clunked the car locked, put the key in my other jeans pocket, then double-checked each door. After making out a narrow deer track, I set off over uneven terrain for the forest that would lead me to the lake, where I aimed to take pictures before either clouds or evening descended. It was only two o'clock. I should be fine.

At first I'd thought it was a crow, squawking once, twice. But then I caught movement, in the distance to my right, in a small clearing at the bottom of a gentle slope. I stopped and leaned against a tree. The sound of a scritch, followed by a high-pitched grunt came from a guy in a plaid shirt and ball cap. He had a shovel in his hand and appeared to be digging a hole. A pretty deep one. I thought he must be a forester planting a tree, so quickly took my cell from my pocket to catch him in action. Dark-haired and bearded, he'd make a terrific addition to my "Occupations" file.

I took a picture and dropped it in the cloud, amazed I could do that in this remote spot. Perhaps I wasn't as far from a town as I'd thought. When the guy turned a little toward me, I took another. Again, it went into the cloud. But, in reality, I was too far away and needed a zoom lens for decent clear photographs. After unclasping the rucksack's belt, in order to take out my camera, I noticed the long package on the ground, a few feet from the man. It didn't look like a tree. More like bed sheets, or a rolled-up rug. The man stopped his digging and grunting, dropped the shovel and went over to the roll. Bending at the knees, he hooked one arm under and the other over and, with some effort, half-hauled it up.

Walking backward, he dragged it awkwardly to the hole.

Perhaps the forester had come across a dead deer, and this was how they disposed of them. But the bundle was the wrong shape and size for a deer, or a fox, or a much-loved dog. When I leaned forward to get a better look, the weight of the backpack and the twig that snapped beneath my boot sent me veering toward another tree.

The man's head twisted and the roll fell from his arms, the wrap unraveling at one end. He stood facing me now, with one hand beneath the peak of his cap, shading his eyes. I wasn't going to move, but then I couldn't have without some effort, stuck as I was at a 45-degree angle against the tree. If I kept real still, he'd think it was a creature and he'd go back to work. My heart pounded in the silence of the forest as his gaze settled on my rust-red jacket amongst the dark tree trunks. Brown, green, anything in my trunk would have been safer.

When my eyes focused properly on the scene, I saw first the hair and then the face lying on its side by the hole. Male, light curly hair. My knees buckled. Stay still, I told myself… but then the guy wiped his brow and began walking my way. Stay still, or run? He was getting nearer. I couldn't decide. Run, I thought, and on the weakest of legs managed to push myself upright. And then I ran. Past tree after tree, over the soft forest floor, I moved as fast as my limbs and my heavy pack allowed. There was a slight upward incline, but on rubbery legs it felt like the steepest of mountains, not helped by the slippery leaves underfoot. I looked back and saw he was gaining ground. I wanted to scream but didn't have the breath. Let there be others here, I prayed, but I'd seen just that one vehicle.

Beyond the trees, on the bumpy stretch that led to my car, I grew wearier and less agile and then tripped with a jolt and fell against a wiry shrub. Pushing myself up again as quickly as I could, but clumsily, I felt the backpack, caught on the bush, slip from me, then watched it tumble and roll over and over back down the slope. The guy caught the falling bag, but it knocked him with force and so he too fell, allowing me to get nearer the road. I heard him cursing, and I heard myself panting noisily, as I moved in slow motion, or so it felt, petrified that any second his hand would land on me.

There, through my tears and hair, was Matt's car, just yards away. I took the key from my pocket, pressed the fob and fell against the driver's door. As I pulled at the handle, I saw he was close to the road and approaching fast. Thirty, forty feet away. I screamed loudly, just at the moment he lifted a phone and took a photograph.

'Go to the police!' he shouted, clearly out of breath as he lumbered forward. 'And you'll end up like him! But not before your family does!'

I jumped in the car, pushed the key in the ignition, and when the engine began humming, and without checking for traffic, I put the car in gear, wrenched the steering wheel to the right and slammed the accelerator. In the mirror I watched him trying to catch up, photographing the car, then slowly shrinking in size as I sped off.

I drove faster than I'd normally feel comfortable with on the narrow winding roads the UK is filled with, expecting the black car to appear in my mirror. Less than two miles on, I reached civilization: a small town that had looked much farther on the map. Sobbing with relief but still trembling, I drove into the parking lot of a large superstore and got out of the vehicle as fast as I could. Surrounded by people –

wonderful real people – I reached into my jeans for my cell. It wasn't there. I checked my jacket, then inside the vehicle, under the seats, in the cracks, willing it to appear but it didn't. I must have dropped it in the chase, one of the times I'd stumbled.

I locked the car and went inside the store, where I looked for directions to the restrooms. Once in the ladies, inside a stall, I closed the toilet lid and fell heavily onto it. Shaking and quietly crying, I sat there far longer than I'd intended. It felt like a safe place. Other women came and went. He couldn't get to me here. Would he be outside, in the store? Would he be waiting by my car? In the car, somehow? Should I call the police? No phone. Wherever he was, whoever he was, he now had my credit cards, my address book, and most likely my cell phone too. And he'd work out from the phone that I'd have access to the photos of him I'd taken. Could he delete them from my cloud without a password? I had no idea, but I'd find out once I got to my Mac. Perhaps I'd email them to myself… something like that. I shivered, remembering his threat. He really could find me and my family, if he discovered I'd gone to the police.

After twenty minutes or so I left the cubicle, looking both ways, then washed my hands and stared into the mirror; my hair wild and no brush to tame it. And if I did report it to the police… well, what exactly did I have? Obviously, he wouldn't bury the body in that spot, not now, and he'd be sure to leave no trace of evidence that he'd been there. My distant pictures would hardly show that a crime had taken place, since I hadn't even gotten the body in them. There'd be DNA, for sure – his, the dead guy's – but could I lead the cops back to that exact spot? There'd been several small clearings, just like that one. I'd have no information regarding the car, other than its color.

And as for identifying him from the photos, what with the cap, that could prove impossible.

I didn't want to leave the security of the store, but knew my only course of action was to go pick up my things, get myself on the highway and head directly home. I buttoned my coat and pulled the collar up, tucking as much hair inside as I could in a futile attempt to disguise myself. Then, with head down, my stomach constricted and the car key clutched tight to use as a weapon, I dove into a cluster of customers all exiting at the same time.

THIRTY-FOUR

I handed the pages back to Ben, too appalled to say anything, except, 'So that's why Matt got rid of his car.'

'Yeah. Said he didn't want the guy spotting it in Oxford. OK if I show you the photos? Isabella printed them out, then deleted them from her laptop.' He slid them across my desk. 'We've had them blown up.'

I sat motionless but churned up, taking in the first photo, in which a man was digging a hole. The figure was small and in the distance, and could have been Terence with shorter hair, but it could also have been lots of other men. He was wearing a checked shirt I wouldn't have expected to see Terence in, along with blue jeans. In the second photo, the man was half facing the camera. Oh, Jesus. Terence, definitely. I felt a wave of disgust, then fear. The fear that was never far from the surface now. As Bella had written, there was no sign of the wrapped figure.

'Who was he?' I asked. 'The dead man.'

'Formerly, he'd been Corporal Wayne Dearlove. Thirty-seven. Served with Terence, or rather, under him.'

'Married? Children?'

'Neither.'

'Well, that's something. Do you know… why?'

'No, but we're interviewing his colleagues, as well as Casales's senior officers. There'd been some discipline issues, complaints. We do know Casales was suddenly allowed permanent leave, on health grounds.'

'Psychological?'

Ben nodded. 'The corporal, Dearlove, had also left the army. Became something of a depressed loner and talked about travelling. So, although he was missing, no one was sure he hadn't headed off to Thailand, or just dropped out of society.'

I took a couple of deep breaths and wrapped arms around my middle. 'So, I'm guessing there was no ambush? That Terence wasn't injured, you know, physically?'

'No. No, he wasn't.'

'Huh.'

'I'm sorry to do this to you, Edie. Can I fetch you some water?'

'I'm all right, thanks. Have you been able to find him, the corporal, at this spot?'

'We have found him, as a matter of fact, but not there. Casales ended up burying him under a concrete floor in a garage he'd built, entirely by himself according to neighbours, on the side of his semi-detached house in a village in Surrey. Some of them thought it odd, starting a job like that late in the year. We did too, so we started excavating.'

'Bloody hell.' I didn't know what was more of a surprise: that Terence had a semi in a village, or that he'd built a garage.

'Terence's village is near Mike's, and not far from Caroline's place. Seems the Thames-side apartment is one of three properties he owns. The third, in Brighton, is a house he inherited but apparently has never used, or, according to the tenant, ever visited.' Ben gave me a sympathetic look. 'This is a lot to take in.'

'Where was the guy, Wayne, actually…'

'Killed? We don't know. Waiting on forensics. The victim had lived in Kent, up to when he'd gone missing.'

'Northumberland's a long way from Kent.'

'Caroline said the family had once holidayed in the National Park up there. I suspect Casales thought it a good remote spot to dispose of the body.'

But then Bella had caught him in the act, forcing him to drive all the way back to the place poor Wayne ended up in. Terence must have been terrified, I thought, for the length of those motorways, that Bella had reported him and his car registration. 'How was he killed?' I asked. 'The same way as…'

'Isabella? No, he wasn't stabbed, but there may have been an altercation, then a blow to the head. Again, we're waiting on forensics. Also…' He looked at me, as though wondering whether to tell me more, then took a deep breath. 'Forensics are working on possible traces of Dearlove found in Terence's chest freezer. He must have stashed him there while building the garage.'

I just shook my head. It got worse and worse, but I had to know.

Ben put the photos and Bella's account away. 'When I spoke to Terence's ex-wife, she was extremely forthcoming. Told me he was never that nice a fella. That she fell for his romantic and passionate traits, while blocking out the not-so-savoury ones. Anyway, things were bearable and they had the boys, but then, after he left the army, he became a foul-tempered and occasionally brutal bully. Hit the boys a few times, before she kicked him out.'

'Oh God, Alfie…'

'Doesn't bear thinking about. Caroline tried to get him into therapy but he wasn't having it. She said her brother thought Terence should be sectioned.'

'Wow.' I suddenly felt sorry for Caroline. 'And is Barnaby really at school in Oxfordshire?'

'Nope. Both are at home, day boys at a private school. Also... well, there's something I think you should be aware of.'

I took a deep breath. 'Go on.'

'We discovered Terence had booked three flights to Spain for last Saturday evening. One for himself, one for Maeve Casales and one for Alfie Casales. Malaga.'

I put my head in my hands on the desk. 'He lost his other family, so decided to take this one?'

'Something like that.' He pulled a further item from his folder and pushed it across my desk. 'I wasn't sure whether to show you this, but since you're keen to know everything.'

Now what? I suddenly wasn't sure I could take more. It was one of the two photos of Bella that Mike had given me. And which Terence had given him. The less formal one where she was smiling and outdoors. There was the roof and partial front windscreen of a car. She seemed to be leaning against it in a rust-red jacket. The jacket in her story? 'What?' I asked Ben.

'Have a closer look.'

I picked it up and took in her face, eyes and mouth. 'Oh Lord,' I whispered, 'she's not smiling.' I looked up at him. 'She's screaming. I can't believe I didn't notice. God, I'm so useless.'

'None of us noticed, Edie. And no, you're not.'

He tucked the picture away and said, 'Oh yeah, almost forgot. We heard from Jack Bevington this morning.'

'What!'

'He'll be popping in for a formal interview and to make a statement later, but he called the incident room from his dad's place to say he had been at the scene of the crime. Said he'd planned on surprising you and had arrived a bit early.'

'And?'

'He saw Nadya's brother leave and had expected the girls and Matt to arrive to take over, but when they didn't he became curious and went around the back, hopped over a few fences, spotted the broken window and went and looked through it. He saw Isabella lying there and was about to check if she was still alive, when he heard the women arrive. Worried that they and the police would think he'd attacked her, he panicked, shut the door and ran. Told us he threw the shoes away before leaving for Portugal.'

'Not realising how clever you are these days.'

'Exactly.'

'I have to say I'm relieved about Jack. To know I'm not that bad a judge of character. Oh, and what about the watch? Mike's watch?'

'We reckon Terence planted it. Mike told us Terence had asked for a few things back before sacking him. The watch, the hat you found and a black coat.'

I felt cold and rubbed at my arms.

'We are keeping a close eye on you, Edie. All of you.'

'I know. Thank you.'

They had someone accompanying Maeve everywhere, and others watching our house, the shop and Alfie's nursery. Not that Terence could ever penetrate Twinkle Toes, with its ever-changing entry code, and the password you have to announce to the member of staff who comes and lets you in through two locked doors.

'Duty of care and all that,' he added. He quickly checked his watch. 'I'm afraid I'm going to have to head back. Bevington's due in half an hour.'

'Well, thanks.'

'Call anytime,' he said, standing. 'Got anyone who could come and be with you?'

'I'll be fine.'

* * *

We picked Alfie up and went straight home, where I watched CBeebies with Alfie, and Maeve went, accompanied, back to the Bodleian.

Late afternoon, she returned with Hector, who'd had a personality transplant since being temporarily dumped. He helped lay the table, while Maeve cooked, and he played with Alfie, and most surprising of all, just as we were about to eat, produced a bottle of wine. I'd been wanting to tell Maeve about Jack's return, but hadn't found the right moment. She'd been in shock since Saturday and was still wobbly. Once Alfie was asleep, maybe.

'Smells yummy,' I said, pulling up a chair.

'It's just thrown-together Moroccan,' said Maeve. 'No time to make a tagine.'

'You're brilliant,' Hector told her. 'Red wine, anyone? It's a rather good merlot.'

'Can I have Coke?' Alfie asked.

'Absolutely not,' said his mum.

'Gan lets me have Coke.'

'Just the odd sip,' I said.

Maeve shook her head in despair. 'It's water only with meals, sweetie, and fruit juice when you're out. You know that's the rule and so does Gran.'

'I hate water.'

'No you don't,' I chipped in, although it did seem unfair, what with Hector filling our wine glasses. 'But maybe Gran could put a splash of juice in the water. Mummy wouldn't mind that.'

'Yes, she would.' Maeve kissed Alfie's head and handed him his beaker.

While we dug into the amazingly good stew, Hector told political anecdotes and Alfie asked over and over for chicken nuggets. 'Shall I?' I mouthed to Maeve, pointing at the freezer. She nodded miserably, and I got up and put four under the grill. At least we're all here, I thought, and compared to the past five days, I felt relatively happy again. If Terence hadn't been about to swing through a windowpane, Tarzan like, and slash us all to pieces, I'd have felt even happier.

When the doorbell rang, I called the plain clothes guys outside. 'A visitor,' I was told, helpfully, and I went and opened the door.

'Hi,' said Jack, looking decidedly nervous.

'Oh,' I replied. 'I heard you were back.'

'How are you?' he asked.

'I've been better.'

'I'm, er, here to apologise.'

'You'd better come in then.'

I took him through to the back room, where Alfie cried, 'Jack!', Hector looked disappointed, and Maeve dropped her fork and covered the table in stew.

'Hi, Alfie. Hi, everybody,' Jack said. 'I just wanted to come and see how you all were. And to give you this, Maeve. It's a CD I made, in Portugal. Dedicated to you.'

As she got up from the table, he smiled tentatively, but on reaching him, she slapped his face, quite hard. Hard enough to make me jump. 'Coward!' she said. 'How could you leave Mum on her own to deal with all that? You were supposed to be partners!'

I was not only shocked, but completely moved.

'I know,' Jack said, head bowed, hand on his cheek. 'I know. I'm really sorry.'

She took the CD and threw it at the wall. 'And no, I don't want that. So just fuck off!'

'Maeve, please,' I said, realising this was, after all, about her hurt feelings. Another man had tricked her and let her down. Poor Jack. He'd just been too scared to hang around and be accused of a murder he hadn't committed.

'It's OK, Edie,' he said. 'I'll go.'

'I think it'll be in everyone's interest if you don't come here again,' Hector said.

Everyone's, or Hector's?

'I'll see you out,' I said, leading Jack down the hall.

By the front door, he put a hand on my shoulder. 'I got an anonymous message,' he whispered, 'through my letterbox, the day after Bella died. It told me I'd been spotted at the scene of the crime, at the house, and there was a witness to verify it. I don't know how, or where he saw me.' Jack took a deep breath. 'Then it said if I disappeared, this witness would stay quiet. And…'

'And what?'

'And nothing bad would happen to Edie and her family.'

'Shit.'

'I had to think quickly when I spotted Bella and heard the women arriving, so I made that call to you saying I was passing Matt's house.' Jack shook his head. 'Dumbest thing I ever did.'

I opened the door for him. 'Lesson learned, I guess. Listen, I'll call you for a chat tomorrow. Oh, and don't run off again.' I nodded towards the back room. 'She likes you a lot, you know.'

'Cool,' he said, almost smiling. 'And, no, I won't.'

I closed the door and sighed an exhausted sigh.

Back in the deadly quiet back room, Maeve stared into space and Hector was knocking back more merlot. The atmosphere was dark and depressing and I longed for things to be normal again. They would be, I told myself. They would.

On seeing me, Alfie picked up his beaker of water. 'Don't want that,' he said, throwing it at the wall. 'Puck off!'

Maeve didn't react, or even notice. Poor Alfie. This couldn't be much fun for him. I remembered his nuggets and pulled them from the grill and added ketchup. From a cupboard I took blackcurrant juice, and from the fridge sparkling water. I mixed them in a new beaker and handed it to Alfie.

'Hey, little man,' I said, stroking his head and lifting him out of his chair. 'Want to eat in front of the TV? Maybe we'll find something on ketchup?'

THIRTY-FIVE

Four days later, with no cheating-partner clients in the pipeline, I sat half-watching *Homes Under the Hammer* in the office, wondering if business would always be this slow, and if I'd survive. This time it was two upbeat brothers, who'd left their jobs to become full-time property developers. Maybe I could buy a property at auction, like they did. Make a killing. No, not killing.

I opened another window on the laptop and looked up Oxford estate agents. I'd arrange a valuation – no time like the present, as Dad always said. I'd been thinking about him a lot recently, and all his cheering clichés. But as I reached for the landline, it rang and made me jump. I'd been jumping a lot recently. I let it ring while I clicked back to *HUTH* and paused it, just as the guys were to be told what their little terraced property was worth now they'd made it look like every other renovated house in the series – beige carpets, white walls and marble-effect worktops. Really, how hard could that be?

Picking up the receiver, I gave a squeaky, 'Hello?', then cleared my throat. I hadn't spoken for a while.

'Edie?' asked Terence.

It was like someone had given me an electric shock.

'It's me,' he said. He breathed in shakily. 'I'm… I'm in a bad way. I don't know what to do.'

I swallowed hard. 'Hand yourself in.'

'I have no one. No one in the entire world I can turn to. Can you imagine how that feels, Edie?' He sniffed and did the shaky breathing again.

'Where are you?' I asked, reaching for my mobile. I had to text or ring DS Ben but was all fingers and thumbs. If I hadn't been on the landline, I'd have shot downstairs for help. Although it was cordless, I knew from experience that the signal didn't stretch that far. I felt trapped, tethered to the spot.

'There's just you,' he went on in a rasping half-whisper. For a moment, I thought it might be a prankster. 'The one person I felt I could call.'

'Go to the nearest police station, Terence.'

He began sobbing into my ear, as I tried with a trembling hand to find Ben in my mobile contacts. 'I can't,' he said.

'So what's the alternative?' I found Ben and pressed call. 'A life on the run?'

Terence sniffed. 'Full of guilt and remorse,' he said in a strangled voice. 'I know, I know. But I don't… know. I can't…'

I covered the mouthpiece so he wouldn't hear Ben's voicemail message, then when it had finished, I held my iPhone close to the earpiece of the handset, as it hopefully recorded him. How I wished Emily or Naz would pop up, so I could scribble an SOS message, or just be with a human.

'You haven't asked me if I'm alone, Terence.'

'Huh,' he said, not quite a laugh. 'That's because I know you are.'

I looked around my tiny room. 'How?'

'I broke in, several weeks back, and… I'm sorry, Edie. I'm so very sorry. You're such a lovely person, and I'm a shit.'

'Where are you?' I tried again. 'Are you in London?'

'No.'

'Oxford?'

'Would you meet me?' he asked, almost pleaded. The voice I'd loved so recently now repelled me, as did the idea of seeing him again, ever.

'Just you, Edie? I can't go to the police on my own. I need you to help me do it.'

'Why would I risk that? You've killed two people.'

'The first was an accident. A sort of fight-gone-wrong situation.'

I moved the mobile phone even closer. 'Well,' I said, 'that makes me feel much safer.'

'Come and meet me, Edie. I have no reason to hurt you, not now I've lost everything, everyone. I'll turn myself in, I promise. I just need you to help me. And I want to explain, to apologise. I behaved atrociously the other day… with you. I'm so terribly sorry. And you're right, I can't be on the run for ever.' He sobbed again, then sniffed. 'Please.'

'Tell me where you are.'

'You have to come alone.'

'I… will. Just tell me where.'

He took a deep shudder of a breath. 'No calling PC Plod.'

'I won't.'

'Or fucking Mike.'

'No. I promise.'

'No taxi.'

'I'll drive, or bus, or walk. But not to a remote spot.'

'I won't hurt you, Edie. You know that? I adore you… and I adore–'

'Don't!'

'I'd never have harmed them. I just wanted a family again. My family. You could have joined us in Spain. It would have been marvellous.'

I wanted to kill him down the phone. Perhaps one day there'd be a way of doing that. 'Where are you?'

He went quiet and I prayed he wouldn't hang up. 'Cat Burger in five minutes,' he said. 'Absolutely no longer, or I won't be there.' Then he ended the call.

'Fuck, fuck, fuck,' I whispered, trying Ben again and getting his voicemail again. I realised, just before leaving a message, that Terence could be listening in via some device in my office, so I grabbed my bag and coat and ran, almost tumbled, down to the shop. 'Oscar,' I panted. He was serving and ignored me, so I shouted, 'Oscar!' which got his attention. 'Phone 999 and tell the police to go to Cat Burger on Cowley Road ASAP, if they want to catch Terence Casales.'

Oscar turned pale, said, 'Fuck,' apologised to the woman he was serving and retrieved his phone. 'Edie, where are you going?' he called out as I made for the door.

'Cat Burger!' I shouted from outside. If Terence had said the top of the multi-storey car park, I wouldn't have gone, obviously. I hadn't completely lost my mind. But Cat Burger would have people in and around it, and once there, I'd work out what to do… stall him, whatever, before the police arrived. I had around three minutes to get there, I reckoned, but first I dialled 999 myself. Belt and braces – another one of Dad's.

I spoke quickly and breathlessly, to one woman, then another, and once assured that the police would be there in minutes, I began walking briskly, then broke into a run. At the junction of Cowley Road and James Street, as I hovered on tiptoe, waiting for a car to pass, I felt a strong arm under my ribs and a solid body against my back. I gasped, winded.

'Not a peep, Edie,' came Terence's firm, unemotional voice. Not Oscar, as I'd first thought, running after me to stop me doing something daft. How stupid not to have brought someone with me. Oscar, Naz, Emily even. Before I had time to alert the two Asian women across the street, I was bent over and shoved onto the driver's seat of a car, then shunted across to the passenger seat, my head hitting something en route. Tears stung my eyes, and it was then, just as Terence's door clunked shut, and too late for anyone to hear, that I managed a scream. Terence pushed my head down, then again, then finally told me to sit in the footwell of the passenger seat. He lifted the lever and pushed the seat back to make room, then strapped himself in and put his foot down. Please don't let him kill a hapless student on a bike. A child. He screeched to a halt at the junction with Iffley Road, and rolled the car around to the left, forcing my cheek to collide with the gearstick.

'Move your fucking head,' he said, pushing me away.

I whimpered, I begged him to stop.

'Edie, Edie, just shut it. I need to concentrate.'

'Let me out?' I pleaded, hands covering my head as I knelt on the floor, squashed into the small space, elbows on the passenger seat. 'I won't tell anyone! I promise!'

He revved the accelerator a little harder. 'You're pathetic, Edie. Look at you. A private investigator? What a joke. You couldn't see what was right under your nose.'

'You're right,' I shouted over the engine. He was right. I prayed to God and my dad to save me, and if they did I'd never put my family in danger again. We seemed to be going uphill. Up Rose Hill presumably.

'What the fuck!' yelled Terence. He slammed the brakes on and my head hit the glove compartment, so hard I saw stars. 'What's that fucking taxi doing?' He honked the horn three times. 'Fucking move!' he shouted.

I felt another bump. Had something hit us in the rear?

'What the… Shit, shit, shit.'

Terence wiggled the gearstick and reversed, bashing into something. Then he went forward and crashed into something else. Back and forth he went, bump, bump, like he was on the dodgems.

'You're a fucking lunatic, Terence,' I said, sobbing with the pains in my head, my cheek. 'Not to mention a psychopath!'

'You think I don't know that?'

'Just stop!' I screamed, and he did.

'Please,' he said, opening the car door and jumping out. 'Tell Maeve I love her.'

I held my breath, waiting for him to jump back in, then someone was calling out. 'Miss? Miss? Are you in there? Are you in the boot?'

Naz? Lovely, lovely Naz? I raised my head and smiled at him, causing him to scream loudly. Then I saw a large bald guy approaching us from the taxi behind and when the two of them had opened my door and helped me out, I spotted Terence running up Rose Hill, reminding me very much of the jogger in Middle Thing.

Naz pulled his phone out and called the police with Terence's location, then looked at my face. 'Oh, my God, miss. Let me take you to A & E?'

'Good idea,' I said, knees buckling. The bald guy caught me.

THIRTY-SIX

"DS Ben", my phone told me. I was in my office, two days later. Outside the shop stood a uniformed policeman, again. Inside my office sat Naz, who'd been an uncomfortable recipient of my gratitude for the past fifteen minutes, and who, I could tell, just wanted to go.

'Hi, Ben,' I said, waving Naz off with a final mouthed, 'Thank you.' I'd buy him a gift of some kind. But what? I knew that when he wasn't driving taxis or reading dictionaries, Naz played computer games. Maybe I'd get him a voucher from that shop in town, the one that young, and not-so-young men with pale faces came out of.

'Edie Fox?' Ben asked.

'No, the Duchess of Malfi.'

'This is Detective Sergeant Ben Watson,' he went on regardless. I assumed, ingeniously, that he had someone with him. 'I'm just ringing firstly to ask if you're OK, following your ordeal.'

'Yes, thank you.' He already knew that. He'd been round to see me.

'That's good to hear. Um, I also have to inform you that a body was discovered yesterday in the water in the Canary Wharf area.'

My heart stopped. 'Just tell me quickly.'

'It's been identified by his ex-wife as that of Terence Casales.'

I sank back in my chair.

'We wanted to be certain before informing you.'

'How did he…?'

'No foul play is suspected, at this moment in time, but a post-mortem should reveal the cause of death in due course.'

'OK.'

'Will you be all right, Miss Fox? I could arrange for a family liaison officer to come and be with you?'

'I'm fine,' I told him. 'But thank you. See you soon for a proper chat?'

'Yes, absolutely. That will definitely be the case. Goodbye, Miss Fox.'

I switched the phone off and hit play on the laptop.

'In the current market,' said a woman in a suit, 'I would put a resale value of eighty-five thousand, five hundred pounds on this property.'

Was that all? The uncle and nephew had bought it for £68,000 – Nottingham house prices being low – and spent ten grand and three months of their lives on it. Then there'd have been legal fees and auction fees of, say, two thousand. I quickly worked out that they'd made… well, not much profit at all. Maybe property development wasn't for me.

Lunch, I remembered, and I closed the laptop and stood up, only to find I had no strength in my legs. Terence. Dead. I sagged back into the chair and tried to experience relief and joy. But neither of those were happening. Perhaps in a day or two. I really should eat.

That would help. Then I'd go and find Maeve and tell her. I stood up and the buzzer went, doing what it always does, scaring the life out of me. I looked at the screen and saw a goatee and messy brown hair.

'Hi, Mike.'

'Are you busy?'

'Snowed under, but come on up.'

* * *

'I'm so not cut out for this job,' I said, halfway through a Cat Burger salad that wasn't proving too satisfying. 'Too gullible.'

'Oh, I think you're pretty good, for a novice.'

'What kind of private eye gets almost raped and then abducted?'

'There's room for improvement, it's true. You're handy with a guitar, I'll say that.'

'Cheers.' I suddenly craved salty carbs and asked if I could pinch some of his chips.

'We tend to call them fries,' he said, Mike-Smith like, 'where I'm from.'

'What, Skegness?' I laughed. 'You mispronounced vitamins, you know, when you were American Mike.' I dipped three chips/fries in mayonnaise and ate them. Delicious.

'Yeah, and thanks for sharing that with my now deceased, thank God, boss.' I'd told him about Terence in the office and we'd hugged and I'd even cried. 'It was one of the litany of errors he presented me with before sacking me, threatening to kill me, and then threatening to kill my sisters too, if I didn't do a damned good job of disappearing.'

'He seemed to be fond of that threat.'

'Isabella?'

'Yep. Jack, too. And it's Bella, by the way, not Isabella.'

'Yeah, well, if Terence had mentioned that vital fact.'

'It's odd that he didn't. I mean, he must have seen her personal emails and texts. Mind you, I almost never sign those with my name. Just a couple of kisses.'

'Girls do that.'

'We do.' I asked a passing waitress for another Coke and some chocolate ice cream.

'Make that two,' said Mike.

'So,' I asked, 'how exactly did you meet Terence? You never said before you went away.' Mike had been up in Lincolnshire spending time with his family. They'd been through a lot, what with the police hunt and all the press speculation.

'We came across each other a few times on this circular route; he ran it, I sometimes ran, sometimes cycled. Seemed like a really nice guy. One day he mentioned this ex-girlfriend, American, that he was keen to trace. Felt things had ended badly and he wanted to apologise. I liked the idea of passing as a wealthy Yank and enjoyed creating our background story.'

I pulled a face. 'If you don't mind me saying, it was a bit overly detailed. Convoluted. For example, you shouldn't have made up fake Cindy.'

'I shouldn't have done a lot of things.'

'And who was the Ruth Smith I spoke to?'

Mike stopped chewing and stared at me. 'You called her?'

'Of course. She was elderly and demented, and had no idea what I was talking about.'

'That's bizarre,' he said. 'I just made up the number, like I did Cindy's. And it turned out to be not only a real one, but an old lady's?'

I gave him a disappointed look. 'Sloppy.'

Mike nodded. 'I'll know better next time.'

'Next time you go undercover for a murderer?'

'No, but I was think–'

'And what was all that Lauren Bacall rubbish?' I asked, my head jumping around and landing on all his faults. 'I mean, it was almost harassment. And anyway, I'm nothing like her.'

'Maybe I meant Humphrey Bogart.'

'Ha ha.'

Mike took a deep breath. 'I'm sorry, Edie, for all that crap. It's just that I was short of money and Terence was mentioning large sums. I love acting. Seemed like a no-brainer.'

'Little did you know.'

'No. Not until I phoned him, following my burger with you, to ask if Isabella had any pet names or abbreviations. He completely lost it when I told him you'd mentioned the name Izzie. He said, "I fucking told you she goes by Bella!" He hadn't, I swear. That was his slip-up, not mine. Anyway, that was when the threats began.' Mike folded his arms and shook his shaggy head. 'What a psychopath.'

'I called Terence that,' I said. My head and arms still hurt from the knocks they'd received in his car, the bruises were growing bigger by the day and I'd had to tell Alfie I'd fallen off my bike. 'But, I don't know,' I added. 'I'm reluctant to label him.' I leaned forward and lowered my voice. 'There's the genetic issue to consider. I wouldn't want Maeve overly worrying every time Alfie kicks little Mabel at nursery, or pours water over Sadiq's painting because it's better than his.'

Mike's eyes widened. 'He does that?'

I leaned back. 'He's three.'

'But still…'

I thought about Alfie and what a tricky time he'd been through, getting attached to a grandfather who'd now disappeared. Maeve, I recalled, had played up after Bloody Greg left, but not for long. She'd been older, though, and most of her friends had temporary 'step-parents' flowing in and out of their lives.

'So, how's little Sandra?' Mike said.

'Who?'

He frowned then laughed. 'I mean Edie, of course. I heard from Ben that you'd found her.'

'She's fine. And she's called Bidget. Alfie renamed her. He adores her, actually we all do. So thanks.'

'Yeah, she was always such a sweetie.'

'Oh, God. Sorry, Mike. You don't want her back, do you?'

'No, no. Sounds like she's very happy.'

'She is,' I said, relieved.

We ate our ice creams in silence for a while, then I asked, 'Why Sandra?'

Mike grinned. 'Because I couldn't call her Bullock?'

'Ah, right. Big fan?'

'Huge.' He dabbed away ice cream and balled up the serviette. 'So, what's next? For you?'

'I don't know. As I said, I'm not sure I'm cut out for crime busting. And this first experience has shaken up my family, and… oh, I don't know, maybe I'm too trusting, or not cynical enough. And I don't think I'm very observant, not like Emily.'

'She's wicked.'

'She is.'

'Why not take her on? I reckon we'd make a good team, the three of us.'

I choked on my wafer, making my eyes water. 'Pardon?'

'Sorry,' he said, 'but how about it? Wilder Fox Investigators? I'd be the undercover guy.'

'You might need to do a course,' I said, obviously not taking him seriously.

He beamed brightly at me. 'You too. Self-defence, at least.'

Now that was a good idea. It was great seeing Mike again, even this different Mike, and there were still lots of things I wanted to ask. 'There's only one minor problem with this plan of yours,' I told him. 'Not enough work coming in to support us all.'

'It would just be a case of effective marketing. I could do that.'

I wiped ketchup off my hands and eyed him suspiciously. 'Perhaps I should get to know Mike Wilder a bit better before leaping into business with him?'

'Fair enough, but don't take too long deciding. I've got Scorsese calling me daily.'

'I'm sure you do.' It was strange hearing the flat vowels and Lincolnshire dialect – the 'tek' instead of 'take' – but I was slowly getting used to it, just as I was getting used to the beard he'd now trimmed to a goatee.

'One thing,' he said. 'We'll need better premises.'

'Stop!' I told him, and he looked hurt. But then he was an actor. 'I'll think about it, all right?'

THIRTY-SEVEN

The weather was fittingly grey and wet as we congregated in the small waiting room. The boys had the puffy eyes of teens dragged early from their beds. Terence's equally bewildered-looking mother had been glammed up, perhaps by the nursing-home staff. She had white permed hair, blue eye shadow and pink lipstick, and pretty features. In all those weeks Terence had only mentioned her once as being, 'Away with the fairies.' Not completely, it appeared, since Maeve was currently making her laugh, an arm linked through hers. For Maeve to meet her other grandmother was the main reason we were here. Although there were her half-brothers too.

I'd caught my breath on seeing seventeen-year-old Barnaby, the spitting image of young Terence. I went over and talked to both the boys, fearing frostiness but receiving smiles and politeness. 'Nice to meet you,' each said, and we talked for a while about the weather and school. Fair-haired Theo, the youngest, was the chattiest, the most outgoing, and it was he who crossed the room to talk to Maeve. Caroline, a tall blonde woman in a rebellious red suit, looked my way. We shifted closer, introduced ourselves, and I gave her my condolences.

'He wasn't all bad,' she whispered, as we were led out of the room by a man in a black coat.

'He was,' said Theo.

Caroline shrugged. 'You're right, he was an arsehole.' She slapped a hand to her mouth and whispered, 'Sorry.'

'Did you bring the gin?' asked Terence's mother beside her.

'In my bag,' said Caroline. 'Do you need it now?'

Yes please, I wanted to say.

But there was no time for gin, for we were suddenly standing in drizzle and lined up behind the assorted employees – no military pallbearers for Terence – carrying the coffin. Then the funeral party, all six of us, entered the chapel of the crematorium to the strains of *Tainted Love.* I reeled slightly, on hearing it.

'His favourite,' Caroline whispered over her shoulder. 'I've always hated it.'

'I think it's brilliant,' said Maeve with a twirly finger and a sexy wiggle that made her stumble on her heels and curse. Theo giggled and his grandmother asked again about gin.

The young male celebrant, who'd be conducting the service, was picking at sleepy dust and frowning at his notes. He gestured towards the coffin as it passed. 'Is this Doris Turner?' he whispered to Caroline.

* * *

The moment we got in the car, Maeve burst into tears. 'That was so sad,' she sobbed. 'The worst day of my life.'

'Oh, love,' I said, not entirely convinced. Maeve had been the star act at the wake, held in a rather nice Surrey pub, so close to the crematorium it would never go out of business. She'd told the group funny anecdotes about her son. She'd made sure Granny was included and talked her into switching to tea, and she'd spent ages talking to Caroline and the boys about the pros and cons of going to Oxford. And all on one glass of white wine, as far as I could tell.

I handed Maeve tissue after tissue as tears and snot poured from her. 'Do you think he cared about me at all?' she asked. 'Because I thought he loved me. I loved him, I really did, even though we'd only just met.'

I squeezed her shoulder. 'Remember, he did say to tell you he loved you.'

'Yeah, I know. I expect it was a soul thing. Like recognising each other from previous lives?'

'Maybe,' I said, although that might mean Terence turning up in Maeve's future lives, and we really couldn't have that. I leaned across and gave her an awkward hug.

'What was that all for?' she asked, as we both buckled up.

'The funeral?'

'Him. Dad. Coming into our lives and fucking us up. I mean, why did any of that need to happen? To us? We were fine before.'

'We were,' I said, unhelpfully, unable to understand it myself. I'd secretly cried too, in my room, at the office. Mostly for Maeve, since Alfie was already forgetting Terence. But the tears had also been for me, and for Isabella. Today I could have cried for those boys, acting blasé throughout the funeral.

Maeve turned to me, two thick mascara streaks reaching her mouth. 'I mean, what was the point?'

THIRTY-EIGHT

Two weeks later I woke up on Astrid's sofa. Jonathan was walking away from me, saying, 'Tea, Edie. Drink it while it's hot.'

I sat myself up and when he waved from the door, waved back. 'Thanks,' I croaked to Astrid's thoughtful husband. Why she had lovers I'd never fathom.

Someone had covered me with a duvet but I had no recollection of falling asleep. I did recall downing a variety of cocktails, then coming back to Astrid's house and having a little smoke and the two of us talking for hours. My head pounded and I looked around for my bag to take painkillers, but it wasn't there. Even wrecked, Astrid would clear away glasses, ashtrays and stray bags before turning in. I drank half the weak tea, found my things, then took myself home to shower and change before heading to the office.

* * *

I woke with a start when the buzzer buzzed loudly and rudely, around four. I lifted my head off the desk, wondering, while palpitating, if there was a volume control.

'Hi, Maeve,' I said, releasing the door. She ran, as she always did, up the stairs.

'Are you OK?' I asked, seeing her flushed cheeks and wild eyes.

She seemed unable to speak and instead gave me a formal-looking envelope, already open. I yawned, took the letter out, rubbed my eyes, then read its contents. All the while Maeve paced back and forth across the tiny room.

'What the heck?' I said on finishing it.

Maeve stopped pacing and glared at me. 'Do you think it's for real?'

That it wasn't hadn't occurred to me, so I reread the contents. "Meredith and Hall", said the heading. Solicitors. Maeve, I was pretty sure it said in semi-accessible English, was a beneficiary of the will of Terence Miguel Casales. Not only had she been left sole ownership of a property in Brighton, address supplied, but there'd be more to come after the London and Surrey houses had been sold and all other bequests blah, blah. It was heavy on the legalese and ran to a second page, but I got the gist. And it really did look kosher. Headed paper, a great flourish of a signature.

'I think it is,' I said, giving it back with a shaky hand. My head felt light, I had butterflies. Please, I thought, please don't let her say she doesn't want anything of her father's, or that she'd give it all to a cat sanctuary, or worse, her half-brothers. 'I could google them?' I offered.

'I already did.'

'And?'

While my heart pounded painfully, Maeve stopped pacing and stared through the window. 'Yeah, they're real. Real solicitors. I spoke to the woman who sent the letter.'

'So why are you worried?' I asked, going over to her.

'Because I just don't trust him,' she said, turning to me, eyes welling up, 'of course.'

'But he's dead, love,' I said, giving her a hug and smelling L'Occitane Roses et Reines. Suddenly I felt hopeful. If she was still wearing the perfume Terence gave her, perhaps she'd keep his house.

'But that might not stop him. What if he owed gazillions and there's nothing left in the estate?'

I felt myself calming down. Maeve wasn't sounding like a masochistic philanthropist, and surely Terence didn't owe as much as he owned? It would all be fine. Better than fine. I'd no longer have to worry about my daughter's future security, or Alfie's most probably. So long as Maeve was wise with her inheritance. 'See,' I said. 'I told you he loved you.'

She blew her nose into a tissue and shoved it in a pocket, then grinned at the letter. 'Maybe he did after all.'

'He did.'

She wiped away tears and quickly rallied, then we high-fived and had a proper hug.

'I was thinking,' she said, eyes still wild but a happy wild, 'walking over here.' She sat down in the client chair.

'What about?'

'About what I want to do with my life. About how I know for sure I'll go mad doing a doctorate.'

'But you're so clever, Maeve. So academic.'

'Funny thing is, it turns out I'm not. I don't know, maybe I'm still suffering from baby brain, or it's all too much, being a single mother and studying.'

'But you're not doing badly, are you?'

'Kind of.' Back came the bad wild eyes. 'Obviously, I got a bit caught up with… him.'

I guessed she meant Terence, not Jack. 'Understandably,' I said, rubbing her back. 'And besides, we all did. So, what, you want to drop out?'

'Yes.'

'And do what? I mean the Brighton house and the money will be useful, but won't last forever.'

'I think we're sent here to do something we're passionate about, Mum. Don't you?'

'Passionate's a strong word, but, yes, I suppose so.'

The happy eyes returned. 'And that's why I want to open a café.'

'Oh, Maeve,' I said, 'don't you think Oxford's got enough of those? I mean, look at the Cowley Road, the High Street, Jericho...'

'Not in Oxford,' she said with a sneer. 'In Brighton, of course, where the house is!'

'Oh, I see…' I walked around the desk to my chair, needing to sit down. All I could think of was Alfie, and never seeing him, or rarely. Maeve too. How could she think of upping sticks like that?

'I looked at the house on Street View, and I tell you, Mum, it's huge. A huge Victorian semi. Mansions, they call them on Rightmove.'

'Well,' I said, 'you have been busy.' I started shuffling some papers on my desk, then opened a drawer and put them in, unnecessarily.

'Are you OK, Mum? Look, I just did it on my phone, on my way here.' She got it out of her pocket.

'I'm fine.' I opened my laptop and checked my emails, pretended to read something, tapped a few keys.

'Oh my God!' Maeve cried out. 'You don't seriously think I'd move to Brighton without you?'

'What?'

'Of course you'd have to come. I mean, how could I run a café and look after Alfie?'

'Really?'

'No, honestly, Mum, I would not go without you. And there are five bedrooms in this mansion. Or six if you count the one the sitting tenant's in.'

'Sitting tenant?'

'Yeah, a woman, the solicitor told me. But she's seventy or something. I expect she'll die soon. Anyway, how am I going to cope with a place that size?'

'But I've got… this,' I said, looking around.

'You think people don't cheat on their partners in Brighton? Or get stabbed in kitchens?'

I flinched.

'Sorry. Sorry. But you know it's got a bigger population, and besides you'd only be based there. There is this thing called the internet? And Brighton's so cool. You'd love it.'

'Would I?' I'd been there just the once, after A levels. I'd got sunburn and an STD. I was dying to see the house on Maeve's phone, but was playing it cool. 'I'll think about it,' I told her.

‘OK. Want to come and pick Alfie up with me?’ She stood and plonked a black felt hat on her head. It wasn’t unlike Mike’s hat, which took me back to that bedroom and Terence and... no, no, mustn’t go there.

I wondered whether to stay in my office and digest the news and check out the solicitors. Go online, perhaps, and look up “Brighton mansions”. It was all very exciting, and a wonderful antidote to the darkness that had been Terence, his death and his funeral. Hopefully, the Brighton house wouldn’t be inextricably linked to her father, in Maeve’s mind.

I closed the laptop. ‘Yes,’ I said. ‘I will come.’

Maeve whooped. ‘That’s fantastic! I promise you won’t regret it!’

‘To nursery, dummy.’

‘Oh.’

I laughed and gave her another hug. ‘Congratulations, love. You deserve everything he’s left you, you know that?’

‘I guess,’ she said.

* * *

The route to Twinkle Toes took us past the end of our street, where I looked down towards the red door and did a quick calculation. I could invest the capital and maybe take the interest each month. We passed two pubs I’d had hundreds of good times in, with partners, friends, and way, way back, my sister. All those people, no longer around. In London, scattered over the globe, dead. Some were still there, though, and I saw one approaching. Mags and I used to be good friends, moaning about our jobs and our men. She’d been slim and gorgeous at twenty-six, twenty-seven, but time hadn’t been her friend. I wondered, as we drew closer, if she remembered coming to the Bullingdon with me that time I’d thrown a bra at Greg, the one I’d found in my car: size 32A. ‘What is she, twelve?’ I’d shouted, completely drunk on Dutch-courage vodka. Mags, also pissed, had thrown the remains of Greg’s pint in his face, and we'd both been escorted out. Now, she and I did that fake-smiley-'Hi!' thing when we passed, speeding up slightly to avoid conversation.

Over the road was my favourite Italian deli, and the best charity shop in town, and the community centre with its reggae nights, flea markets, and the art classes Maeve had been to as a child. We passed the natural health place, where I'd far too often had needles stuck in me to mend a broken heart. Then there was Cat Burger, of course. More recent, but still…

I stopped and turned around at one point, looking back and trying to feel attachment to it all. But, actually, I couldn't. Not much, at any rate. It's funny how quickly that happens, once you've made up your mind to move on.

Maeve took a call and hung around by the nursery gate. When I came out with Alfie, who was burbling away about Lucy, his new favourite teacher, Maeve was still on the phone. 'No, honestly, hon,' she was saying, 'there'd be plenty of room for us all. It's got a million bedrooms.'

Hector. My heart sank. I took Alfie's hand and crossed the street, Maeve following and talking about the café idea.

'Of course there'd be loads of customers. It's Brighton!'

With a bit of luck, I thought, Hector would be legally tied to Oxford by his trust fund.

'And you're such a brilliant cook,' Maeve was saying, 'that I think we could really make a success of it.'

Had I ever seen Hector cook? It would hardly be his thing, a café. Not unless he got to sound off about politics to the customers, pulling up a chair and cornering them.

'OK, well have a think,' Maeve was saying. 'Gotta go. Talk to you later. Yeah, miss you too. Bye, Jack.'

Jack?

Jack!

I wasn't sure anything else could shock me, but this had. Why had the normally open Maeve kept quiet about it? Embarrassment? No, not Maeve.

We turned onto the Cowley Road. Would they really need me in Brighton? Probably not. And would I, truthfully, want to be there? Surely you'd have to know a place well to operate as an investigator. We passed a "Pub Quiz" sign. It had been ages since I'd been to one of those. Maybe I could get another team together. Astrid and Mike. And Emily, if she wasn't barred. Had the sun just come out? For some reason, life suddenly felt lighter. "Zumba", said another sign, "Thursdays 7pm". After three years of devoted grannyhood, perhaps I could consider the idea of having fun again, untethered.

I'd been thinking of saying no to Mike's proposition, but now wasn't sure. I handed Alfie over to Maeve and got my phone out. Still thinking about it, I messaged him, adding a silly emoji. Suddenly and unexpectedly I had options, and I was going to keep them open.

If you enjoyed this book, please let others know by leaving a quick review on Amazon. Also, if you spot anything untoward in the paperback, get in touch. We strive for the best quality and appreciate reader feedback.

editor@thebookfolks.com

www.thebookfolks.com

Also in this series

THE RUNAWAY HUSBAND (Book 2)

Edie Fox is secretly resentful of her glamorous new client, Jessica Relish, who comes into her Oxford detective agency searching for her missing husband. But when the much younger, and apparently handsome and charming Hugh turns up dead in a wood, Edie's jealousy vanishes, and she quickens the search to find out what happened to him.

To be released early summer 2023!

Other great light-hearted mysteries

THE WIFE'S BOYFRIEND
by Robert McCracken

Charlie Geddis is thrown out by his wife but, determined to win her back, decides to prove that her new boyfriend, a property developer with a lot of assets, is in fact a lying crook. In the process, he becomes embroiled in a web of bribes, infidelities and possibly a murder!

FREE with Kindle Unlimited and available in paperback!

NEAR MISS
by Traude Ailinger

After being nearly hit by a car, fashion journalist Amy Thornton decides to visit the driver, who ends up in hospital after evading her. Curious about this strange man she becomes convinced she's unveiled a murder plot. But it won't be so easy to persuade Scottish detective DI Russell McCord.

FREE with Kindle Unlimited and available in paperback!

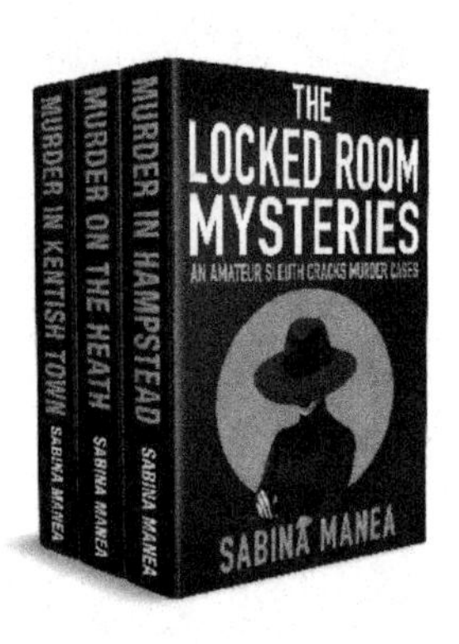

THE LOCKED ROOM MYSTERIES
by Sabina Manea

Perfect for fans of classic whodunits, this collection is comprised of the first three books in Sabina Manea's popular amateur sleuth series: Murder in Hampstead, Murder on the Heath and Murder in Kentish Town. Set in bohemian north London, canny amateur sleuth Lucia Steer steps in to solve seemingly impossible crimes where the police fail.

FREE with Kindle Unlimited and available individually in paperback!

THE
BOOK
FOLKS

Printed in Great Britain
by Amazon

26646934R00148